THE SUICIDE DETECTIVE

W.L. BACH

ENDURE ALL PUBLISHING LLC

ISBN Print 979-8-9879630-4-3

ISBN ebook 979-8-9879630-5-0

Book cover design by Getcovers.com

Printed in the United States of America

Author's Note

When I write a book, I start with the big ideas I want to convey to the reader, and from those I build the story. In this book, I had several concepts I wanted to explore: the terrible epidemic of veteran suicide, the unbelievable loyalty of working dogs and service dogs, and the bravery and sacrifice of our female veterans and our Special Operations Forces. I have firsthand experience with all of these as a veteran of Iraq and Afghanistan.

Beyond telling a compelling tale, I hope that you as a reader take away a better understanding of veteran issues, and if you feel moved to highlight these in your corner of the world and remind people of the sacrifice of the few to defend the many, I would be grateful.

If you are local to Western Colorado, you will notice that I took some liberties with the timeline of this story. That is, a few of the venues in this book did not exist when this story was set in time. I did this as I know these venues well and wanted you as the reader to feel the authenticity of these places.

Dedication

Dedicated to those military and veteran families who have lost their service member to suicide. Our nation's heart goes out to you.

Also dedicated to those brave military working dogs who save lives every day and whose actions embody the term loyalty. I saw firsthand the amazing contributions that our canine partners made in Iraq. They are true heroes.

1

Sergeant Amber Downing was sweating nervously through her uniform even though it was a cool fall evening in Baghdad. It was the first time she and her military working dog had been assigned to work with Special Ops personnel, and she didn't know what to expect. Normally the two of them supported the infantry brigade deployed to Baghdad on rotation, but a request had come through the chain of command for a dog handler and a canine that could chase down insurgents who fled from a target; they called it squirter control. The Spec Ops boys had their own dogs, but two of them had been hurt recently when a suicide bomber blew himself up as the dogs cornered him in the back of a house.

Razor trotted on his black nylon leash, sniffing the air, ready for action. He looked up at his handler constantly, ready to execute any command she gave him. Sergeant Downing looked down at Razor and picked up her pace. She was to meet the Operational Detachment Alpha or ODA Team at 0200 and board a helicopter to the target. The elite Army Special Forces soldiers always ran their missions in the wee hours. It was 0130 as she and Razor hustled across the darkened airfield to the blacked-out MH-47 behemoths lined up in a row.

Normally she was not allowed on this side of the airfield. It's where they kept all the secret aircraft, spy planes and drones. She came to a chain-link fence topped with razor wire. A gate was manned by a soldier carrying a nasty-looking short machine gun illuminated by a crackling blue light on the fence. She presented her ID, he checked it against a roster on a clipboard and waved her through. Razor was pulling at the leash, ready to get to work.

She knocked on the faded green door to the prefab metal building that the sentry had pointed to. Master Sergeant Jimmy Parnell opened the door and waved her and Razor in. He was tall and lanky with leathery skin and deep set eyes. He held coffee in a styrofoam cup. The rest of the assault team were standing around the room checking their weapons, talking quietly and looking at photos of the target area on the wall. They had that look of men ready for action.

Parnell spoke to her in a deep Texas drawl, "Any questions from the brief?"

"Nope," she said, patting Razor on the head to calm him. She had attended the mission brief that afternoon and Parnell let her go get some chow before the mission.

"Is that dog good at squirter control?"

She patted Razor, "Did you hear about the mission south of Baghdad last month? A guy jumped out the window of a target building with three pounds of Semtex, $12,000 in cash and a severed head in a bag."

"Yeah I heard about that one," Parnell said, "Crazy Iraq shit."

"Well Razor was on that one; he chased the guy down a back alley, chomped his Achilles and held on until the soldiers arrived. Yeah he's good, real good."

"Great. You and the dog sit next to me in the front of the Chinook. We'll land right next to the target and the assault team will move out the back first. You follow me to the entrance to the compound. If we have a squirter, I'll give you the description and direction and you and the dog do your thing."

"His name is Razor," she said, looking Parnell in the eye.

"Razor, got it. Let's load up," Parnell said loudly to the men in the room. The soldiers acknowledged the command, strapped on their helmets and walked out the green door towards the big helicopter that was already spinning its rotors on the tarmac like a giant dragon awakening.

Downing followed Parnell with her M4 rifle slung over her left shoulder and Razor on her right. She jingled along the apron with the standard loadout of 210 rounds of ammunition, her body armor, flashlight, water bottles and a small knife. Razor was trained as an attack canine and wore a special vest that held a GPS tracker, camera and microphone so Downing could communicate with him and watch his actions. "First on, last off!" Parnell yelled at her over his shoulder above the din of the huge motors. She nodded, gave Razor a tug and together they walked up the ramp of the rumbling Chinook. She smiled inwardly. *This is why I joined the Army—the opportunity to work with dogs, to be part of something big and important, to have the chance to do some good in this messed up world.*

The metal ramp at the rear of the MH-47 was slick with oil and Razor's paws slipped until Amber gave him a small tug on the leash. Together they walked to the front of the helicopter in the cabin, dimly lit with red lights. The aircrew had set up folding aluminum and canvas bench seats along each side of the huge machine, leaving the center open. She took a seat at the end of the row behind the pilots, fastened the lap belt and snapped a carabiner onto Razor's harness, connecting him to an aluminum seat post. Parnell sat beside her as the rest of the assault force filed in and filled up the back of the cavernous helicopter. The ramp went up like the closing of a giant's mouth. With that, the big helo rumbled down the runway, and lifted off to the north into the black sky.

Razor tucked in tight between Amber's boots underneath the seat, staring up at her with dark eyes. She knew exactly what that meant—he was looking for confirmation that everything was going to be alright. If she was afraid, he would feed on that and become anxious. She rubbed his ears and tried to slow her breathing. This was not his first helicopter ride, but he always looked nervous as the 10,000 moving parts squealed and hissed. The huge aircraft probably sounded to Razor like an unnatural contraption ready to come apart at any minute.

After 25 minutes, Amber saw a small yellow light illuminate next to the ramp. She felt the helo decelerate, bank and start to turn in a slow arc. The special forces soldiers began to check their weapons, tighten helmets and prepare for the landing. The big machine shuddered as it descended quickly. Amber knew they were trying to land near the target and catch the terrorists by surprise—a quick landing was part of the plan. The big black ramp door began to open before the helo landed, revealing the faint lights of distant villages and farms. Suddenly the wheels touched down with a bump. The Special Forces soldiers quickly released their lap belts and rushed out the back of the aircraft into the inky night. Amber stood up, patted Razor to calm him and followed Parnell down the ramp into the darkness. The unmistakable smell of the Iraq war hit her; the burning of garbage, the poor sewage systems, the scent of death and explosives.

The assault team blew the outer gate off the hinges with a deafening C-4 charge and stormed inside the two-story brick building. Astute intelligence work had determined that the compound was a terrorist logistics facility. Gunfire erupted inside the house as the SF soldiers methodically cleared the lower floor interior rooms, then fought their way upstairs. Amber kept Razor close, he tugged at the leash at the sound of gunfire—sensing he was about to go to work. Sure enough, as Parnell was talking on his headset to the assault team, they reported that a single squirter had escaped out the back door of the building and jumped the brick wall surrounding the compound, heading north through open fields toward a maze of date palms. If the squirter made the cover of the dense date palm grove, he was lost to them.

Parnell spoke to Amber over the inner squad radio, "Dog 1, this is Honcho, we've got a squirter escaping behind the target, last seen heading east.

"Roger Honcho, I'm on it." Amber ran Razor to the side of the compound, pointed east, gave him the action command and let Razor off the leash. The speed, agility and drive of a well-trained Belgian Malinois almost defies gravity. Sprinting through the field, Razor picked up the scent of the man first—his nose was over 500 times more sensitive than a human. He smelled sweat, dirty clothes, a whiff of explosives, footprints in the dust, and most of all, fear. His incredible hearing sensed thrashing in the bushes 300 feet ahead. He turned course slightly, put his head down and sprinted like a cheetah.

Standing near the side of the compound, Amber was tracking Razor on a special electronic tablet. The screen background was a detailed topographic map of the area. Razor's GPS collar was reflected as a blue dot, moving quickly east across the screen. When the blue dot stopped, Amber knew what happened next. Her heart raced as she visualized Razor executing the training they had practiced together for over a year.

Razor could see the target now. The man ran 50 yards ahead through waist-high fields, approaching a stand of trees. The sight of the target gave Razor a final burst of energy—he closed the gap in less than five seconds. The man had just made it to the edge of the date palm farm. He stopped to catch his breath, standing for a moment with his hands on his hips, looking back towards the dim lights of the compound. Suddenly two yellow eyes came barreling towards him out of the dark field. Before he had time to turn and run, Razor leaped at full speed, hitting the man at nearly 20 mph with a mouth full of teeth. The man tried to raise the pistol he was carrying—Razor was trained to attack the weapon first. He clamped on the man's right arm, pulling him violently to the ground. With a shake of his dark head, Razor's teeth tore to the bone, the man screamed loudly and dropped the pistol.

Amber saw the blue dot stop on the screen. She pushed a button on the tablet and a second window appeared next to the map—the camera mounted on Razor's back activated. It was nearly impossible to see anything but a shaky blur while he was running, but now she could see the terrorist on his back, as Razor tore at the man's arm. "Legs, legs," yelled Amber over the microphone that Razor wore on his head. Immediately Razor let go of the man's arm and sunk his teeth into an ankle. *He won't be running now,* she thought.

Through the jerky camera, Amber saw the man on his back reach to his waist with his good hand and pull out a long dagger as Razor tore into his lower leg. She yelled "Weapon!" to Razor, but it was too late, the man swung the knife and stuck it in Razor's back. The camera went dead. Before Parnell could tell her it was too dangerous, Staff Sergeant Amber Downing took off sprinting across the field.

2

April 2012, Grand Junction, Colorado

Amber walked down the sterile hallway that smelled faintly of bleach and the odor sent her mind back to the military hospital in Ramstein Germany. She would walk the hallways in her wing of the hospital constantly wondering, *Why did this happen and why him?* The answers never came, but there was something in the asking of the questions and the slow, deliberate movement down the slick linoleum-clad hospital floor that had given her a grip on life.

Nikita, sensing her master was drifting, nudged Amber's hand with her wet black nose. Amber snapped back to the present at the touch from her service dog. "Alright girl, let's get to work," she said aloud, speaking to herself and Nikita.

The Grand Junction VA Medical Center in Western Colorado had largely avoided the stigma of unresponsive service that larger VA hospitals were known for, where veterans waited months for care, or died before they could be treated. Although there was a high percentage of Veterans in Grand Junction and the surrounding western slope of Colorado, their numbers didn't compare to the huge population of Veterans in the larger cities of Denver and Salt Lake City that served as east and west bookends to little Grand Junction.

In addition to the patient care and medical staff at the Grand Junction VA Medical Center, there was a largely unknown office in the basement that performed data analysis for the medical center. Due in part to her disability from her military service, Amber had landed the data analyst position after the Army put her out on a medical retirement. Although the job was as boring as they come, it was close to her hometown of Montrose and she didn't have to deal with other people and patients. It suited her. The leadership of the VA facility hadn't hired anyone into her position for over two years due to budget problems, but the local state congressman representing Grand Junction got a whiff of the vacancy and badgered the Department of Veterans Affairs in D.C. to fund it.

The management at the Grand Junction VA Medical Center didn't know how to utilize the position, so they just threw random projects at her: How many male patients under the age of 50 had undergone knee replacement surgery in the last five years? What demographic of veterans used prescription pain pills the most? (Everyone thought it was Vietnam vets, but it turned out to be post 9/11 vets). What percentage of female vets sought psychiatric help versus their male counterparts? Amber's favorite project was a request to figure out how many service dogs on average entered the VA during the year. It turned out that on average, 17 service dogs entered the Grand Junction VA every day.

There was one other desk in the basement office she occupied, but it was not used. She was glad for the solitude—it gave her an opportunity to let Nikita roam the empty space without bothering anyone. Nikita, a lean and ultra-attentive brown and black German

Shepherd, would lay under Amber's desk until either one of them got restless and needed to move.

Amber spun her chair around after an hour of work and grabbed a small stuffed duck on her desk. Nikita immediately sprang to attention, her eyes ablaze with readiness; it was game time. Amber tossed the duck into the far corner of the carpeted room, and Nikita sprinted for it. As Nikita rushed back with the duck, Amber had a vision of her battle-buddy, Razor, sprinting towards a target in Iraq. She pushed that memory quickly out of her mind.

At noon, Amber walked up the stairs from the basement to the cafe. The food wasn't great, but it was her one chance to be around people during the day—she rarely had any visitors to the basement. It was a slow Friday at the cafe. Nikita raised her nose at the smell of hamburgers sizzling on the grill. A few old vets were sitting at tables, sipping coffee waiting for an appointment or just hanging out.

Amber walked up to the counter where Sheri was taking orders today. Sheri usually worked Monday, Wednesday and Friday. Nikita lifted her head towards the counter, smelling Sheri's hand. "Hey Nikita, come here sweet girl," Sheri said, pulling out a dog treat from a bin below the register. Nikita reached her long nose across the counter and gently took the biscuit in her mouth. Sheri was Amber's only friend at the VA. They both grew up in the ranching and farming community of Montrose south of Grand Junction, although Sheri was about 10 years older than Amber.

"How is your dad doing, Sheri?" The last time they talked, Sheri had revealed that her father was not doing well.

Sheri reached across the counter to pet Nikita on the head before answering. "I think I'm going to have to put him in a home, but I know it will kill him. He fell down in his kitchen last week, broke his wrist. I worry about him so much."

"I'm so sorry, Sheri," Amber said. "Is there anything I can do?"

"No ... but thanks for asking, Amber. What'll it be - the usual?"

"Yes, thanks."

Sheri rang up a BLT, fries and a bottle of water. After paying, Amber picked out a table by the window. Nikita curled up under the protection of the table and rested her head on Amber's foot.

The cafe was empty now except for two vets at a corner table nursing coffees. One vet with a Marine Corps ballcap kept turning his head and looking at her. Finally he stood and walked over to her table. Nikita immediately stood up and faced the man. She was trained as a Post Traumatic Stress Disorder or PTSD service dog for Amber, but she had deep instincts to guard and protect. Amber reached down, patted her head and said in a soothing voice, "It's okay, girl."

The vet stopped at the table and Amber set her sandwich down. "I worked with German Shepherds in Vietnam," he said, looking at Nikita but speaking to Amber. "They are wonderful, loyal dogs. Do you mind if I pet him?"

Nikita wore a vest with "SERVICE DOG" and "DO NOT PET" patches, but Amber had a hard time telling people, especially veterans, that they couldn't touch her. Nikita's sparkling brown, soulful eyes and silver-black mane seemed to attract people. It was that deep connection man had with wolves and now dogs that drew people to her. As he stuck out his hand, Nikita laid her ears back—she wasn't afraid of him. On rare occasions, Nikita growled at someone and showed her formidable teeth. She wasn't supposed to do that as a service dog, but Amber knew that deep down there was a fiercely loyal streak in Nikita that sometimes sensed danger. Amber could live with the occasional wolf bubbling to the surface. The service dog trainer where Amber had been given Nikita had suggested she select a Golden Retriever. "They are so sweet," he had implored. But she was undeterred. She chose the German Shepherd. *Sometimes you need a dog that's not all sweetness,* she thought to herself, remembering Razor.

The USMC veteran stopped petting Nikita and turned to Amber. "A Shepherd saved my life in Nam. I was on a perimeter patrol at our firebase and a Viet Cong soldier was hiding by the fence. My dog Angel, running ahead of me, sniffed out the intruder and I was able to get the drop on 'im before he could raise his weapon. How long have you had 'im?" he asked.

"She's a female...I've had her for a year now." Almost everyone assumed Nikita was a male. Amber knew that female German Shepherds could be high strung, but she fell in love with Nikita during the first visit to the service dog training facility. The old vet nodded and returned to his seat. Amber waved at Sheri and headed downstairs.

Back at her desk, Amber noticed a new email from her supervisor, John Hutson, labeled "Important". He asked her to come up to his office that afternoon to discuss a new project. She was immediately curious; all previous tasks had been sent to her by email. She clipped the leash on Nikita and headed up the stairs, wondering what was up.

3

Sprinting through the open field strewn with water bottles and old tires, Amber raced toward Razor, her heart pounding. She knew Parnell wouldn't send out troops to help Razor until the target house was cleared. That could take another fifteen minutes. Razor couldn't wait that long. Her headset crackled, "Dog 1, this is Honcho, where are you?" It was Parnell.

"Razor is down ... I'm heading in his direction behind the compound," she responded in short breaths as she ran.

"Negative, Dog 1, return to the compound, we'll send out a team to help the dog."

"I'm almost there, Honcho, I'll retrieve him and return."

Parnell was furious. He couldn't risk having Amber killed or captured. It would be a disaster. "Goddammit, Dog 1, get your ass back here NOW!"

Amber ignored the order, she was almost there. She could see Razor lying near the edge of a stand of trees. She rushed up to him, yanked off her small backpack and pulled out the canine medic kit from her vest. Kneeling beside him, she could see sticky blood trickling out of his left side through matted hair and pooling into the dark soil. He didn't raise his head—he just looked up at her with those golden eyes. She tore open the kit, pulled out a large bandage saturated with a coagulant and placed it over the wound. "You're going to be OKAY, boy," she spoke soothingly to him. She grabbed a roll of heavy gauze and began to wrap it tight around Razor's waist, putting pressure on the dressing and holding it in place. Razor kept his eyes on her the whole time. Suddenly, he growled.

4

APRIL 2012, GRAND JUNCTION, COLORADO

Amber walked upstairs with a little trepidation. She had never been called to her boss's office. Nikita's claws made a clicking sound as her paws sought purchase on the freshly waxed floor. *What kind of project would be labeled Important?* She had no reason to be nervous, but she also didn't like the way John looked at her.

John Hutson was the GJ VA Hospital Administrator. As far as everyone knew, he had no medical background. In fact, he had been a Navy Corpsman in the Gulf War, though he rarely spoke of it and kept no Navy memorabilia in his office. He'd moved up through the byzantine ranks of the federal employment system and landed the slot as head of the Grand Junction VA after a stint as a staffer at VA headquarters in D.C. A short, round man, John had only been on the job for a year.

Hutson's secretary, a petite blonde with long nails painted with dark pink flamingos, waved Amber into the office. Amber had never been to this suite before. The door was open, but she knocked anyway. John looked up from his computer, stared at her a split second, noticed Nikita then looked back at Amber. Amber was used to that look that men often gave her. She'd become an expert at reading it in the

Army. Most men saw her as a beautiful woman first and a soldier second. She was blessed with high cheekbones, piercing blue eyes, long sand-colored hair and a figure she was not able to hide. Hutson had been looking her up and down, but quickly tried to retreat to his 'professional' demeanor.

"Amber, sit down, please," John said, standing up and pointing to one of two chairs in front of his gaudy metal and glass desk. She chose the seat on the right as it allowed Nikita, who always heeled on the left, to easily lay down next to her. Amber was on alert—*Why am I here?*

"I have a project for you," said the administrator, sitting up in his chair and leaning forward. His feet were dangling off the ground in his chair, Amber noticed, so he could appear taller at his desk. He waited a moment, deciding how to proceed, fiddling with a pen on his desk. "Given the situation with your fiancé, I wanted to discuss this with you in person."

Amber tried to hide it, but her heart began to race and she went flush. Only a handful of people knew that her fiancé had committed suicide. *It must be in my VA medical file,* she thought with some trepidation. *Does he have access to my medical file?*

John leaned forward trying to gauge her reaction. "We've been tasked with collecting data on veteran suicides in this area. I know this is sensitive for you..." he paused and waited for her to respond.

"Thank you, Mr. Hutson."

"Call me John, please," he said with a phony smile that Amber found cheesy.

"Thank you, John ... the issue of my fiancé's death is difficult for me, but the subject of suicide is not. I'm passionate about doing anything I can to stem the tide of suicides among veterans. I'm all ears, so what've you got for me?" She made herself sound a lot more enthusiastic than she was.

"The job is to collect information on suicides in this geographic area. Headquarters has given us data fields to be collected. It's mostly innocuous facts like date, time, location of the veteran ... stuff like that. But there are also a few, shall I say, sensitive data fields," he said, clasping his hands together on the desk.

"Such as?" Amber asked, sensing that she was not going to like his answer.

"Well ... they want to know how the veteran committed suicide ... you know, gunshot, overdose, etc. There's also a data field that I objected to, but they insist we just do our best. They want us to try and determine *why* the veteran committed suicide." He let that sit in the air to see how Amber reacted.

"John, that is completely unreasonable, if not totally unknowable," Amber protested, wondering what kind of an idiot would come up with that request.

"I know, Amber, we pushed back on this, but Headquarters is insistent that we at least try to get some information for each veteran. That's why I wanted to talk this out with you," he said, sitting back in his chair, glancing down at her legs and waiting for her to respond.

"I don't know how I would even approach that, John," she said, as her gut tightened thinking about how she would have to dig into the details of each suicide.

"No, I get it. All I ask is that you make an attempt, OK? Just read the files, do your best, talk to people who knew the veteran, that sort of thing." He made it sound like she was going to interview people for a job, not delve into the darkest elements of the tortured human psyche.

She didn't know what to say. Did he even have a clue what this would entail? How it would force Amber to walk across the chasm of Chris's death every day? Amber was, if anything, meticulous and thorough. She would have to talk to the family, friends and former military teammates to try to get to the bottom of the reason for the suicides. Just the thought of the task made her head spin.

"How far back do they want us to go?" she asked, afraid it might reach back to Vietnam or something crazy like that.

John put his hands flat on the desk, clearly sensing Amber's anxiety. "It only goes back five years. I think they're interested in the effects of the last years of the Afghanistan and Iraq wars."

Five years was not too bad, thought Amber. "How many veteran suicides are we looking at in this area?" she asked, getting to the heart of the matter.

John rearranged the papers on his desk before answering. "A hundred and forty two. If you finish one a day, you could be done in six months." He obviously had no idea what it would take to try to understand why these people took their own lives. She realized there was no use arguing with him.

"So I assume they gave us six months to finish this?" she asked cynically, seeing in her mind's eye how her summer would now go.

"They actually gave us eight months. I'm giving you seven—that'll leave me a month to review your data and come back to you with any questions. So I need your completed project on October 1st. I'll send you the spreadsheet right now." He turned to his computer, clicked a few buttons and sent it to Amber. "Well that's it. Anything else I can do for you?" he asked, staring too long at her chest.

"No, thanks," she said, standing up, with Nikita following her lead. "I'll let you know if I hit any snags." Walking back downstairs to her cubicle, Amber knew she would have to move past denial if she was going to be able to get started on this. She sat down at her desk, opened her laptop and saw the email from John. Then it hit her, *another poor schmuck at the VA in San Diego would be contacting me to understand what happened to Chris*. Just the thought of that conversation made her despair. She closed the laptop. It was Friday. *I'm outta here.*

5

April 2012, Montrose, Colorado

Amber punched the steering wheel in anger. The hard plastic wheel left a dent in her knuckle and hurt like hell. Nikita stuck her head into the front seat wondering what was going on. "You have got to be kidding me!" Amber said out loud. "Of all the tasks they could have given me." She started the truck and drove out of the VA Medical Center parking lot. "I guess I could just quit," she said looking back at Nikita. Nikita turned her head slightly, as if trying to understand what her master was saying. Amber sighed, turned on the I-70 bypass towards Montrose and headed home. As she mulled over the project or the possibility of quitting her job, it came to her. She couldn't quit, she never quit at anything. She would complete the project with the same detachment she used in the Army when dealing with anything that bothered her.

It took Amber nearly an hour to drive home, but she liked living near her hometown of Montrose. The little farming and ranching community where she'd grown up had become a bustling hub on the Western Slope and the gateway to Telluride and Crested Butte for tourists, skiers and lovers of outdoor sports. Many of the newcomers had relocated from the Denver area, California and Texas, enticed by the lower cost of living and to escape big city traffic and crime. She'd purchased a small log cabin on five acres nestled into the foothills of the Uncompahgre Plateau just north of town. The pinyon pine-covered yard gave Nikita a great place to run and chase rabbits. It felt like home to her.

The beginning of spring brought hope for warmer weather to the area, but patches of snow covered the ground in the shade of trees as Amber drove up her long gravel driveway. Two deer darted in front of her truck as she approached the small cabin, causing Nikita to bark. On the way home from work, she'd called her friend Hannah—they would meet for burgers and drinks at The Horsefly Brewing Company at 7:30. Amber wanted some company after the turn of events at work today. The thought of the pending project put a knot in her gut.

She opened the back door of her Toyota Tacoma and Nikita jumped out like she was on fire and raced around the house to make her rounds and check for animals on her property. It occurred to Amber that she had paid for the house, but Nikita owned it. Nikita knew every dip, valley, rock, bush and tree. She defended the property from other animals and people. Like it or not, Amber knew that's what you get with a German Shepherd.

Amber opened the front door which led immediately to a stairway to the main floor. She left her coat on a hook by the door, walked up the stairs and felt the chill in the cabin. The old cast iron wood stove was cold. Amber sat on the weathered wood floor next to the stove and set about building a small fire. *This might be my last fire of the year,* she thought. The whole cabin was one square room with stairs on the right side leading down to the home's entrance and garage underneath. The main floor above the garage held the kitchen, two small bedrooms, the bathroom and a small living room. The high peaked roof allowed room for a bank of south-facing windows on the front of the cabin that picked up the morning sun and a partial view of the San Juan Mountains. The small deck in front of the windows was her favorite place to hang out when the weather was fine. It was a simple cabin, clad in local timber, but it felt homey and safe to Amber.

After she got the fire roaring, Amber opened the front door and yelled for Nikita. There were mountain lions, bobcats, lynx, coyotes and even bears in the area. She never left Nikita out for too long by herself. "Come on, girl!" she called out. In a few moments Nikita came running from behind the cabin with an enthusiasm that reminded Amber of Razor.

She stepped into the cabin and Nikita shot ahead of her, stopping at her bowl and staring up at Amber with big brown eyes. Anyone who thinks dogs can't communicate well hasn't spent enough time with them. Amber poured out a cup and a half of kibble into Nikita's bowl, gave her water, then poured herself a glass of white wine and sat down on the couch facing the windows and mountains.

Nikita wolfed down her food then came bounding out of the kitchen, leaped up and curled on the couch, setting her paws on Amber's lap, staring out the window scanning for animals. Amber called it deer TV. She set her hand on Nikita's back and began to stroke her thick fur. She finally allowed herself to think about the conversation with her boss and the looming project again. *How was she ever going to approach those people who lost a loved one to suicide? Hey, you don't know me, but I was just wondering why your son killed himself? The sheer audacity of the senior managers who came up with this absurd task was amazing.* Finally, one positive thought came to her about the project: *Maybe somehow this data will be put to use to prevent veteran suicides. I hope to hell this doesn't just go into some big circular file at VA Headquarters.*

As much as she tried, she couldn't help but let her thoughts drift to Chris. They'd met in Baghdad where he was assigned to an infantry brigade. He'd sat down next to her one day at the chow hall and started up a conversation, without trying to hit on her.

She remembered how he'd set his cardboard tray down and politely asked, "Do you mind if I sit here?"

She was feeling down after a recent mission where she had seen a small boy hit and killed by a car driven by an insurgent who fled from a checkpoint. She was not in a great mood for conversation. "Knock yourself out."

"I can't tell if this is chicken or one of the pigeons flying around here," he smiled at her, poking at his meat with a plastic fork.

"Well, it sure beats T-Rats," she said, hinting that she didn't really want to have a conversation.

"You got that right. I'm Chris, by the way. Chris Hawkins."

She turned reluctantly to get a better look at him. He was about 5'11", lean, with short cropped sandy hair, and the kindest eyes she had ever seen. They were golden and reminded Amber of the sun glinting off a brown trout wiggling at the end of her fly line.

"I'm Amber," she said, "Staff Sergeant Amber Downing." He was charming, sweet and funny. He had grown up in San Diego as a self-described surf bum, defied everyone's expectations and joined the Army after two years in college. He felt he was wasting his time studying chemistry and wanted to get out and make a difference in the world.

They started eating dinner together at the chow hall whenever they weren't in the field. He was a good listener and was really interested in Amber's life and work as a military working dog handler. After nine months together in Iraq, he ordered a ring from the States and proposed to her. It's hard to find natural beauty in a bustling industrial military base in the Green Zone of Iraq, but she and Chris would meet out in a barren field and watch the sunset whenever they could. It was there that he proposed to her. They had never even spent a night together, living in separate barracks, but she had a gut feeling he was the one for her.

***

Amber looked at her watch; it was 7 p.m.—time to head to the brewery to meet Hannah. She whistled for Nikita, who leaped off the couch, sensing that there was an imminent car ride. Together they drove down the dark forest road to downtown Montrose.

Amber stepped into the brew pub and scanned the room, looking for her friend. She saw several heads turn to look at her. Either her service dog or her looks always drew unwanted attention. She spotted Hannah at a corner table near the window, nodded and made her way through the busy restaurant, Nikita faithfully at her side.

"Hello, girl," Hannah said as she stood and bent down to give Nikita a pat on the head. Nikita ignored her and found a tasty crumb under the table. The two women embraced and sat down.

Hannah was wearing a sexy, tight-fitting wool dress and a colorful scarf. Her green eyes sparkled and her short black hair was cut perfectly. *She always dresses so nice.* Amber was wearing blue jeans and a sweatshirt. There were already two glasses of red wine on the table—Hannah had come early and ordered, knowing that Amber liked her merlot.

"How've you been? What's going on at work? Don't let me forget; I want to tell you about this new adventure we have to do." Hannah shot out a staccato of questions. She had an exuberant personality that contrasted with Amber's more somber demeanor.

The two friends had met years ago when they were both on active duty in the Army stationed at Fort Bragg serving as military police officers. Amber had been training to be a military working dog handler and Hannah was working security on base. Amber had signed up for a 10K running race on base, ran into Hannah at the start and the two became instant friends. When Amber received orders to Iraq as a military working dog handler, Hannah herself received orders to Iraq to work in the security forces one month later. After overlapping tours in Iraq, they both got out of the Army about the same time. Hannah decided to settle in Montrose after Amber had described what a great little town it was—Hannah was done with big cities.

Amber wanted to talk to Hannah about the new project at work, but she knew Chris's suicide would come up. When a fellow MP had taken his own life at Fort Bragg, Hannah had confided privately to Amber that she thought the soldier was weak. The two women had very different views on suicide. Amber plunged ahead, she needed to talk this out. "Well, to be honest, Hannah, I'm struggling with a new project they gave me."

"What've they tasked you with this time? Counting how many crutches they gave out this year?" Amber felt that Hannah demeaned her job at the VA and thought it was beneath her abilities. Hannah had tried to convince her to join the Montrose Police Department as a dog handler, since Amber had the training and experience from the Army, but Amber didn't want to carry a gun anymore and deal with confrontations. She'd had enough of that in Iraq.

"No, they gave me a crazy task to track veteran suicides in our area for the last five years."

Hannah's face tightened as she took a sip of wine to hide it. The issue of Chris's suicide had been difficult for both of them, but for different reasons. "But that's not the bad part," continued Amber, taking a sip of her wine. "They expect me to figure out *why* each veteran committed suicide!"

"What? That is insane, girl. What are they smoking up there in Grand Junction?"

"This actually comes from VA Headquarters. So every poor sap like me at a VA hospital has to deal with this."

Amber shook her head in dismay. Hannah reached across the table and put her hand on Amber's. "Hey, hey, Amber, you can do this, girl. Look at everything you've done. This is just a paperwork drill. There's no bullets flying, right? This isn't Iraq. You can do this with one arm tied behind your back!" For all of Hannah's encouragement, Amber knew this was a terrible project for her. It would immerse her in the inscrutable darkness of suicide for God knew how long.

"Hey, remember I suggested we go whitewater rafting this summer? We live so close to all this fantastic outdoor adventure, we need to take advantage of it. I found this non-profit, Warriors on the Cataract, they take veterans down the Colorado and Green Rivers, what do you say?" Hannah's enthusiasm was refreshing to Amber. She had a constant thirst for new adventures. Amber admired her attitude and wished she could be a little more on top of things like Hannah was.

Amber smiled, "Yeah, okay, that sounds fun; let's plan it. How's work for you, anyway?"

"I'm still on patrol. I mostly do traffic stops and accidents—there's never a dull moment. Once in a while I pull over some crackhead, but mostly it's little old ladies driving too slow or high school kids showing off."

"And how's Brian doing?" Amber asked. Brian Dixon was a cop in Grand Junction and Hannah's on-again, off-again boyfriend. Hannah and Brian had met in the Army at Military Police (MP) school and kept up the relationship. Amber wasn't fond of him—she thought Brian was too controlling and jealous—but she tried to keep her feelings to herself. She would never tell Hannah her thoughts about Brian, but she figured Hannah already knew.

"He's been promoted to sergeant. I mentioned our possible raft trip this summer and he wants to come along."

Oh boy, thought Amber. *Here we go again. Will he ever let Hannah off the leash?* Amber didn't respond, out of respect for her friend. She would have liked to say, "Tell him to take a hike, this is a girl's trip, for once." But she kept her thoughts to herself.

The two friends planned to meet again next week. Despite Hannah's unbounded optimism, Amber didn't feel any better about the upcoming work project. She drove up the dark driveway, opened the door and plunked down on the couch. Nikita curled up next to her as Amber stared at the red embers glowing in the wood stove. Amber recalled the conversation with her friend. Hannah had tried to give her encouragement about the new project, but Amber sensed something else in Hannah's eyes when she heard about the project, something she couldn't pin down. Amber fell asleep wondering about that just as a pack of coyotes trotted silently through her property on the hunt.

6

SEPTEMBER 2008, SALADIN PROVINCE, IRAQ

When Razor growled, Amber stopped wrapping the medical tape around his chest, turned to look over her shoulder, and immediately felt a blow to the back of her head before she could see anything. At the same moment, Master Sergeant Parnell's team completed the assault on the compound. Parnell ordered the Explosive Ordnance Disposal operators to check the place for booby traps and for the exploitation team to follow up behind EOD when the house was clear to gather any intelligence or evidence they could find.

Parnell barked orders to one of his fire team leaders over the radio. In a few seconds, three soldiers ran out the front door and met Parnell. He gave them a quick brief on where Sergeant Downing had headed after her dog, they nodded and followed Parnell, running behind the compound and into the fields. It was a black night, but Parnell could see the edge of the palm forest where the squirter would have aimed for. He looked back at the soldiers, pointed to the treeline and sped up.

They reached the trees, spread out and started to search around the ground with red lens flashlights, looking for clues. Sergeant Johnson's excited voice came over the radio, "I've got the dog."

Parnell and the other three closed in on Razor. Johnson, a high school wrestling champion from Oklahoma, was kneeling over the dog. He saw a wound dressing on the dog's side that had been partially placed by Sergeant Downing. Copper-scented blood oozed slowly from the wound, yet the dog remained alive.

"Any of you guys know how to IV a dog?" Johnson asked, looking at the soldiers standing over him.

"Yeah, I watched a dog handler do it once," said Sergeant Thompson. "I'll do it." Thompson grew up in foster care in Alabama. He was the only black soldier in the Company, and the radioman. He was also trained as a medic.

"Give me some light, guys," Thompson said as he kneeled down and took out his own IV bag from a pouch. Next he pulled out a needle and rubber tubing, found a vein on the dog's paw, and plunged the needle into Razor. "Hold this up," he told Johnson, handing him the IV bag as he plugged the fluid into the hose leading to Razor's paw.

Parnell and the other two soldiers were scanning the edge of the forest, looking for any sign of where Downing had gone. Parnell spotted a flashlight lying near the base of a tree—definitely Downing's Army issued light. He shined his light between the trees and saw a clear path through the murky palm forest. Twilight was just around the corner. He had a big decision to make.

The man walked through the dark stand of trees with Amber slumped over his shoulder. *This is a great opportunity, inshallah,* thought Khalid Al Thine or KAT as he was known to US intelligence. KAT was a mid-level operative with Al Qaeda in Iraq, known as AQI, for short, to the Americans. KAT was moving up the chain of command fast due to his cunning and ruthlessness. Two weeks ago he had organized the bombing of a busload of Shia school girls. That earned him instant infamy in the eyes of the Americans, which automatically led to his promotion within the murky and fluid ranks of AQI.

KAT assessed his wounds. That devil hound had torn up his wrist and ankle, but he could still move. He had taken a chance with this soldier, it was an opportunity too good to pass up. He'd crept up on her as she was concentrating on the dog's wounds. He was within five feet of her when the dog lifted his head and growled. He'd lunged and whacked the soldier on the back of her head with the butt of his pistol before she could turn and face him. The wounded dog lay motionless, growling at the man he had fought with, but clearly unable to stand. *Good, let him bleed out and suffer.* He grabbed the soldier under her arms and dragged her into the dense forest of trees. He had to move fast now. He knew the soldiers would be coming.

7

April 2012, Grand Junction, Colorado

B ack in her underground VA office on Monday, Amber checked email, made a pot of coffee, fiddled with her lumbar seat knob, checked the calendar and adjusted the temperature in the room—basically anything to avoid starting the project that her boss had given her. Finally, when she could no longer procrastinate, she opened the spreadsheet from VA Headquarters. She stared at it for a good minute. *How do you eat an elephant? One bite at a time.*

Amber sighed and started to review the data fields. She moved to the top of the spreadsheet and scrolled down to get a sense of the 142 names, noting that about three quarters of the names appeared to be men. Even though this was a drop in the bucket of all veteran suicides, she was still shocked at the pages and pages of names from this remote part of Colorado and Utah.

Next she moved back to the top of the spreadsheet and studied each of the data fields. Several of the columns along the left side were already filled in by VA Headquarters, *thank goodness.* These were easily accessible data from the service member's record or VA file. They included rank, date of birth, age, branch of service, social security number, next of kin, last contact for next of kin, place of death and date of death. As she moved right, she saw that most of those remaining columns were blank. This was the information they expected her to gather.

She began to closely study these headings. The first was the location of death. They already had a column for the place of death, so what was this? She scrolled to the bottom where there was an explanation and instructions for each data field. Place of death refers to the city, town, state, etc. where the service member died. For the location of death, they wanted the exact physical location: bedroom, bathroom, backyard, garage, county park … *geez who came up with this?*

Next up was the method. *What a lousy word. It sounds so sterile.* She read the instructions again. Here they wanted to know how the service member committed suicide. The instructions laid out the requirement to capture as much detail as possible for each method. As examples they listed the following, "Gunshot to the right side of the head using a Colt .45 semi-automatic, overdose of oxycontin prescribed by Doctor XX, driving a 1979 Ford Pinto over a cliff. *You've got to be shitting me!*

The next column made her heart sink: reason for suicide. *Here the idiots expect me to get into the mind of the service member.* The examples they gave made her want to laugh and cry at the same time: service member was overcome by PTSD, service member was unable to deal with a moral injury. *Moral injury? She needed to study that more.* Service member was unable to cope with a failed relationship, service member was unable to integrate back into civilian society. *I've got a combination of all of these,* she thought with a measure of gallows humor.

The last column was labeled contributing factors. Here again they expected her to be part sleuth and part psychiatrist. The examples given were alcohol abuse, prescription drug dependence, illegal drug use, divorce, bankruptcy, etc. Amber stood up and walked around the small office deep in thought. Nikita immediately stood up from under the desk, stretched her long legs and walked beside Amber as if glued to her left side. She finally realized that very little of the information she had to collect was available online. She had been holding to an irrational hope that somehow she would be able to complete this project without talking to friends and families of the service member. Now she knew that was not going to work. The true implications of the project hit her like a blast of cold air. She sat back down at her desk and put her head in her hands. Sensing Amber's distress, Nikita put her wet nose next to Amber's face and licked her ear.

After a few minutes of denial, Amber recovered her composure. *I can do this,* she told herself, "There are no bullets flying, you can do this girl," she recalled Hannah's words. She opened the spreadsheet and studied the first name on the alphabetical list: Appleton, Jason, Marine, age 24, died December 2010 in Moab, UT. The parents were listed as next of kin, with an address and phone number in Moab. Before she called them, Amber had an idea to search the internet for any news articles relating to the death or funeral that might provide information and insight. She punched in Jason Appleton US Marine and landed on a page full of entries. She scrolled until she found an article in the *Moab Sun News* listing an obituary for Appleton containing the highlights of his short life and a picture of him in Marine dress blues. He looked so young with a proud smile and a high and tight. There was no mention of suicide in the obituary—there never is. The article stated that he died at home, so that was one piece she needed. There wasn't much more useful information. She had to make the first call, but before she did, Amber kneeled down and gave Nikita a hug. "We can do this together," she whispered to her best friend.

A woman's voice answered the phone. "Hello, Mrs. Appleton?"

"Yes."

"My name is Amber Downing from the VA Medical Center in Grand Junction. We're trying to reduce suicides among veterans and I wonder if I might speak with you about Jason for a moment." She had come up with that introduction as a more meaningful way to approach the next of kin. She couldn't just say, "I'm tasked with collecting some information to fill out a stupid spreadsheet."

There was silence for a moment before Mrs. Appleton spoke. "What exactly can I help you with, Amber?"

Amber went on, using her own script. "In order for us to develop improved strategies to prevent veteran suicides, we need to better understand the suicides of our brothers and sisters. I was in the Army for 10 years, Mrs. Appleton, and am very passionate about preventing veteran suicides. I've seen too many, including my own fiancé." She hadn't planned to mention Chris, it just sort of came out in her attempt to build trust with Mrs. Appleton. A knot formed in her stomach.

Again there was a momentary silence before Jason's mother spoke. "I'm sorry, dear, but what do you need from me?"

"If you could help me understand a few things, it might make a difference someday for another veteran." There was no response, so Amber continued, figuring she would start with the most important issue. "Do you have any idea why your son took his own life?"

There was another painful pause. Amber was sure the woman had hung up or maybe even fainted. Finally, Mrs. Appleton spoke. "Jason's convoy was attacked in Afghanistan. He survived the blast but came home with a traumatic brain injury. He just wasn't the same. I thought he was on the mend until that day in December. It was the anniversary of the blast. I think he felt guilty about surviving when most of his squad was killed."

The next question made Amber's stomach turn thinking about it. She could imagine the black despair she would feel if someone asked her this about Chris. Finally Amber spoke softly, "Thank you so much, ma'am, that will help a lot. In the newspaper, it said Jason died at home. Can you give me any more information about how he died?" She wasn't sure if that was the best way to phrase the question, but she would work on it for next time.

"He shot himself, dear ... with a shotgun to the chest." Amber could hear the pain in the mother's voice. *I'm not going to ask any more ridiculous questions like the make and model of the shotgun,* she thought. But she did need to know the location.

"Did it happen in your home?" she asked, trying to soften the question and give Mrs. Appleton the space to answer as she wanted.

"No, it was in the backyard, behind the barn."

Amber waited a few moments. "I am so sorry for your loss, Mrs. Appleton. If there is anything I can do for you, I'll leave you my number so you can get in touch with me."

Amber put the phone down as a swirl of emotions coursed through her body. The obituary picture of Corporal Appleton was still up on her computer screen. She stared at the young Marine, envisioning him graduating boot camp with great pride as his family stood around and gave him hugs and congratulations and took him out to dinner at a Mexican restaurant with his sister and cousins. She wished she had a way to honor his life beyond just detailing his death. Then an idea came to her. *I'll keep a separate electronic folder just for me on each of these veterans. I'll put their picture in the file and anything I think is important that is not part of the official project.* She quickly created the separate file system and built the first entry page for Jason Appleton. After copying and pasting his newspaper photo, she typed some notes from the obituary and her conversation with his mother. She ended the entry with these questions of her own: *Did he receive proper treatment for his PTSD and TBI? Why was he living at home? Was his disability so bad that his parents had to take care of him? Was he in contact with any of his Marine buddies? Did he leave a note or confide in anyone before the suicide?* She had so many questions, she could have gone on for two pages, but she stopped, realizing she had 141 more suicides to study. *Heaven help me!*

Thoughts of Chris started to squeeze into her consciousness, like black sludge seeping under a door, but she couldn't let them in, not now, not here. She had to stay focused. She couldn't think of him and complete this work—she might come off the rails.

She looked at her watch; it was 2 p.m.—she'd worked right through lunch. She grabbed a power bar from her desk and a bottle of water for a quick snack, then took Nikita out back to a grassy spot behind the hospital for a break. It gave her some time to process that first data entry as Nikita ran around, sniffed the grass and chased birds that lazily lifted off as she ran at them. Amber felt pretty good about the call to Mrs. Appleton. It had gone better than she'd expected. But in her gut she knew for every case that seemed easy, another would tear her heart out.

8

SEPTEMBER 2008, SALADIN PROVINCE, IRAQ

Amber awoke groggy, feeling like a hammer was pounding on the inside of her head. She surveyed the room. Cement basement, filthy, rusty metal drums along the walls, a stale odor of death. Flecks of dust floated in the air, spotlighted by the stream of light pouring in from a high window. She heard footsteps on the low floor above. *Where am I? What happened?* Then she remembered. Helping Razor, the growl, a blow to her head, then darkness.

She tried to move, but her left arm was chained to the cement wall. Her right arm was free, a bottle of water sat at her side. She reached for the bottle, her arm stiff, like something was out of joint. She grabbed it, bit the dirty cap with her teeth and twisted it off. The water was warm, but clean. She gulped down half the bottle then set it on the ground.

A door creaked to her right, and she turned to see a man in an Arab robe walking toward her. Short beard, flowing Arab head covering, beads in his right hand. Dead eyes.

He walked over, pulled a folding chair off the wall and sat down in front of her. He stared at her a moment, then spoke in decent English with a thick accent, "Inshallah, you are our prisoner."

"Where is my dog?" she asked, feeling suddenly dizzy.

"I left your heathen animal to die by my wound. You, however, are valuable to us."

She squeezed her eyes shut, thinking of Razor bleeding out in that dirty field. *Show no emotion to these assholes.*

"No harm will come to you, if you will do as I direct," he said sitting in front of her, rolling his black beads between his fingers, his eyes like two chips of charcoal.

Amber looked at him for a moment then shook her head in regret and disgust for letting herself get captured like this.

"Your soldiers have been killing my people who have been captured," he said. "You are lucky, I will not do the same to you, you will be a bargaining chip."

Amber's regret was giving way to anger. "Americans don't kill unarmed civilians, that's how I know you're lying about everything," she spat.

A smile started at one corner of his mouth and rose into a smirk, "You Americans are so self-righteous. You think you are always the good guys. Believe me, this is a fact, your soldiers are murderers."

He stood up, reached into a cardboard box, took out another bottle of water and set it on the ground next to Amber. Then he was gone.

Amber pulled at the chain and cuff on her wrist. It wouldn't loosen. She looked around the dirt floor for anything she could use. Nothing, the floor had been swept.

What did he say about soldiers killing unarmed civilians? Impossible. He's trying to mess with my head, get me to cave and cooperate. It won't happen.

9

May 2012, Grand Junction, Colorado

Back in the office, Amber was ready to get back to the project. No delay tactics this time, she fired up a cup of coffee and got right to work. Her next case was Jerry Arnold, an Army sergeant who had been deployed to Iraq like her, but unlike her Baghdad tour, Arnold spent half his deployment out west in Al Qa'im, a wild town on the border with Syria that was home to a strong Al Qaeda presence. Later in his deployment, his unit was posted to Baghdad. She started with a Google search and found a few tidbits: his mother lives in Fruita, just 12 miles down the road, he was a high school football star quarterback and much loved by the community, he was in the infantry, and was 26 years old when he took his life. Amber copied his high school yearbook photo and pasted it into her private file. She stared at his picture, trying to see how his life had come undone so quickly. There were no clues. She picked up the phone.

It rang seven times and Amber was about to hang up when a deep female voice said, "Hello."

"Hello, is this Mrs. Arnold?"

"Yes."

"My name is Amber Downing. I'm a former soldier and now work here at the VA Medical Center in Grand Junction. We're conducting a study to try and reduce veteran suicides. I was hoping I would be able to ask you a few questions about your son Jerry."

"Listen, lady, I don't know who you are and whatever you tell me over the phone means nothing. For all I know you're a scammer or a reporter."

"I totally get it, Mrs. Arnold. If you would allow me, I will come to your home and present my credentials. You can also look me up under the staff on the Grand Junction VA website." Amber hadn't intended to set up a face-to-face interview, but she understood why Jerry's mother would be reluctant to talk to a stranger over the phone.

She waited for Mrs. Arnold to finally speak. "I guess that'll be OK. You can come by this afternoon, better to get this over with. I don't want to be layin' in my bed all night wonderin' what you're up to. I don't get much sleep anyways, after what happened to my Jerry."

"I understand. Thank you very much, Mrs. Arnold. I have your address here in the system. I'll come by about 3 p.m."

Amber started a file on the next veteran, a Navy petty officer who served on several aircraft carriers. But she kept thinking about the meeting with the soldier's mother that afternoon. A knot built up in her gut the more she thought about asking those hyper-sensitive questions face-to-face with Mrs. Arnold. *What if she got angry at the questions? How would I cope with that?* Those feelings of angst opened the basement door to the terrible questions she'd tried to bury as deep as she could: *Why did Chris take his own life? Could I have done anything to prevent it? Was our love not good enough? Didn't I matter to him? How could he leave me alone like this?* She recognized the ascending self-pity in her questions but was unable to deal with it. His death had left a red gash in her life. Tears welled up in the corners of her deep blue eyes and rolled down her cheeks.

Nikita sensed something was amiss in Amber's increased heart rate, the long breaths, and the tears; she knew by training and instinct that something was wrong with her master. She sat up and put her head on Amber's lap. Dogs actually have several distinct facial expressions, particularly seen in their eyes. In their 30,000 years of living with man, they have learned how to sense human emotions. Amber smiled at the soft, wet nose on her lap. She bent over and gave Nikita a kiss and rubbed her ears. "Thank you girl, thank you."

Mrs. Arnold lived down 23 ½ road. *Who comes up with half a road as an address?* Amber thought. This part of Fruita was built on dry, brown adobe clay. There were very few trees or plants as she drove east up the thin dirt road, dust swirling in her wake. The place looked like the surface of the moon minus the craters. She passed a few scattered manufactured homes with beat-up old trucks in the yard, until she came to a small white, mid-century farmhouse. A four-foot chain link fence ran around the gravel landscape. A few brightly colored yard gnomes guarded the battered house. Amber checked the address again on her phone—this was it. She pulled into the short driveway and parked. *Should I bring Nikita in? I could use her support, but I don't want to throw off Mrs. Arnold. What if she has a house cat who wouldn't appreciate a big German Shepherd on her territory?* She decided she needed her best friend with her regardless.

Mrs. Arnold answered the door as if she'd been waiting behind it, ready to swing it open. She was a large woman, not overweight, just linebacker big. *No wonder her son was a star on the football team.* She wore an apron over blue jeans and a green sweater—flecks of flour dusted her brown hair. She looked at Amber and Nikita then back to Amber. "Come in, please." *First hurdle complete.*

She led them into a small living room that had a nice view of the Book Cliff Mountains. The tall red rock faces looked like a shelf of books. The place smelled faintly of cookies baking. Mrs. Arnold motioned for Amber to sit in the armchair, which she did, making sure Nikita lay down next to her. Mrs. Arnold ignored Nikita. Amber found people either gushed over her service dog or ignored Nikita completely—there was very little middle ground.

"Thank you so much for seeing me, Mrs. Arnold," Amber began, breathing deeply to calm her nerves. "This is my VA ID card," she said, handing the card that hung on a lanyard around her neck to Jerry's mother. Mrs. Arnold glanced at it and nodded.

"As I mentioned on the phone, we're trying to prevent veteran suicides by gathering key information that can help us establish new programs and strategies."

"OK, what was your name again?" Mrs. Arnold interrupted before Amber could finish her introduction.

"Amber."

"Amber, right, here's the thing, I don't believe for a minute that my son Jerry killed himself," she tossed out, waiting for Amber to respond. Amber was momentarily stunned; she hadn't anticipated this line, but tried to recover quickly.

"Can you explain a bit more, ma'am?" She wanted to make sure the mother wasn't a nutter who couldn't handle the truth of her son's suicide.

Mrs. Arnold looked intently at Amber for a moment, like she was deciding whether to trust her. "Jerry was doing alright. He had some hard times in Iraq, but he was upbeat at the time. He had applied to the Transportation Security Administration (TSA), he was about to be honored by his high school and have his football jersey number retired. Do those sound like telltale signs of suicide?" she asked, throwing her hands up in the air.

Amber was about to give the pat answer about how we never know with suicides, thinking immediately about Chris, but decided to ask more. "Can you tell me how he died then?"

Mrs. Arnold looked down at the faded carpet for a moment before speaking in a quiet voice. "He was found at the end of this dirt road, three miles from here. Someone had put a pistol in his mouth and pulled the trigger, blowing his whole face off. The police found his fingerprints on the gun, so they ruled it a suicide. Lazy bastards. Are you asking me to believe that my son put a pistol in his mouth and pulled the trigger?" she asked, throwing her hands in the air as her voice rose.

"This is difficult, Mrs. Arnold, but let me ask you a few questions," Amber interjected before the woman shut down on her or became too emotional.

"Did he leave a note?"

"No."

"Did they find his car at the scene?"

"Ya see, that's another thing, his car was still here. Why would he walk three miles down the road? The whole damn thing didn't make sense."

"Did they perform an autopsy?"

"No, they ruled it a suicide so there was no need."

Amber could see why Mrs. Arnold was having a hard time accepting that her son had killed himself. Some of the facts even gave Amber pause, but a veteran with diagnosed PTSD was far more likely to commit suicide than be secretly murdered—that just didn't make sense, no matter how convinced Mrs. Arnold was. Nevertheless, Amber wanted to see if she could get to the bottom of this for the mother's sake.

"Did Jerry leave behind his records from the Army? He might have a box or file with his citations, evaluation reports, personnel files and official papers. I can't promise anything, but I'd be happy to study them to get a better picture of your son—maybe it'll provide some insights on his death."

"Yes, as a matter of fact he did have a plastic file case with all of that information. Come with me, I'll show you where it is." Mrs. Arnold stood up and beckoned Amber to follow her down the hallway cluttered with family pictures. Nikita stood and walked alongside Amber.

"This is his room," said Jerry's mother, opening the door. "He was living here while saving up money for his own place. My husband died five years ago, so there was plenty of room in the house."

Amber stepped in and realized the room was probably unchanged from when Jerry had been in high school. There was a shelf above the window filled with shiny plastic football trophies, and the other wall was covered with pictures of football teams pinned into the drywall. The bedspread was an orange Denver Broncos blanket with a football shaped pillow. A TV was set up in one corner on a stand with a video game controller attached. Amber looked around, trying to develop a better sense of Jerry. "Where did he keep his military files?" she asked, turning back to Mrs. Arnold.

"He kept them right here in his closet on the top shelf," she said, sliding the closet door open. She rummaged around the shelf, then turned back to Amber, ashen. "They're gone! This is where he always kept them! I haven't looked here since his death." She looked stupefied. "It makes no sense. Where could they be? They were here before he died - I saw them. The police came by after they found him and searched his room, but why would they take anything?"

On the drive back to the VA, Amber thought about the meeting. She would bet money that Jerry had committed suicide, but she had to admit there were some strange things in this case, not the least of which was the missing files from Jerry's time in the Army. *What could have happened to them? Mrs. Arnold seemed convinced they were in the closet before his death. Did someone take them? Had Jerry moved them? If so, why?*

Amber could have headed home, it was late afternoon, but something was bugging her. She returned to the VA and went down to her basement office, Nikita in tow. The fact that Sergeant Arnold had killed himself by putting a pistol in his mouth seemed strange to Amber. *Why put a pistol in your mouth? Why not put it to the side of your head?* There was something awful and punitive about putting a big metal pistol in your mouth and pulling the trigger.

Back in her office, she started to search for information on suicides by firearm. She found that 70 percent of men and 49 percent of women use firearms to commit suicide. But there was very little data available on how victims used the firearms. She did find two studies, both of which showed that placement of the gun in the mouth was used in less than one percent of suicides. "What was going on with

Arnold?" she said aloud as she shut down her laptop and the pair headed home for the night.

10

Sergeant Thompson handed the satellite handset to Master Sergeant Parnell. As the radio operator, Thompson had been keeping the Special Operations Tactical Operations Center informed of their progress. "The colonel wants to speak with you, Jimmy," said Thompson, the biggest man in the unit. The use of first names among special operations forces was common. The bond they created with each other was unique within the U.S. military.

Parnell took the handset, "Jackal, this is Honcho, over."

"Honcho, this is Jackal, what's the status there?"

"Sir, our dog handler is missing. We found her working dog with a stab wound. I assume the dog handler has been taken captive or killed."

"Don't assume anything, Honcho, just give me the facts."

"Yes sir. I found a trail leading through a palm grove. Some of the dog handler's gear was on the ground like it had been ditched by someone. It appears she walked or was dragged through the forest."

"Roger, Honcho, we should have eyes above you in a few minutes." Parnell knew they would be directing the closest unmanned aerial vehicle, or UAV, to hover over their site and look for Downing.

"What's your next move, Honcho?"

"Sir, I'd like to pursue this trail through the palm grove. She was less than 30 minutes ahead of us. If we hustle, we may catch up with her and her possible captor."

There was quiet on the line as the colonel thought about the plan. He didn't want to let the small team stumble into an ambush. On the other hand, the capture of a US soldier by Al Qaeda was unthinkable.

"Permission granted, Honcho. We'll track you with a UAV over-flight. Report to me every 20 minutes."

"Sir, one more thing ... the working dog is injured, but may be able to lead us to Downing. He's lost a lot of blood, but he's our best chance at finding her with his keen senses."

The colonel hesitated again. He had incredible respect for the working dogs who had saved so many of his soldiers' lives with their heroic efforts. He knew the implications of what Parnell was request-ing, "Honcho, use the dog to find our soldier."

"Roger all, sir. Honcho out."

Parnell turned to his team, which had formed a tactical perimeter around Razor. "Guys, bring it in." The soldiers moved close to Parnell in a tight circle so he could talk quietly to them and share the plan. "Downing is missing, may have been captured or killed. We're going to patrol through that palm forest to see if we can locate her. She's only half an hour ahead of us. We have a good chance of catching up to her." He paused to see their reaction—they all knew that walking into an ambush was a big risk. The team all nodded in agreement. They would do whatever they could to recover one of their own.

"We need to bring the dog—he's our best chance of finding her by scent. Can the dog walk?"

"I've given him the full IV bag, but he's lost a lot of blood," said Thompson.

"I guess we have our answer," Johnson said, looking over Jimmy's shoulder. They all turned to see Razor get up on his feet and give a soft growl, as if to say, "What are you guys waiting for, let's roll."

11

May 2012, Montrose, Colorado

On her way home from work, Amber texted Hannah and suggested they meet for drinks at Phelanie's, the town's take on a speakeasy. The bar posted the daily verbal password on social media so customers could gain entrance. It was a smart marketing ploy. The place was all dark wood with dim lights and artwork reminiscent of the ambiance of a speakeasy from the Great Gatsby era. It was 6:30 p.m. as Amber arrived first this time and grabbed seats in the back corner, where deep leather chairs and a dark couch surrounded a small table. It was a place to drink, not eat, although you could order a meat and cheese plate. Amber sat down, hoping for a few minutes of alone time before Hannah and Brian showed up. Nikita laid down between Amber's seat and the couch, putting her head on Amber's feet. The story of Jerry Arnold was still rattling through her head. Time for a drink. She looked up and one of the servers dressed in 1920 period garb caught her eye and came over. He approached the table but stopped to look at Nikita when he spotted her on the ground. Nikita gave a low growl at the intruder.

"Beautiful dog, what's his name?"

Amber looked at the mid-thirties man with dark wavy hair and sharp cheekbones. "Her name is Nikita," she said, noticing the spark in his copper-colored eyes.

"I love German Shepherds—so smart and loyal. My name is Tony. What can I get for you?" he asked, looking up from Nikita and taken aback by Amber's beautiful face.

"I'll take a smoked old-fashioned, please." She knew that drink would be prepared at her table and she wanted to see this waiter make it for her. She immediately liked anyone who loved German Shepherds.

Tony left and returned shortly, pushing an ornate drink cart with a bottle of whiskey, a small torch, a glass, some wood chips and ice. Amber sat up to watch the creation. He proceeded to pour the whiskey over a large ball of ice in the glass, light a small piece of wood with the torch, get it smoking, and place it in the glass with a lid to capture the smoked flavor. Amber smiled as he passed her the smoky concoction, taking a slow sip. "Delicious!" she exclaimed, looking over the glass at Tony.

A big smile spread across his face, "Yeah, that's my favorite drink. It's not a fruity thing, but it has a rich taste." He was about to ask Amber how long she had lived in the area when Brian and Hannah arrived.

"Amber, you look wonderful," Hannah gushed as she leaned in to give Amber what looked like a fake hug to Tony. She slung her oversized purse on the couch and sat next to Amber.

Brian stood ramrod straight and nodded at Amber with a look that said, "I know you don't like me, and I don't care," taking a seat next to Hannah. Tony took their drink orders, stole a furtive glance at Amber and headed back to the bar, to gather their drink orders.

"How is that project coming?" Hannah asked almost immediately. Brian was studying the pictures on the wall, appearing to not pay attention to the conversation.

"It's really hard to sort out these suicides. It's emotionally draining for me. I've not been getting much sleep since I started." Amber would not confide this to most people, but she trusted Hannah, a fellow female veteran.

"You can't let this effect you like that," Hannah said, moving closer to Amber with what sounded like real concern in her voice. As a police officer, she knew how hard it was to leave the stress from her work at her front door.

"I know, I know. This last case has really got me puzzled, though," Amber said, taking a sip of her old-fashioned."

"What's the problem with it?" Hannah asked.

"It's strange, the mother wouldn't talk to me over the phone. When I went out to her place in Fruita, she claimed her son didn't kill himself and suggested he'd been murdered." Amber noticed Brian suddenly put down his phone and turned to listen intently. *Brian's with the Grand Junction PD so he's probably interested in the notion of a homicide,* she thought.

"What made her think it was murder?" asked Hannah, stealing a glance at Brian.

"It was just a series of things that didn't line up, according to the mother. At first I thought she was in denial, but I have to say that a few of the facts of the case are just plain weird."

Brian interjected, "Parents are always in denial about suicide—seen it many times. I'm sure the department investigated thoroughly. Believe me, if there was a hint of foul play, they would've started a line of inquiry." Brian was always quick to insert his opinion, thought Amber ... a little too quick. He seemed almost upset that Amber would believe anything about the mother's story.

Later that night, Amber sat on her back porch with a cup of Sleepy Time tea in her hand. Nikita prowled the deck, her senses alert to the presence of anything beyond her vision in the darkened tree line. Amber had been holding off thoughts of Chris all day, but finally the wall came down. Jerry Arnold's story had taken a wrecking ball to her defenses. Intuitively, she sensed that self-pity would not lead anywhere good, but it was so hard to think of the good times they'd had together without deep, visceral regret at the way it all ended.

She thought back to their last time together at the hospital in Baghdad. She had been focused on seeing Razor and heading back to the States for treatment. Chris had seemed distracted when he visited her, and she sensed something was wrong. He was distant and too emotional. *Had she missed it?* she wondered. *Maybe Chris was feeling overwhelmed about the loss of the men in his platoon?* But maybe it had been something else? She thought it possible that she had not seen something dark in him, something she should have seen as a fellow soldier. *Maybe she was blinded by love and didn't want to see the struggle below the surface.* She tried to shake off the feeling that the signs of suicide had been there all along, but deep down she remembered the occasional distance he would put between them, as if his head was off in a cloud; the times he was depressed after a mission had gone bad; the times she heard from some of his fellow soldiers that he awoke in the wee hours and walked around the barracks at night, checking and re-checking that the doors and windows were locked. He always joked that he was a light sleeper, but now she knew it was more than that, so much more.

12

MAY 2012, GRAND JUNCTION, COLORADO

The next day she had a voicemail from her boss, John. He wanted an update on her progress with the suicide data collection. She made a mental note to call him back, even though he was only a few floors above her office. She didn't need any more of his leering looks. She decided she wouldn't mention anything about Jerry Arnold or the visit to his mother. She didn't want John to micro-manage how she handled the project.

She worked through two more cases before lunch. One was a female Air Force Tech Sergeant who'd served two tours in Iraq. When her husband left her shortly after she redeployed, she overdosed on painkillers. The second was a Navy sailor who jumped in front of a bus after he was kicked out of the Navy for failing his second trip to alcohol rehab. There was enough information about these two cases in the media and service record files that she didn't have to contact the families. But she still put all the extra information she gathered about them into her binder. It was the case after lunch that caught her attention.

Henry Lopez was an Army soldier who'd killed himself with a firearm after a combat tour in Iraq. There was no clear indication about why he had committed suicide. He'd been evaluated by the VA after his service and referred to a specialist, but not diagnosed with PTSD or traumatic brain injury. There was nothing in the media archives or his service record that indicated a motive for suicide. Amber decided she would have to make a call to the family on this one.

She noticed that the contact number for the family was another local area code. She took a big breath, exhaled and made the call. After a few rings, she heard a female voice say, "Hola." Amber didn't speak Spanish but had learned a few phrases in the Army.

"Hola, mi nombre es Amber. I work for the Grand Junction VA. I would like to ask you a few questions about Henry. Are you his madre?" She hoped her Spanglish wasn't insulting to the woman.

"Si, si, he was my son," the woman said with an accent. Obviously she spoke good English. "What do you want to know?" Amber had her questions about Sergeant Lopez's suicide ready, but decided she couldn't do it over the phone with this mother, too much would be lost in translation.

"We're trying to reduce veteran suicides and I wanted to ask you if I could come to your home? It would only take a few minutes."

There was a pause on the line, but then the mother answered, "Si, si, whatever I can do to help."

Amber gave herself 30 minutes to make the drive and meet the mother. After they'd hung up, she realized she hadn't even asked the woman her name. *What kind of insensitive bureaucrat am I?*

She followed the address to a neighborhood of small 1940ish homes on the east side of town. She drove slowly up to a row of shabby shotgun houses with iron bars on the windows and located the address for Mrs. Lopez. It was the last house in the row, faded yellow with a sagging roof and a few chickens pecking at the dirt in the side yard. Amber parked on the street and knocked on the door.

A short woman in a bright yellow dress opened the door. Her long black hair hung loosely down her back. Her face was striking, with a sharp nose and large brown eyes.

"Hello, Mrs. Lopez, I'm Amber Downing from the Veterans Affairs hospital here in town." Nikita stood quietly at her side, raising her nose to sniff the smells coming from the home.

"Si, si, come inside please." Amber and Nikita stepped into a small but well-organized living room. She was obviously a devout Catholic, as Amber noted crosses on the walls and a brightly colored picture of the Virgin Mary hung above the alcove leading to the kitchen.

"Please sit down. Would you care for some coffee?" Mrs. Lopez asked.

"That would be lovely, thank you."

Amber took a seat on the small couch and Nikita lay down next to her feet while Mrs. Lopez attended to the coffee. Within a few minutes, she brought a tray with two coffees and a plate of warm cookies. Amber took a cup and one cookie. "Thank you, Mrs. Lopez. May I ask your first name?"

"Maria," she said, placing the tray on the table between them and taking a seat in a rocker covered with what looked like a handmade quilt. Amber sipped the coffee. It was instant, but with a cinnamon flavor that was surprisingly good.

"Mrs. Lopez ... Maria, as I mentioned on the phone we are conducting a study to try and reduce veteran suicides. I know this might be difficult for you, but I would like to ask you a few questions about your son's death."

Maria looked at her hands for a moment before speaking. "OK," she nodded.

Amber decided to start with something relatively easy. "Where did your son die, Maria?"

Mrs. Lopez looked up at Amber with eyes like black steel. "The police found him in a park near here. He had a pistol in his hand. They said it was his. I didn't know he owned a gun."

"Was he troubled about anything? Divorce, break up with a girlfriend, anything that would have upset him at the time?"

"No, no, he was happy. He had just been hired by the post office, everything was good. He was living with me until he could get his own apartment near here so he could keep an eye on his mother. He was a good boy."

Amber tried a different tack, "When Henry came back from Iraq, did you notice anything different in him, any way he might have changed?"

Maria thought for a moment, looked out the window and spoke as if to another person. "He was quieter and more withdrawn after he came home. He wouldn't talk about his time in Iraq with me. I know he had some troubles though."

"Is there a Mr. Lopez?" Amber asked, reaching down and petting Nikita, more for her own benefit.

"He left after Henry died. It was unbearable for him. He drank too much and lost his job. I haven't seen him in nine months."

The black ripples from suicide spread poison and touch everyone, Amber thought. "Did Henry keep his files and records from the Army?"

"After he died, someone ransacked his storage unit. They tore up everything and stole his military files ... so strange."

A tingle went up Amber's spine. *Two stolen boxes of files?*

"The thing is, Henry made a copy of all his records and left them here with me for safekeeping in case he ever lost them."

"So you still have the copies?" Amber asked, trying to subdue her excitement.

"Si, si, I have them in my bedroom."

Amber sat forward in her chair. "Maria, I know this is a big request, but may I borrow those files? I would like to see if there is anything in his military or medical records that would give us more information about his death."

Maria took a sip of coffee to hide the pain that was breaking through her calm demeanor. She stared over the cup at Amber as if to get a read on her before answering.

"OK, but I have a request."

"Of course, just name it."

"I want you to promise me that you will find out why my son died."

Amber was stunned for a moment, with thoughts of her fiancé's suicide racing through her head. She was close to him and had no idea why he'd killed himself; how was she going to make a promise to this mother who had lost so much?

She reached down and scratched Nikita's nose before answering, "I promise, Maria, I will find out for you." *Why did I say that?* She immediately envisioned herself having to come back to this home and telling Maria that she had no clue why her son had died. Her gut wrenched at the thought of that conversation. She didn't know how she was going to keep this promise, only that she had to, for Maria, for Chris and for herself.

On the drive back to the VA, she looked over at the file box on the floor of her truck. Was there a hidden clue in there to help explain Sergeant Lopez's death? The fact that two soldiers who both died by suicide might have had their military records stolen was bordering on an unbelievable coincidence.

13

The black shadow on the leash ahead of him stopped. Pino halted and bent to one knee to look at something on the ground that Razor was pawing and licking. The rest of the team knelt quietly behind him, each man taking up a field of fire to provide 360 degree security for the element. Parnell was next in line behind Pino so that the point man could easily relay what he saw to the team leader and Parnell could give him directions and guidance when needed. The object in the trail would be a perfect booby trap by its location and placement. Pino studied the object from different angles. Out of caution, he would normally not touch it, but an American soldier was missing—he picked it up.

Aquino, or Pino, as he was known to his friends, was the point man for Parnell's fire team. He grew up in the jungles near Mindanao and came to the United States at 12 years old, when his American father, a Navy sailor, married his Filipino mother and adopted him. The spry Filipino soldier was a natural in the field. It was a dark night, near total blackness under the heavy canopy of the date palm forest. The team all wore night vision goggles, but with little ambient light, it was hard to make out a path, even with the goggles. Fortunately, Razor was at Pino's side. Pino was not a trained military dog handler, but he understood animals.

Parnell crept up to see why Pino had stopped. "Whadya got, Pino?" he asked in his low drawl.

Pino held up a light blue Nalgene water bottle for Parnell to see. "It must have fallen from her pack," he whispered. "Razor found it."

Parnell nodded silently, took the water bottle, motioned for Pino to turn around and placed the bottle inside Pino's backpack. Parnell had no doubt now that they were on her track.

Pino whispered, "Good boy" to the dog and with the military working dog surged ahead, straining on the leash following an invisible scent. Razor followed a trail through the palm forest so faint that it was invisible to the naked eye. As a boy in the jungles of the southern Philippines, Pino had learned to track animals. Now he and Razor were tracking a more dangerous prey, one more cunning and ruthless than any wild beast he had hunted under the thick triple canopy jungle of his homeland.

Pino set the pace for the fire team. He moved like a cat in the wild, with a powerful yet fluid gait. He was not only tracking Downing and her captor, he was just as focused on not leading the fire team into an ambush or, heaven forbid, an improvised explosive device (IED). The Al Qaeda terrorist network in Iraq had employed explosively formed projectile IED's to devastating effect against the Allies. Every soldier in Iraq feared those more than any enemy encounter. The insurgents they knew they could beat - the hidden land mines, not so much. It was no easy thing to spot an IED or booby trap, but Pino knew all the signs: disturbed earth, footprints, evidence of digging, the presence of wires, an obvious spot for the enemy to set off a command-detonated

IED with a cell phone, or an object left in the trail that was booby trapped and would set off the IED when it was picked up. That's why he had taken so long to observe Downing's water bottle, to ensure it wasn't an initiator for an IED.

After twenty minutes of tracking, Razor led the soldiers to the far edge of the palm forest. He was sniffing the ground and trying to tug Pino into the clearing beyond the trees. Pino pulled Razor back into the cover of the treeline and raised his right arm slowly with a fist, signaling for the fire team to quietly take a knee. They had to move fast to recover a hostage, but this open field presented Pino with a big decision—keep moving now and risk exposing the fire team to an ambush in the open, or hold here and wait for direction from Parnell or higher headquarters. Against his gut feeling, Pino took a knee.

Pino made Razor lay down, he wanted to check on the dog's wound and dressing. He lifted the dressing and examined the gash and noted blood had soaked through the dressing, but it looked like the compression bandage was holding on. He tied off Razor's leash to a small tree then moved to his stomach and crept forward to the edge of the forest. Beyond the trees, there was an open field of crops that looked like wheat. On the other side, maybe 500 yards away, Pino could see a building. At this distance he couldn't make out what type of building, but he figured it to be some sort of farmhouse. A glimmer of light shone from inside. Nothing was a sure thing in this life, but Pino knew the faint trail Razor had followed through the dense trees led to that structure, and Sergeant Downing. He was sure of it.

14

Three months before Amber's capture

KAT and two AQI foot soldiers had been scouting the dusty, narrow road near the west of Baghdad for days. The American soldiers often flew helicopters in and out of the Green Zone, the large, high-walled protected security area in the heart of Baghdad. But the Americans still had to roll out in vehicle convoys every day. The soldiers frequently changed their routes and made it hard for KAT and his band of die-hard AQI terrorists to set up a proper IED ambush, but there were a few choke points that the convoys still had to pass through in the city. KAT and his men had been watching one of the main vehicle gates outside the Green Zone for three days, pretending to be simple street vendors. Eventually they saw a pattern—the soldiers made a sharp turn north on Abu Bakr Road every third or fourth day. They would set up there.

KAT preferred command detonated IEDs, which were set off when a cell phone signal initiated the detonation in the device. The pressure-activated mines were too easy to defeat. The soldiers could just run a big minesweeper vehicle in front of the convoy and blow those up. The cell phone-activated IEDs allowed KAT to detonate the explosives at just the right time, catching a vehicle in the middle of an ambush and causing maximum carnage.

KAT was patient; he knew what it took to defeat the infidels. A week ago he and his men had placed two old waste bins near the location they had chosen for the vehicle ambush. They let the cans sit there for six days so the soldiers would get used to seeing the trash cans as innocuous objects when they passed by them. On the last day, KAT pulled the waste bins in at 0100, filled them with two large explosively-formed projectiles, and set them back on the street. KAT knew from his observations that the soldiers would be passing that narrow road the following evening.

He stationed one man near the gate, dressed as a beggar, to report to him when the convoy left the Green Zone. He situated another man in a burned-out, abandoned building near the turn leading to Abu Bakr Road, to text him when and if the soldiers came toward his ambush site. It was a well thought out plan.

At 0230 in the morning, Captain Reynolds ordered his convoy to line up and stage at the western gate of the Green Zone. He and some of his platoon were tasked to deliver ammunition, food and medical supplies to one of the smaller fire bases located to the west of Baghdad. Several of the men in his platoon were out on another mission, so Captain Reynolds had requested two additional soldiers from the Infantry Brigade in Baghdad to supplement his crew. Reynolds was a large man, an officer from New Jersey who had been a lacrosse player at West Point. His men, mostly from the South, made fun of his thick Jersey accent behind his back. He was on his second tour to

Iraq and hated leaving Becky and their two-year-old daughter back at Fort Hood. His men knew him as a calm leader under fire and an officer who would not put them at undue risk. Reynolds led from the front in an armored HUMVEE. Behind him was the behemoth mine-resistant ambush-protected vehicle, or MRAP, followed by two more HUMVEEs. Reynolds had instructed his men to stuff all the supplies into the MRAP so they wouldn't have to bring an unarmored supply truck with them. The longer the convoy, the more exposed it was to the enemy.

At 0305 Reynolds keyed the radio handset and came over the secure radio net initiating a radio check to each of the vehicles, "Ranger 2, 3 and 4, this is Ranger 1, radio check, over."

"Ranger 2, roger."

"Ranger 3, loud and clear."

"Ranger 4, roger."

As they rolled out the gate in the dim light of a new moon, Reynolds thought he saw an old beggar in rags lying near the wall next to the gate. At 0309, Reynolds made the turn down Abu Bakr Road and the rest of the convoy followed. It wasn't the quickest way to their destination, but he used it periodically to keep the enemy guessing.

At 0314, the convoy passed a narrowing in the road where two trash bins sat leaning against a damaged brick building with garbage spilling out of them. From his vantage point in a small balcony across the street, KAT let the lead HUMVEE and the MRAP pass, then he punched the call button on his cell phone, detonating the huge explosion just as the second HUMVEE passed the kill zone, and cutting the convoy in half. Molten steel traveling at up to 2,000 feet per second sliced through the HUMVEE, shredding the soldiers inside.

Sgt. Henry Lopez, the driver of the HUMVEE right behind the blast, immediately yelled into the radio for the whole convoy to hear, "IED blast just took out Ranger 3! It's flipped onto its left side. We're gonna stop and pull out our soldiers."

Capt. Reynolds took a deep breath before shouting further directions to the remaining three vehicles over the radio. "Ranger 2, provide rear security for Ranger 3, I'll cover the street area in front of us." The rear armored door to the MRAP opened and three soldiers from Ranger 2 jumped out, took cover next to the large armored carrier and sighted their weapons back down the alley they had come from so the troops from Ranger 4 behind them could retrieve the dead and wounded from the stricken Ranger 3 HUMVEE. The blast had kicked up a massive dust cloud. Blood and fuel poured out of the damaged vehicle and soaked into the hot, dusty Baghdad road making it look like a scene from Dante's Inferno.

Sgt. Henry Lopez, Corporal Jerry Arnold and Master Sgt. John Holmes jumped out of Ranger 4 and ran to the destroyed HUMVEE. They knew that Al Qaeda liked to start an ambush with a vehicle IED then finish it with terrorists shooting down from windows and rooftops with AK-47's and rocket-propelled grenades as the American soldiers recovered their injured comrades. It was eerily quiet as they raced across the open alley to the HUMVEE, which was spewing black smoke from its engine compartment.

Lopez and Arnold reached the upturned vehicle first and started to pull the gunner, Corporal Smith, out from his turret. Smith was slouched over in his harness, his head drooping towards the ground, his arms dangling loosely as the HUMVEE lay on its side. Lopez lifted Smith under the shoulders in the turret while Arnold unfastened his harness. Smith slid into Lopez's arms, missing both his legs above the knees. Lopez laid him on the ground. "Dios Mio!" he whispered to himself.

Holmes had moved to the other side and was trying to open one of the doors on the high side of the upturned vehicle. "Get over here and help me with these other guys," he yelled to Lopez and Arnold over the radio. Lopez grabbed the tourniquet from his medical pouch, slipped it over Smith's right leg and cinched it down to stop the bleeding. Arnold pulled out his own tourniquet and cranked it down on Smith's other leg. It was all they could do for now—they needed to help Holmes with the other soldiers.

Lopez and Arnold stood up together and ran to the other side of the smoking HUMVEE where Master Sergeant Holmes was holding the front passenger side door open looking down into the truck at the other two soldiers trapped inside. The upturned passenger side of the vehicle was completely demolished where the molten steel from the EFP had shredded the HUMVEE, destroying everything in its path.

Lopez got to the door first and looked down on his two friends in the front seat. What he saw was a horror beyond imagination. His two platoon mates were hardly recognizable as humans. The inside of the HUMVEE was splattered with their body parts, blood and pieces of their equipment. Arnold appeared at his side, took one look down, turned and puked up his guts. Holmes yelled into the radio, "I've got two dead and one wounded, we need help now!"

15

MAY 2012, MONTROSE AND GRAND JUNCTION, COLORADO

L ast night Amber had a hard time getting to sleep, as thoughts of her meeting with Maria Lopez spun through her mind. What most intrigued her, and kept her awake last night, was the box of Sergeant Lopez's records. The fact that the military files of Arnold and Lopez had both gone missing and that the two had both killed themselves with a pistol in the mouth was just too much of a coincidence for Amber. Someone must have been trying to get their hands on those records or make sure no one else saw them—she couldn't think of another explanation. But why? If Lopez hadn't made a copy of his records for his mother to keep, there would have been nothing to potentially tie these two strange suicides together.

Spring arrived in Montrose and with it came the winds, sweeping away the dank debris winter had left rotting on the ground. Amber woke up to find her folding chairs strewn across her back deck. She'd heard the old cabin straining against the wind last night, like a schooner in a gale. Nikita was standing over her food bowl, head set slightly to one side, giving Amber an unmistakable signal. She poured kibble in her bowl and started up a pot of coffee. She sat on the back deck sipping black coffee and eating a bowl of oatmeal with berries while Nikita ran her trap lines around the property, marking her territory and discovering which animals had visited her domain last night. She smelled the usual: rabbits, deer and coyote.

A thought of the server, Tony, at Phelanie's drifted into Amber's mind. He was nice, he loved dogs, plus he was good-looking. She smiled inwardly as she thought about him. She considered making another trip to that bar soon, but then Chris floated into her mind—was she being disloyal to him, to his memory? When would she be able to move on and meet someone else … if ever? She pushed those unanswerable thoughts out of her head and focused on her work.

Two hours later, she was logging on to her computer at work. She checked her emails for any action items but found only a bunch of VA announcements and junk news that she quickly scanned and deleted. She pulled the brown metal filing case out from under her desk. *Let's see who you were, Sergeant Lopez.*

The box contained two fat files: copies of his medical record and his service record. She started with the service record file. Born in 1983, Henry Lopez had enlisted in 2001 after high school. *This is interesting*, she thought, he'd enlisted into the Army National Guard. The National Guard units had taken rotations to Iraq and Afghanistan, like the regular Army units, she knew, but she had assumed Lopez was regular Army. She wanted to know what unit he was with. She scanned more documents until she saw he'd been assigned to Charlie Company of the 157th Infantry Battalion. Their headquarters unit was in Colorado Springs, but there were companies located in Grand Junction, Fort Lupton, Alamosa and Windsor. She knew that most of the National Guard troops were part-timers, but there were a few full-time soldiers. She discovered that Lopez was a full-time soldier. It looked like he had spent all of his five years in the Army assigned to the same unit—not uncommon in the National Guard.

Next she reviewed his training record. After infantry training he had attended a variety of schools and courses over his career, including heavy weapons, cold weather training, HUMVEE driver/gunner and several leadership courses. The National Guard had done a good job of training and preparing him for leadership positions.

She then dug into Lopez's promotion history to see what his supervisors thought of him. She thumbed through his periodic evaluations, noting that he had advanced up the ranks early to sergeant. His superiors had thought him a highly competent soldier and recommended him for promotion at every step, until she read his last report. It was the evaluation covering the time of his last deployment to Iraq. Amber whistled and said, "Wow." His last evaluation was a career killer. The senior rater, a Master Sergeant John Holmes, had tanked his last report, saying he was insubordinate and not fit to be a leader in the Army. There were no specifics in the write-up to shed light on what had caused Holmes to make disparaging remarks about Lopez, but the intent was clear enough—get him out of the Army.

Amber set the report down and reached out to pet Nikita, who was lying under her desk. She looked up and sighed as Amber scratched her ears. *What happened to you in Iraq, Sergeant Lopez?* She had no idea, but one thing she was sure of—whatever it was, it had something to do with his suicide.

Amber felt her stomach growl—it was lunchtime. She walked up the stairs and out the back door to let Nikita sniff the grass and do her business before they headed to the cafe. Sheri looked up from behind the cash register, nodded and smiled as Amber and Nikita stepped into the cafe. The place was empty.

"Hey, Amber, long time no see," said her best friend at the VA from behind the cafe counter.

"I've been crazy busy, Sheri. I've got this new project I'm trying to work through."

"What's it about? Didn't you tell me they mostly give you silly projects?"

Amber looked around to make sure the cafe was empty before answering. "It's a data collection project on the suicides of veterans in this area for the last five years."

Sheri grimaced. When they had become friends last year, Amber had told her about Chris's suicide. Sheri instantly realized why she hadn't seen Amber for a while. "Wow, sorry to hear you got stuck with that. Doesn't seem like a good one for you..." she left the words hanging.

"It's all right, Sheri. I did go through a period of denial, but then just started to get on with it. I hate to say it, but it's been very interesting, even if it is a bit gruesome."

She ordered a BLT, fries and iced tea and sat in the corner with her back to the wall, so she could see everyone in the cafe. After Iraq, it made her extremely anxious to have anyone behind her. It was after 1 o'clock and most customers had already eaten. Sheri stepped from behind the counter and walked over to the table. She was older than Amber, in her mid-forties, her long blonde hair hung in a ponytail, and she wore an apron over blue jeans and a T-shirt. Her husband Ed, a Marine, had been killed during the early days of the war in Afghanistan by an IED. She'd never remarried and raised their daughter Meghan by herself. Her left arm below the elbow was missing. Amber had never asked about it and Sheri never spoke of it. She sat down at Amber's table, always available to speak frankly to her friend.

"So how are you really doing, Amber? This project has to be hard for you, with what happened to Chris and all..."

"I'm fine, really." Amber threw up her well-constructed defenses whenever anyone brought up the subject of Chris. She couldn't think about it, couldn't dwell on it, had to move on. But this was her good friend, someone she trusted, someone she could talk to. She let her guard down, a bit.

After a moment's pause, she sighed and said, "Well, to be honest, this project has given me something to think about besides Chris. It's ironic, but as I dig into these veteran suicides, I'm forgetting some of my own troubles, at least for a while," she said, taking a sip of her iced tea.

"I'm glad to hear it, really glad," said Sheri as she reached her hand across the table and rested it on Amber's arm for a moment. "You've had a lotta bad breaks, honey, way more than your share, and I just want you to know I'm here for you, OK?" She squeezed Amber's arm gently.

Amber didn't like to think about her past, but suddenly the unfairness and reality of it all hit her. *Dammit,* she thought, unable to hold back the emotions. Scenes of Iraq, her captivity, Razor, her fiancé; all of it crashed into her mind. Sheri's kind touch had cracked her defenses. She couldn't talk, and tears came to her deep blue eyes and rolled down her smooth cheeks. Sheri stood up, moved next to Amber and wrapped her arm around her, letting Amber sob into her shoulder as Sheri gently rubbed her back, "It's gonna be alright, Amber, I promise."

16

Parnell knelt in the soft soil inside the treeline with Thompson's radio handset to his ear. He punched the talk button, "Jackal, this is Honcho, over."

After a few seconds, the colonel's voice came over the handset speaker, "Honcho, this is Jackal, what's the status of your patrol, over."

"Sir, we've tracked Downing's path through the date palm forest to a clearing. We found her Nalgene bottle on the trail. The dog is all over her scent. We're staged at the edge of a clearing. There's a house across the field that may be where she's being held. Request permission to recon the house and assault if it looks like Downing is inside, over."

The colonel paused before answering. "Permission granted. We have you on visual with the UAV. We'll have it focus on that house. You have 52 minutes until twilight. If you don't recover her by then, you need to extract before it gets light. I'll put a helo right in that field 52 minutes from now to extract your team."

"Yes sir, copy all," Parnell said as he handed the mic back to Thompson. Pino was lying down in the dirt at the edge of the field, watching the house. Parnell tapped his leg and Pino turned around to see the master sergeant give him a signal to come to him. Thompson and Johnson huddled closer so they could hear Parnell give the orders. "OK, we've got permission to recon that house and assault it if we think Downing is inside. There's only four of us, so we stay together, assault together. The colonel gave us 52 minutes until first light so we need to move out now. Any questions?" Parnell looked at his team; they had rehearsed for contingencies like this for years, so no one had any questions. "Pino, take us to that house."

Pino, nodded. They all looked at each other one time before stepping out of the protection of the cover. Every man knew two things: they couldn't leave Downing with the enemy and they may be in for a fight. Parnell looked each man in the eye, nodded and they stood up as one and started to move slowly across the open field toward the dim building.

Pino picked out the route for the team, staying in a low irrigation ditch to keep their silhouettes out of view from the building. The cold water sloshing in the bottom of the ditch caused their boots to make a soft sucking sound as they lifted each foot carefully out of the mud to avoid alerting anyone in the house. Pino found a low berm about 25 yards from the building. He stopped the patrol there to peek over the top of the rise. He saw a dim light inside. There was one door visible on this side of the building, he figured there had to be another door on the back or side of the structure. There were two windows on either side of the door. As he looked at the house, he saw a figure pass in front of both windows carrying a rifle. He crept backwards to let Parnell know what he had seen.

The master sergeant was huddled in a circle with the other two. "There's a door on this side of the house and two windows. I saw an armed male figure pass in front of the windows."

"Any sign of Downing?" Parnell asked. He knew he had to have some cause to enter the building, or the colonel would tear him a new one.

"No, I could creep around the whole house, get a better picture of what we've got?" Pino asked expectantly, looking up at the big Texan.

Parnell looked at his watch. They'd already used 25 minutes moving quietly across the field. They only had 27 minutes before twilight and the colonel dropped a helicopter in the field to extract them. It was a risk, but one worth taking. "We don't have time, guys. We have to go in that door and take our chances. It looks like a one-story building—we can take it easily with surprise on our side. The dog led us here; he knows Downing's scent. This has got to be the place."

"What about the dog?" asked Thompson.

"Better leave him here, he's injured," Parnell said, sizing up his men to get a gauge on their readiness. He saw steel eyes staring back at him. Parnell nodded and the men stood up as one and started the final movement to the target.

Pino looked at Razor and saw blood dripping from his bandages. "You stay here, boy, don't move." The black-nosed Malinois had an anxious look on his face. Being left behind was his worst fear.

The team reached the front of the house and ducked under the windows on either side of the door before standing up, two men on each side of the entry point, ready for an assault. They hadn't brought all the tools and explosives for a forced entry on this foray. Parnell was hoping the door was unlocked, or they could kick it in. Parnell and

Pino were stacked on the door knob side and Thompson and Johnson were on the hinge side. Parnell reached for the knob and turned it slowly—it was open. He nodded at the men, raised his M4 assault rifle to eye level with one hand and pushed open the door.

The first thing Parnell saw was the bloody body on the table covered with cuts, bruises and torture marks. Some poor collaborator—who knew? As he slid down the wall to get away from the door, Pino was right behind him scanning the barely lit room with his weapon sight. Sliding along the opposite wall, Thompson and Johnson opened fire at a man who stepped into the room with a pistol in his hand. They each double-tapped the man—one shot to the chest and one to the head. The man fell flat on his face, blood pooling in large dark circles around his head, the weapon tumbling out of his hand. Knowing that surprise was gone now, the two teams rushed through the rest of the house, clearing four other rooms. Downing was nowhere to be seen. Moving back to the front room, Thompson bent down to pick up the pistol from the man he'd shot. It wasn't a pistol, but a portable drill with a nasty-looking bloody drill bit. Parnell stepped over to look.

Thompson knew he'd made a mistake. "Jimmy, I screwed up. Look here," he said to Parnell, holding up the portable drill.

"Don't worry about it, Thompson, that shithead was torturing this poor sap with the drill. As far as I'm concerned, you were protecting that guy." They turned to look at the tortured captive. Johnson already had his hand on the bloody man's arm, searching for a pulse. "He's dead."

"You guys see any signs of Downing here?" Parnell asked.

"No, just a bunch of bomb-making tools and torture devices," said Pino with disgust in his voice. "We should blow this whole piece of shit house up—it's clearly an AQI safe house. Downing might have been here."

Parnell nodded, he'd let the colonel know what they'd found, and recommend an air strike on this house of horrors.

⸺◈⸺

Amber sat against the basement wall thinking how she was going to get out of this mess. She tried not to think of Razor, hoping and praying he was alive. She couldn't bear the thought of losing her loyal partner. She pushed those dark thoughts out of her head. She had to keep her focus on escaping. Reaching for the water bottle, she saw it was empty, and that's when she heard gunfire above. She knew she was in a basement below a building, maybe a hidden basement. She yelled out, but her dry, parched throat felt like sandpaper and she could only squeak. A door above her slammed open and KAT came running down the stairs into the basement brandishing a pistol in his hand.

"Up!" he whispered loudly to Downing, putting the pistol to her head and with his other hand unlocking the chain binding her to the wall. She stood up on wobbly legs as KAT shoved the pistol into her back. "If you make a noise, I will shoot you," he said quietly into her ear. With that, he shoved her toward the other side of the basement, not the way she had come in when she'd been blindfolded and had stumbled down the stairs. In the far corner was a small alcove with a low, horizontal trap door about chest high. KAT bent down under the door and pushed it open, then looked carefully around before stepping back and aiming the gun at Amber. "You go out first, I will have the gun on you. If you try to run, I will gun you down."

Amber stepped under the opening and hoisted herself up. She looked around and thought about running, but below her KAT was aiming the pistol directly at her. With one hand, KAT pulled himself out into the darkness while holding the pistol on her. He motioned with the pistol, and they started walking through a field of head-high crops. *This is my chance to get away*, she thought.

17

MAY 2012, MONTROSE, COLORADO

She had come to dread Memorial Day. Amber knew it was coming in May, but she had ignored the calendar. Now it was here—*denial only works for a short time.* The VA was closed for the Monday holiday so she couldn't go to work. She'd been invited to the memorial service that the American Legion put on at a local cemetery south of town. She knew she should go, but the thought of a ceremony focused on the death of all those veterans made her heart race. It hadn't always been that way. She used to enjoy the solemn holiday, thinking about the veterans from World War I, II and the Vietnam War who had died for their country. But after Iraq and Chris's suicide, she dreaded the holiday. Her wounds were too raw, her experience too fresh. But she knew she should go, so she grabbed Nikita and headed out.

A crowd of veterans and civilians were standing at the edge of the cemetery when Amber pulled up. "Here we go, girl, let's do this," she said, both to Nikita and herself. She walked up to the rear of the assembly, standing in the back so she could see the ceremony but not be seen by anybody. The local Navy Junior ROTC unit paraded the colors and everyone saluted or took their hats off. A retired Navy SEAL Captain began to speak about the importance of honoring our departed veterans. Amber was trying to listen, but her mind was drifting off to Iraq, to a dark little room where she'd been chained to the wall, where she had looked the wolf of fear in the eyes. Her heart rate picked up, and she began to sweat. Nikita, trained to notice her moods, came behind her and put her head between Amber's legs, looking up at her with soulful brown eyes. It was a way Nikita had learned to give a hug. Amber bent down and gave her a pat on the head. "Thank you, girl ... I needed that." Nikita's tail wagged as she lay down between Amber's legs.

The speaker's voice drifted back to Amber's consciousness, "...and we must also remember that on average 22 veterans a day commit suicide. This is a stain on our country, a plague that we must heal. The hidden wounds of war continue to haunt our veterans for years, taking too many of them away from friends and families, wives, husbands, children and comrades. I'm sure everyone here has been touched by this darkness. Please raise your hand if a Veteran close to you has taken their own life." Amber saw a sea of hands go up in front of her. She turned, almost unconsciously, and walked back to her truck, Nikita at her side watching the tears fall from Amber's face onto the fresh, spring grass.

Amber sat in her truck, tears rolling down her face. Nikita moved from her seat in the back to the front. She put her paw on Amber's lap and began to lick her tears away. "Oh, sweet girl, what am I gonna do?" The pain and loneliness were like a knife in her gut. "I've gotta get past this somehow, right, girl?" Nikita cocked her head, trying to understand.

Amber set off for home, but somehow found herself at Phelanie's Speakeasy as if the car had a mind of its own. She sat there in the parking lot with the steering wheel in her hands. *What am I doing here? Maybe he's not working today. Maybe they're closed? I'll just go in for one drink, what can it hurt?* She walked into the dark bar, Nikita at her side as always. The place was empty—it was only noon. She took a seat on a corner couch, as her eyes adjusted and she surreptitiously looked around to see if Tony was working. She didn't see him, but suddenly he emerged from the back room carrying a case of wine to the bar. He glanced her way and smiled as he put the case down clearly recognizing her.

A few moments later, he stepped out from behind the bar and came over to her table. He was wearing blue jeans and a white T-shirt. She'd forgotten that he was tall, maybe six-foot-one, and very athletic looking. "Well, hello girl," he said teasingly to Nikita as he bent down and rubbed her ears. Nikita wagged her tail and licked his hand.

Looking up at Amber, he said, "I didn't get your name the last time you were here."

"It's Amber, Amber Downing."

"Hi again, Amber. I'm Tony."

"I remember," she nodded, thinking he smelled like an evergreen candle.

"So what brings you into the bar on this fine Memorial Day?"

"I thought I'd come by and have a drink," she said, looking up at him and hoping he didn't think she was a lush for drinking at noon.

"Well, your timing is good. We just opened and you have the place to yourself. What can I get you? Another old-fashioned?"

He remembered my drink. "Yeah, that would be great," she said, looking forward to watching him mix the concoction with those deliberate movements of his.

Nikita stood up and stretched while Tony went off to procure the ingredients. Amber looked around the empty bar. The walnut-colored wood paneling and deep red carpet made the place seem old. It reminded her of a pub in England she had once visited.

Within minutes Tony returned with the drink fixings on a small cart. Amber valued his silent work, appreciating how he took his time making the drink. She watched his hands move gently but confidently, lighting the wood on fire, gathering the smoke into the glass, carefully pouring the smoky whiskey and stirring the ice. She looked at his face and couldn't help but see some sadness in his dark eyes. He handed her the dark brown smoky drink. She took a sip, peering at him over the rim and smiling. "It's really good."

"Glad you like it," he said, returning her smile and wiping his hands on a small towel.

Amber didn't want him to leave just yet. "How long have you been working here?"

"Just a year now. I'm a school teacher, but being an educator doesn't make ends meet. I work here nights and weekends." She hadn't seen that coming. Now she was impressed. Her mother had been a school teacher so she knew all about the long hours and poor pay.

"What do you teach?"

"Kids," he said with a twinkle in his eye.

"Yeah, I figured that," she said with a smirk, "But what subject?"

"English. The only job available for English majors that pays. What do you do?"

"I work for the VA hospital in Grand Junction."

"So you're a medical professional?"

She took a sip of the smoky whiskey. "No, I collect statistics and analyze them to try to make meaning out of them." That was the first time she'd ever said that about her job.

"What kind of statistics?" he asked, sitting down across from her, since the bar was still empty.

What kind of data indeed, she thought. "Well, a variety of things, but right now I have a big project related to Veteran suicides." She felt it strangely easy to talk to him.

At the mention of suicide, his face darkened and he shook his head ever so slightly. In that one expression, she knew, somehow, some way, he had been touched by suicide. He hung his head for a moment then lifted it and sighed heavily.

"Is everything OK?" she asked.

He looked like he didn't want to talk about it but Amber was genuinely concerned.

He paused for what seemed like ages and looked directly at her. "My wife died by suicide two years ago."

Amber was stunned. She didn't know how to respond. She didn't want to bring up Chris, but she felt tremendous sorrow for Tony—she knew what he was going through.

"I'm so sorry, Tony, that's terrible. I, my ..." It wouldn't come out. He looked into her eyes and for a second something passed between them, like a silent wavelength of pain, but also of empathy.

Two couples walked through the front door. Tony looked at Amber one more time then nodded and stood to take care of the new customers. Amber stared at her whiskey but didn't feel like drinking it anymore. She looked at Nikita. "Let's go home, girl."

As she stood to leave, Tony came over. "My boss said it's going to be slow today, so he let me off. Do you want to grab a cup of coffee or something?"

She took a deep breath before answering but went with her instinct. "Sure, that would be great."

"We can just walk to San Juan Coffeehouse?" he asked, walking toward the exit with her.

"Sounds good," she nodded. San Juan Coffeehouse was a new venue that served great coffee and delicious food. It was a long narrow building on Main Street with plenty of seating. The couple who ran the place were super nice and always welcomed Nikita.

The place was starting to fill up with many people off work for Memorial Day. They both ordered black coffee and found two comfy seats in the back. Nikita lay down on the floor next to Amber, who sat on a leather couch. Tony sat in the stuffed armchair across from her.

Amber sat back and sipped her steaming coffee, letting Tony open the conversation. Some people thought she was cold because she could stay silent for a long time. In fact, she was always analyzing every situation. It was mostly unconscious, but she knew it could irritate people. She realized that Tony probably wanted to talk about his late wife but didn't know how to open.

She threw him a lifeline. "So how long were you married?"

"Almost four years. We met in college at Western State University."

"What was her name?"

"Angelica," he said, looking down at his feet.

Amber planned to stick to the facts, unless he wanted to talk about the suicide. "Were you married right out of college?"

"No, we dated for a few years. We were both on the mountain bike team and rode together in our spare time after school. How about you, were you ever married?" he asked, sipping his coffee.

She looked down at Nikita and scratched her ears before answering. He sensed it was not an easy question. "I was engaged to a fellow soldier," she said, looking up at him. "He took his own life two years ago." She saw his jaw drop for a moment with the realization that they had both lost their partners to suicide two years ago. Suddenly pain, guilt, anger and even shame came bubbling up for both. It was not a topic that either of them could talk to anyone else about. The shared pain brought shared understanding.

He opened first. "I thought we were both happy and had big plans for a family and all that. I was teaching one day and came home to find her dead from an overdose of painkillers. At least that was what the coroner determined. I took the rest of the semester off, checked myself into a Benedictine monastery in New Mexico and stayed there for three months."

Amber was taken aback, she had never been to a monastery, or met someone who had stayed at one. "What was the monastery like?" Amber asked, sipping her drink.

"Very peaceful, quiet," he said thinking about it. "There was a strict routine which helped me get out of my own head a little bit and focus on the tasks at hand. I volunteered in the garden so I was busy with my hands all the time."

Amber thought her time in the Army after Chris's death was about as far from a monastery as anyone could get. She envied the way Tony had been able to take that much time off to work through his trauma. She realized deep down that she needed something like that. She had never really come to terms with losing Chris and her experience in Iraq.

Tony was patiently anticipating her willingness to share, should she find it within herself. She looked up at the ceiling as if trying to read the lights before answering. "Chris shot himself after a combat tour in Iraq. We were engaged and we ... I was very happy. I don't know what happened. I must have missed some signs. He had a tough tour; we both did. I just didn't see it coming." She had been looking off into space as she talked. Now she looked directly at him.

"If I learned anything at that monastery, it's that you can't blame yourself. If you do, it will be like a lead ball around your neck. Trust me, I carried it for quite a while."

"So, you're free of guilt now?" She regretted asking that as soon as she'd said it. It sounded condescending.

"I'd like to say I'm free, I'd like to be free, but no, I still feel guilty. The thing is, I can now recognize what the feelings are doing to me and use techniques to move past them."

Amber was skeptical. She thought of the word *technique* as some mechanical advantage, like keeping both eyes open when shooting a pistol to optimize your vision.

"What do you mean by technique?" she asked, trying not to sound sarcastic.

"OK, call it meditation, prayer, mindfulness, whatever you want, but you need a way to filter out the unhealthy feelings and focus on something more positive."

Amber wasn't sure if her feelings of guilt were unhealthy or if they were just a natural response to the suicide of her fiancé. At her core, she did realize that her feelings of guilt and pain were holding her back, whether they were natural or not. She was stuck, and she did want to move forward in her life. She just felt she couldn't let go of the guilt right now—somehow it felt disloyal to Chris and his memory, especially since she did not understand his suicide.

She looked up at Tony. The tussle of black hair, the dark eyebrows, the kind eyes, the sharp chin, the strong hands. A feeling stirred within her as she came to the realization of how deeply she longed for an intimate connection.

18

Three months before Amber's capture

Lopez was trying to pull one of the two fellow soldiers from the stricken HUMVEE when a burst of automatic weapons' fire riddled the damaged vehicle from the building above. Lopez jumped for cover to the other side of the vehicle and sprayed the windows above with fire, sending glass and chips of brick falling onto the dusty road. Arnold dropped the other dead soldier he was carrying and returned fire while Holmes reached for his radio handset and yelled at the captain, "We've got effective fire coming from the windows above us!"

Captain Reynolds spoke calmly over the radio to all his troops. "Ranger 4, take your crew, enter that building and suppress the fire. Ranger 2, move into position and provide security for Ranger 3." Three soldiers from the behemoth mine resistant MRAP two of which were augmentees from the infantry brigade, exited out the back door and moved in unison to the stricken HUMVEE and took fields of fire behind the convoy, allowing Holmes, Lopez and Arnold to enter the building.

"Roger all," Holmes answered, then turned to Arnold and Lopez. "You two hold security there," he pointed to a broken wooden door directly below the window where they had received fire. Lopez nodded then ran across the open road and sought cover against the wall of the building next to the door with Arnold following closely behind. Holmes fired into the window to provide cover for their movement. When the team reached the door, Holmes let off a final burst of automatic weapon fire and sprinted to the entry. After catching his breath, Holmes gave Lopez a nod and Lopez kicked in the door and stepped into the darkened opening.

The room was nothing but an alcove with a stairway leading to a second floor. Lopez pointed up with his finger, readied his weapon and started a careful climb up the stairs with the other two soldiers following closely. At the top of the staircase Lopez looked around and saw a narrow hall with several doors, like a series of small apartments. Lopez knew the door to the far right must have window access to the road where they had been receiving fire.

Lopez moved to one side of the door, Arnold covered the other side and Holmes crept up to the door handle. Holmes gave the men a 1,2,3 hand signal then rammed the door with his shoulder, bursting into the small room. Lopez flowed into the room behind Holmes and covered the left side of the room while Arnold flowed to the right of the door. Seated at the opposite wall in front of them was a very old Arab man with a deeply weathered face, gray hair and a close-cropped gray beard. He was sitting in a tattered and overstuffed chair. Standing next to him were two boys. Lopez figured they couldn't have been older than

15. Next to the window was a small table where a rusty and battered AK-47 lay.

Holmes stepped up to the old man and butted him in the face with the stock of his carbine. Blood poured from the man's nose as his head rocked back with the blow and bounced off the wall. Holmes turned back to Arnold and Lopez, who were holding security at the door, and yelled with a savagery that neither of the soldiers had heard before. "These assholes are part of the IED ambush! They're the reason Jones and Jimenez are piles of fucking goo in that HUMVEE. We're going to take these shit birds off the board before any more of our brothers get slaughtered!" He pulled the pistol from his holster and, to the shock of Arnold and Lopez, put the black, cold barrel into the old man's mouth and pulled the trigger. Brains and blood spattered against the brick wall and the man slumped forward in his seat. The two boys screamed.

Lopez bent over and threw up, unable to process what he had just seen. Holmes turned to the two soldiers, his eyes aflame with hatred and a strange sense of satisfaction. "You two take out these other shitheads," he said, pointing his pistol at the two boys, who were now cringing against the wall, crying. Arnold was unable to speak as he stared at the boys. Lopez said, "Sarge, we can't kill these kids! It's murder!"

"Bullshit, they killed our guys, shot at us and will do it again. Do it now!" he demanded.

Lopez shook his head. "I can't do it, Sarge."

"You will do it, you weak bastards," Holmes spat out in a rage, turning his pistol on the two soldiers. "You'll shoot them, or I swear to God, I will drop you both right here." Holmes raised the gun and released the safety. Arnold walked forward in a daze and pulled his pistol out. The boys had slumped against the wall, cowering in fear, huddled next to each other. Lopez watched Arnold look back at him with a pleading look, frozen in place. Holmes fired a shot over Arnold's head. "Do it! Do it now!" Lopez saw Arnold close his eyes as he put the big pistol in the boy's mouth and pulled the trigger.

Lopez slid to the floor, unable to process what he had just seen. Holmes walked over and put his pistol to Lopez's head. "You're next. Either do this, or I will take you out right now. Your choice, soldier." Lopez tried to move, but his hands felt like lead. He couldn't believe what was happening. Suddenly a gun went off. Lopez and Holmes both turned to look at Arnold—he was bent over, the pistol still in his hand, blood pooling around Arnold's feet from the second boy. Lopez stood up, walked over to Arnold, gently pulled the pistol from the boy's mouth and took it away from Arnold. Lopez looked into Arnold's eyes—they were dead pools of pain and regret.

Holmes nodded to the door and Lopez and Arnold, walking like zombies, made their way out the door into the hallway, down the stairs and back out to the alley. Outside the entryway, one of the soldiers from the other unit in Baghdad was holding security for them. Lopez and Arnold passed him without even looking at him. The third soldier from upstairs, the master sergeant, spoke to him, "We killed the terrorists up there, we're all clear here now."

"Do you need me to go up there to collect the weapons?" the soldier asked.

"No, we're all good," said Holmes as he passed the lone soldier and headed back to their HUMVEE.

When Holmes turned the corner in the alley, the soldier hesitated, then proceeded up the stairs. Captain Reynolds had given him an order to collect any enemy weapons. He didn't know the tall master sergeant, but he was not about to disobey the captain. He climbed the stairs, saw the open door to the right and stepped in. The scene before him could not have been more hellish. He lowered his weapon, closed his eyes and fought back the tears. After a brief pause, he stepped back into the hallway, shaking his head as if to knock the images from his mind and stumbled downstairs where he threw up in a corner.

19

MAY 2012, GRAND JUNCTION, COLORADO

At three in the morning, Amber awoke from a nightmare where Lopez, Arnold and their mothers all stared at her as if she had something they all needed. She tried to go back to sleep, but those faces in her dreams wouldn't go away. She moved to the couch, threw a blanket over her head and tried to sleep. Nikita was confused by the change of routine and stuck her wet nose under the blanket, giving Amber a lick on the cheek. "It's OK girl, lie down here," Amber said, pointing to the floor. Nikita reluctantly curled up on the floor next to the couch, perking her ears up at the sound of an owl hooting in the yard.

Back at her desk Tuesday morning, Amber opened her laptop and stared at the other cases she had to resolve. Those would have to wait, she decided, she had to find out more about Lopez and Arnold. She reached for the file folder on Lopez and sorted through the documents until she found the unit he was assigned to: Charlie Company of the 157th Infantry Battalion. She needed to talk to someone in the same National Guard unit as Lopez. Maybe there was a connection she could make or a fellow soldier she could talk to about him. She recalled the meeting with Maria Lopez. "I want you to find out why my son died." She'd made a promise to Lopez's mother, and she intended to keep it.

She typed Charlie Company of the 157 Infantry Battalion into Google and came up with a phone number for the unit in Grand Junction. She dialed it straight away. "Sergeant Garcia, Army National Guard," a female voice greeted after the second ring.

"Hello, my name is Amber Downing, I work here at the VA in Grand Junction. I was hoping there's someone in the unit I could talk to about one of your former soldiers."

"Which soldier are you referring to?"

Amber hesitated, not wanting to scare off Garcia. "Sergeant Henry Lopez."

There was silence on the other end of the line for a few moments. "What do you need to know about him?" Amber sensed the change in Garcia's voice. The friendly tone had become all business.

"VA Headquarters has tasked each VA hospital with collecting data on veteran suicides for the last five years. I'm just trying to gather some basic information about him." Technically, this was true. She'd just left out the part about trying to find out why Lopez died from suicide.

"Well, we're kind of a skeleton crew right now, but I deployed to Iraq with Lopez so I could probably answer a few questions."

"That would be super helpful. Thanks so much, Sergeant Garcia, I'll be over there in about 30 minutes, is that OK?"

"Sure, see you then."

Amber sat back in her chair and thought about the upcoming meeting. She'd have to be very careful about her questions. In her experience, military personnel were very reluctant to share negative information about members of their unit. It was like protecting the family. If Garcia got a whiff that Amber suspected there was something strange about Lopez's suicide, Garcia would throw up a shield wall in a heartbeat.

Amber stopped at a local coffee shop on the way and picked up two lattes. She knew that most soldiers loved their coffee. The long hours and late nights during training and operations were often fueled by a strong Cup of Joe.

The red brick National Guard building loomed large as Amber parked and let Nikita out. She was balancing two coffees in a carrier in one hand and Nikita's leash in the other. She found the entrance and pushed on the red buzzer with her elbow. Garcia's voice came over an intercom. "Present your credentials, please."

Amber dropped the leash, pulled her VA ID card from around her neck and held it to the camera mounted above the doorbell. The door clicked and Amber and Nikita walked in. She stopped inside the doorway and waited. Amber saw a female soldier walking down the hallway toward her.

The woman was a striking Latina soldier with fine, sharp features. She was wearing her battle dress camouflage uniform, with dark hair tucked in a bun behind her head. Amber noted the top of a tattoo on her neck, protruding above the soldier's T-shirt.

"Amber Downing?"

"Yes, nice to meet you, Sergeant Garcia."

The soldier glanced at Nikita but ignored her. "You can call me Isabella."

"Got it, I needed some coffee so I bought you one too."

Isabella smiled, nodded and took the cup Amber handed to her.

"Is there a place we can talk in private?"

Amber noticed the slightest upturn of Isabella's perfect eyebrows when Amber mentioned a private space.

"Sure, follow me." Isabella led them down a white corridor lined with photos of the unit on the walls to an empty conference room on the left. They both sat down, and Nikita curled up under Amber's chair.

"How can I help you, Ms. Downing?"

"As I mentioned, Sergeant Lopez is one of the 142 veteran suicides I have to document. I just happened to notice on the VA spreadsheet that Lopez was assigned to your unit so I was hoping I could just ask a few questions. Can you tell me anything about Lopez?" She left her question vague, hoping Isabella would elaborate on the man.

Garcia took a sip of her coffee and noticeably shifted in her seat. "He was a good soldier, did his time in Iraq, performed well and came home. His suicide was a tragedy. It was a total shock to all of us in the unit."

"You mentioned on the phone that you deployed with him to Iraq."

"That's right," Garcia took a sip of her coffee, warily eyeing Amber.

"So, what was his duty? I'm a former Army MP myself. I was a dog handler working out of Baghdad." Amber figured she should play that card now, maybe get Garcia to trust her more.

"We were running convoys out of the Green Zone to different fire bases. Lopez and his battle buddy, Corporal Arnold were assigned to one of our convoy teams."

"Wait a minute," Amber said, trying to hide the shock in her voice. "You mean Sergeant Lopez and Corporal Jerry Arnold were in the same unit?"

"Yeah, they deployed together in the same platoon. In fact, they were good friends. That's another reason both the suicides were a shock to us. They were such good friends. They had each other to rely on and talk to."

Amber's head was spinning. She took a sip of her coffee and reached down under the table to pet Nikita to help gather her thoughts and calm her mind. *Lopez and Arnold were in the same unit and were friends!* She tried to compose herself.

Amber decided to take a different tack, "How did their deployment go? I was captured for a time by AQI, so I know how a deployment can take a hard turn south."

"You were captured? My God! I can't imagine," Garcia said, leaning forward in her chair. Amber didn't elaborate and Garcia didn't push the issue. Garcia sat back, now more willing to share information with this former soldier who had seen combat and captivity by the enemy. "Most of their convoy runs were straightforward. Maybe every other week there was a TIC." The acronym for 'troops in contact' meant a firefight and brought Amber immediately back to the sights and smells of Iraq. "There was one mission, towards the end of the deployment, that went off the rails. We lost three of our soldiers in an IED attack, good friends of Arnold and Lopez."

Amber sensed she was close to the underlying truth now. "Oh, wow. What happened?"

Garcia looked down at her nails, then her face turned red with anger. "Fucking AQI put an EFP in some trash cans down an alley. They hit the third vehicle in the convoy, a HUMVEE broadside, killing all three soldiers. Two died instantly, one bled out after losing both his legs." Amber sensed the pain in Isabella's voice. Clearly, she knew these soldiers too and suffered from their loss.

"Arnold, Lopez and Master Sergeant Holmes were in the fourth vehicle in the convoy. They were first on scene. Some terrorists fired on them from a window after the IED went off and they assaulted the building and killed all three. Real heroic stuff. They were decorated for bravery."

That was a life-altering event, thought Amber. *Was it enough for two veterans to take their own lives? Who was to say how it affected them? Soldiers had killed themselves for far less trauma than this.* She sensed this incident must have had something to do with the suicides.

Amber recalled seeing or hearing the name of the other soldier, Holmes, somewhere. She racked her brain to remember. Then it came to her: Holmes had signed the last performance evaluation for Lopez, the negative evaluation that was a career killer.

Garcia had given Amber more information than she'd hoped for. It was time to try one more line of questioning, since she had nothing to lose now. "I noticed in Lopez's personnel file that he was given a career-ending evaluation at the end of his last tour? How does a guy decorated for bravery get an evaluation like that?"

Garcia looked confused. "How did you get a copy of that evaluation? Those records are private." Amber quickly realized her mistake. She shouldn't have had the file because it's not a document the VA would normally have access to. Maybe more importantly, the file was not supposed to exist since someone had stolen the originals. Garcia might have nothing to do with that, but Amber couldn't tell her about the missing files of Lopez and Arnold.

"Sergeant Lopez's mother gave me a copy of his last evaluation." she explained, though she didn't want to reveal that she had copies of Lopez's entire service record.

The answer seemed to satisfy Garcia. "Well, personal evaluations are private, as you know, so I don't know what was in his last one - I never saw it. I know he did a great job in Iraq and everyone in the platoon respected him."

"I can tell you; this was a really bad evaluation - it said he was insubordinate, not fit for the Army. It would have been a death knell for his career," Amber pointed out to Garcia, looking for her reaction.

Garcia looked mystified. "That's strange, I wasn't aware of a negative evaluation. Now it makes sense why he got out of the Army. I was trying to talk him into re-enlisting, but he was set on getting out."

Amber sensed Garcia truly was as surprised as she was about the evaluation. She didn't want to push her luck with Garcia. She shrugged as if it would remain a mystery and said, "Well, thanks so much for your time. This will help me close out these two cases."

"What is the VA trying to do with this data, anyway?" Garcia asked as they both stood.

"I honestly don't know. I'm down in the trenches trying to give them good data. My boss says they're going to use the information to try to prevent future veteran suicides."

"Well, I certainly hope so," said Garcia, opening the door for Amber and Nikita.

Amber nodded. "Me too. Thanks again, it was nice to meet you, Isabella."

"Same here, let me know if you need anything else."

Amber hadn't expected Garcia to offer further help. She hoped she wouldn't need it, but something told her she might need to return.

On the drive back to the VA, Amber tried to make sense of the information Garcia had shared. *This changes everything. Two soldiers from the same unit had committed suicide within a few months of each other, and both had used a pistol in the mouth as the method. Then throw in the fact that both of their military service records had apparently disappeared. This is just plain weird.* She thought about taking this information to her boss, John, but quickly dismissed the idea. *He'll tell me I'm working outside the scope of the project and order me not to pursue it anymore.* No, she was going to continue to investigate the Lopez-Arnold connection while working on the remainder of the project.

20

SEPTEMBER 2008, SALADIN PROVINCE, IRAQ

Amber felt the pistol jab into her spine as KAT shoved her through the tall crops behind the safehouse. Amber was glad to be free of the shackle in that dank basement, but she was afraid of where KAT would take her next. She looked up at the stars as her captor urged her to move quicker. She sensed it would be dawn soon; the faintest hint of light was peaking above the horizon to the east. After ten minutes of walking through chest-high fields of wheat, they came to a small clearing where a battered Toyota HiLux sat parked at the end of a dusty dirt road. Aiming the pistol on Amber, KAT zip-tied her hands and pushed her into the back seat of the small pickup truck. Amber knew she had to create a delay somehow, give a rescue team time to find her. That's when she heard it.

Razor stood outside the house pawing the dirt and growling as Parnell and his fire team assaulted the building. Razor was used to being part of the pack that went inside, so he was confused. Why was he left alone outside while the men were inside? Where was his master? He had followed her scent to this building. This was not the routine. He was anxious and upset. He heard shots fired in the house and gave a bark before running to the door the men had gone through, but it was closed. Listening for the men inside, he heard voices, then sprinted around the back of the building looking for another entrance, a way to join the men. That's when he smelled it, the unmistakable scent of his handler near a low basement door. He circled the ground near the door, pawing at the dirt and lifting his nose into the night air. Then he smelled her again, the scent led off into the bushes. Putting his nose to the ground, he sniffed the dark earth, trying to lock in on the smell. He trotted back and forth until he picked up the scent. Now he smelled something else. It was the scent of the man who had hurt him in the forest. The two smells were mixed now. They both led off into the tall bushes. The soldiers had left him behind. His master would never leave him alone on a mission, he always went with her. He put his nose to the ground again, picked up the odors and followed them into the darkness.

In their frantic search before the sun came up and the extraction helo landed, Parnell's team hadn't noticed the well hidden door that led to a basement. After clearing the last room, Parnell motioned for the men to exit back out the front. Parnell walked carefully back out the front door, his weapon at the ready in case an insurgent had sneaked out of the building and moved around to ambush them as they exited through the choke point. When he saw it was clear, he motioned for the other three to follow him out the door. The sun hadn't risen above the horizon yet, but there was an orange glow to the east. He knew the extraction helos would soon arrive—they were out of time.

"Pino, grab the dog, let's move off into the bushes while I talk to the colonel, and we wait for the extract." Pino gave a thumbs up to Parnell and blew a quiet whistle. When Razor didn't respond, Pino started a slow search of the front yard, whistling periodically. He moved around to the rear of the building—still no dog. He pushed his mic button, "The dog is gone, I can't find him."

Parnell, huddling out front with the other two, gave an exasperated order. "Find that damn dog, Pino. We can't lose two members of our team today." Suddenly Parnell heard the distant sound of rotors. The colonel had sent the extraction helicopter at first light as he said he would. Parnell grabbed the VHF radio mic from his radioman. This was not going to be a pleasant call.

"Jackal, this is Honcho."

"Go ahead, Honcho."

"Sir, we did not recover the package, repeat, it was a dry hole. It was a torture house and bomb-making lab. The package could have been here, but we saw no signs. Recommend we take it out."

"Jackal, I understand. Do you have any more indications of the location of the package?"

"Negative. Sir ... one more thing. The dog is missing. When we came out of the house, he was gone." There was silence for a few moments. Parnell expected an ass-chewing.

"Jackal, we're checking with the UAV (unmanned aerial vehicle). If the dog has a tracking collar, we might be able to lock onto it with a drone. Stand by."

The Blackhawk helicopter sent to extract them was visible as a speck low over the horizon out of the south. It would be on the ground in five minutes. Parnell spoke over the intercom to his team, who were huddled in a defensive perimeter off to the side of the house. "That's our ride, ETA five minutes. The colonel is checking with the UAV guys to see if they can get a lock on the dog. Hold tight on boarding the helo until I hear from the colonel."

"Roger all," Thompson answered for the rest of the guys.

Johnson walked out to the best clearing in the field and threw an infrared chemical light on the ground. The Blackhawk pilot would see it as the best place to land, but it would be invisible to anyone without night vision goggles. Five minutes later, the helo began to descend, bank, flare and set on the ground, kicking up a cloud of dust and twigs that covered the area in a brown cloud.

Parnell keyed the handset. "Jackal, this is Honcho, the extraction has landed. Do we have permission to board?"

"Wait one," came the voice of the colonel.

"Damn! We were so close," Parnell whispered under his breath.

Back at the operations center, Colonel Harrison was seated at the plywood desk the Sea Bees had built, with four screens and a bank of phones in front of him. He'd been the Special Operations Task Force Commander for three months now. During that time, he'd barely slept five hours a day, trying to keep up with the multitude of ongoing missions and endless video teleconferences. A soldier ran through the door to his office and stopped quickly in front of his desk. "Sir, we've got a lock on the dog," he said, out of breath. "He's moving at about five miles per hour, heading northwest of the target house."

Colonel Harrison turned in his seat and looked up at his sergeant major, who was standing behind him. The two men had known each other since completing the Special Forces Selection Q-course together, nearly 30 years ago. Sergeant Major Brown had a shaved head and rock-like face. He spoke in a deep voice. "The dog is probably chasing after Downing. What do you want to do Sir, try and intercept the working dog or pull back and see where the dog heads?"

The two men had worked together for so long that they were perfect sounding boards for each other. Colonel Harrison spoke softly. "It's getting light now, if we put the team on the hunt, they could run into trouble. It's only four soldiers. The dog is injured and probably losing blood slowly. On the other hand, we must do everything we can to rescue our soldier and her working dog."

Brown nodded, "Sir, I think you're right. The team has been in the field all night and has already assaulted two buildings. I'd suggest we extract them, keep tracking the dog and see where it goes. We can always insert the team back into the situation if the UAVs or the dog find Downing."

The colonel nodded; he was thinking the same thing. He grabbed the red handset on his desk. "Honcho, this is Jackal, board the extraction helo with your team and stand by for further orders."

***

Parnell acknowledged the command and relayed it over the intercom to his soldiers. He knew it wouldn't go over well. Like him, the guys would want to continue the search. He shook his head in dismay. *Why were they stopping now?* He felt they should keep searching for

Downing. He knew they were close. The rest of the team nodded to Parnell. Pino took the lead and led the men, heads down against the blowing dust, into the side door of the black helicopter.

At that same moment, Razor trotted out of the bush into a small dirt clearing. He sniffed around and saw a pickup truck in front of him about 100 yards down the road. The scent led in that direction. It was getting stronger as he ran toward the truck. Before he could get there, the truck started and pulled out down the barely used dirt road. Razor let out a growl as he tucked his head and sprinted after the truck in the dark.

21

Back in her office, Amber paced the room, "What is going on here?" She said aloud to Nikita who was busy chewing on her stuffed duck. She sat down at her desk to write down everything she'd learned from her discussions with Isabella Garcia, Sergeant Lopez's mother and Corporal Arnold's mother. She started jotting down the facts as she knew them on a piece of paper. Sergeant Lopez and Corporal Arnold had killed themselves within a few months of each other. Both soldiers put a gun in their mouth to commit the suicide, which is very rare and somewhat strange. It turns out that both soldiers were in the same National Guard unit. In addition, the two were assigned to the same convoy platoon in Iraq, conducting the same missions together. According to Sergeant Garcia, there was one bloody operation that went awry that they were both involved in. Three of their teammates were killed in an IED attack, and Arnold and Lopez, along with a Master Sergeant Holmes, assaulted a building, killing three insurgents who were shooting at them. It turns out that Master Sergeant Holmes had either signed or authored a particularly damning evaluation on Sergeant Lopez that killed his career after his last tour to Iraq. Sergeant Garcia was clearly surprised or shocked by that evaluation. In all other respects, it seemed that Sergeant Lopez had been an exemplary soldier, well-liked by his platoon. Another strange coincidence was that the service records of both men were stolen or missing. Apparently, no one knew that Lopez had made a copy of his record and given it to his mother.

Amber stared at the random facts, looking for patterns. She kept coming back to the deadly operation in Iraq. That had to be the key. She knew from personal experience how traumatic an incident like that could be in one's life. What she couldn't piece together, though, was how that one incident had led to the suicides of two soldiers within a short time of each other. She was missing pieces of the puzzle.

Nothing was making sense. She put her notes aside and started working on a few of the other cases in her spreadsheet. Next up was an Air Force airman who'd taken his life after a breakup with his girlfriend. He hadn't been deployed to a war zone but worked as an aircraft mechanic at Tinker Air Force Base. Upon leaving the service, he moved back to his hometown of Delta, Colorado, and worked as a mechanic until taking his life 18 months later. It was tragic like all the others, but at least there was a clear, though senseless, motive. She made a few calls and searched the internet, collecting enough information to close out the case. It was straightforward, if there can be such a thing as a straightforward suicide.

On the drive home, Amber thought about Lopez and Arnold. *It would be good to talk this over with somebody.* Maybe she could bounce her discoveries off Hannah, get her perspective. She made the call. Hannah would meet her for dinner at Camp Robber, a restaurant named for the local Gray Jay that is a bold thief at campsites. They both loved the New Mexico-styled food there and the great service.

The thing about Hannah, Amber thought as she stepped into her truck, *is that she is better at talking than listening.*

Amber arrived first and secured a quiet booth near the back corner of the dining room. Nikita scouted out the diners then curled up under the table, her head resting on Amber's foot as she watched people walk by. Ten minutes later, Hannah walked in, looked around, nodded and headed to Amber's table. She had just finished her shift and was still wearing her dark blue Montrose Police uniform with a 9mm Glock pistol on her black duty belt. Underneath her shirt she wore body armor, making her look a little chunky. Her black hair was in a bun. The two friends hugged. Nikita stood up, gave Hannah a lick on the back of her hand then returned to her safe spot under the table.

"How are you doing, girl?" Hannah asked, sliding into the booth carefully with her kit. Amber looked across the table at her friend. She thought to herself for a moment, why they never talked about Iraq. Maybe it was just too difficult to talk about, too risky to their friendship.

"Everything is good," said Amber, wondering why she used that phony phrase so often when she was feeling the hollow darkness within her most of the time. Some things in your life you just have to fake to endure the day.

The waiter came by, and Amber ordered a margarita. Hannah ordered a coke. Amber figured Hannah didn't want people to see her drinking in uniform. They both ordered the burrito special, Christmas-style, with red and green chili sauce lathered on top. The friends caught up quickly before Hannah changed the subject, "How is that project coming?" she asked. Brian had asked her to see what Amber was doing with the Arnold suicide case. He was obviously interested as a Grand Junction police officer.

"I've been plowing through it, but two cases have thrown me for a loop," Amber said, sipping her drink, hoping she could get a perspective from her friend.

"What do you mean?" Hannah inquired, her expression fraught with anxiety that there were some gruesome suicide details that had gotten into Amber's head. The food arrived and they paused the conversation so the burritos wouldn't get cold. After a few bites, Amber started her story.

"Well, I stumbled on two cases that have a lot in common. The more I dug into them, the more coincidences I found. I just feel like something is off ... I can't put my finger on it."

"Tell me about them," offered Hannah.

And with that, Amber went through all the facts she'd discovered about Lopez and Arnold. Hannah listened quietly, which was rare for her. She usually interjected questions and comments, but tonight she sat without a word. At the end of her story, Amber said, "So what do you think?"

"I wouldn't put too much stock in the missing military files. Guys lose them all the time after getting out. They get misplaced, lost or thrown out during a move," Hannah said, putting down her fork after her last bite of tasty green chili. "I mean, why would someone take them? They're just a bunch of records of a military career and medical records. It doesn't make sense. There's nothing sensitive in there." Amber nodded in agreement but remained silent. She knew Hannah had more to say.

"And this notion that the suicides are connected doesn't make sense either. Soldiers from the same unit kill themselves all the time, especially if they've been in the shit together, I don't see the connection," Hannah said.

That had been in the back of Amber's mind, but she wanted to hear what her friend would say. "I don't have Arnold's record, but I didn't see anything out of the ordinary in Lopez's record, with the exception of the bad evaluation," said Amber, taking a sip of her margarita. "I certainly didn't see anything suspicious that would point to foul play."

The moment hung still as the two friends looked at each other, both in deep thought. "You see, I think maybe you're reading a little too much into this," said Hannah, draining her soda. Amber hadn't expected the mild rebuke from her friend. "Too bad you don't have the other record," said Hannah, "That might fill in the blanks."

"Yeah, that would be helpful, you're right," Amber said, immediately thinking of Arnold's mother and the cold reception she'd gotten when she'd visited. She didn't relish the idea of going back to Mrs. Arnold and asking about the possibility of another copy of the service record. Suddenly she remembered that Mrs. Arnold had been convinced her son's death hadn't been a suicide. At the time, Amber had considered her reaction as the incomprehensible grief of a mother who couldn't fathom the loss of her only son to suicide. It was clear that Hannah didn't see it, but now Amber thought just maybe, there was something going on here.

22

SEPTEMBER 2008, SALADIN PROVINCE, IRAQ

The dented HiLux pickup truck bounced down the rutted farm road in the dim early morning light. KAT knew the Americans would be throwing everything they had at him to find the woman soldier he had in the backseat. It was strange, he thought; they would sacrifice many soldiers to recover one captured soldier. The Americans were not accustomed to death like he had become. He looked down at his mobile phone and saw that he had coverage now. Pushing a few buttons on the flip phone, he made a call while slowing down to reduce the ambient noise. He kept the conversation generic as he had been taught by his senior Al Qaeda mentor.

"Hello," a voice said in Arabic.

"I have a package, meet me at the intersection where your uncle lives."

The voice on the other end was silent for a moment, thinking about the plan they had practiced in case this scenario ever happened. "You mean the crossroads near my uncle who has the farm?"

"Yes, yes, that is the one. Forty-five minutes."

"Inshallah."

KAT stepped on the gas, propelling the battered truck down the bumpy road. In the back, Amber bounced around on the torn-up vinyl seat like a fish in a basket. KAT had instructed her to lay down under the threat of knocking her teeth out. He didn't want her to see where they were going or to have a bystander spot a blonde-haired soldier in the backseat and notify the Americans. He was sure the soldiers were already blanketing the local area with radio messages about a reward for information leading to the recovery of the soldier.

⸺◦⸺

Although her hands were tied, Amber slowly reached them over her head to feel for the door latch. She grabbed the handle and slowly pulled down on it, realizing that it was unlocked and that she could pop it open if the time was right. At this speed she would land on her head and break her neck if she tried to jump out. She slid her hands back down to her waist as she tried to fight back the paralyzing fear that was creeping up her spine. She had to get away from her captor. The image of a video she had seen of AQI terrorists dressed in black standing over a frightened journalist held captive in front of them came to her mind as a terrible reminder of her predicament. The sick bastards cut off the guy's head with a long serrated knife right in front of the camera. It was the most horrible thing she had ever seen. The thought that she might end up in front of a camera as a sensational propaganda video for all the sickos in the world was overwhelming. She closed her eyes and tried to think of any hope she could mine. That's when she remembered Razor. *Had she heard his growl when she was being loaded into the truck? Or was it her imagination ... or maybe another dog?* She instantly recalled the knife wound that KAT had inflicted on Razor. Two thoughts followed—she didn't want an injured Razor to follow her; she couldn't stand to lose him like that, bleeding out somewhere along a dusty road. And second, she would make sure KAT paid a price for hurting Razor.

⁘

The colonel stared at the dark green computer screen, fiddling with the mouse. A female Air Force major from the UAV squadron stood next to him wearing her flight suit with a leather name tag that read *Major Archuleta, USAF.* "Sir, that little dot moving there is the military working dog," she explained, leaning over and pointing to the screen. "We picked up the GPS signal and were able to geo-locate the position and focus our UAV camera on him." The major pointed to a small blip on the screen that was clearly moving down a dirt road.

"Do you have a visual on where he's going or what he might be following?" asked the colonel.

"There are several vehicles heading down that same road ahead of the dog," she said, scrolling out the zoom knob so the colonel could see the bigger picture and the vehicles ahead of the dog. "There are also a few farmhouses ahead of them. The dirt road leads to a more populated area south of Balad. In less than an hour, these vehicles, and presumably the dog, will enter the outskirts of Baghdad where it will be very hard for us to track them in the maze of roads, vehicles, people and animals."

Colonel Harrison scratched the stubble on his chin. He'd been up for 36 hours straight overseeing this mission and several others. He had another tough decision to make: he could drop some troops on that road and have them interdict and search all the vehicles, or he could let the dog continue the hunt and zero in on the target. If he started a random vehicle search, the captor might get wind of the roadblock and slip away into the farmland. If he let the dog continue the chase, the wounded working dog could die from blood loss before he found Downing and the colonel would lose his best lead on the captor. His gut told him to go for the riskier move. He hadn't become Task Force Commander of all special operations forces in Iraq by being timid.

He turned in his chair to Command Sergeant Major Brown, who was standing behind him. "I think the dog is onto her scent. I'm going to let him keep hunting. Have that Blackhawk with Parnell's ODA (Operational Detachment Alpha) team head north and set down in Balad and await further orders. I want that bird turning hot on the tarmac so they can depart on a minute's notice."

Brown nodded and said, "Yes, sir," before stepping out of the office to pass the colonel's orders to the Task Force Operations Officer.

23

MAY 2012, GRAND JUNCTION, COLORADO

A late spring snow drifted like small white butterflies on Amber's windshield as she headed to work, making the world outside her car look like a snow globe. Just when she thought winter was over, Mother Nature planned another slap down. The weather was unpredictable in Western Colorado in the spring, but she'd let the last few days of warm weather lure her into complacency. The wet snow stuck to her wipers and started to build up on the road, covering everything in a layer of dirty gray. Suddenly her cell phone buzzed. She wouldn't have picked it up, but she noticed it was from Maria Lopez.

"Hello?"

"Ms. Downing, this is Maria Lopez. You came to see me about my son."

"Of course, Mrs. Lopez, how can I help you?"

"Well, someone broke into my home last night when I was at bingo. I don't know if they took anything, but they threw my stuff all around."

"Have you called the police?"

"No, I thought I would talk to you first."

"OK, Mrs. Lopez, I'll be there in about 15 minutes."

"Thank you, I'll see you soon."

Amber realized the only reason Mrs. Lopez had called her was because she thought the break-in was somehow connected to her son or his death. She was already in Grand Junction near the VA hospital, so she made a U-turn and headed south towards Maria's home. Ten minutes later, she pulled up next to the chipped curb. Sparkling snow covered the sidewalk and driveway like white glitter but was beginning to melt quickly. Amber decided to leave Nikita in the truck—no telling if broken glass or other dangers were on the floor of Maria's home. She rang the doorbell and Mrs. Lopez answered, wearing a white robe with roses printed on it and fuzzy slippers.

"Come in, dear, it's cold outside," she said, stepping back and closing the door behind Amber. The place was a wreck. The cabinets in the small living room had been opened, the contents thrown all over the floor. Amber gazed around in shock at the condition of the once tidy little home.

"Let me show you the rest of the house," she said, leading Amber down the hallway to the two small bedrooms in the rear of the home. At each entrance, Maria stopped and let Amber see the wreckage in the rooms. Beds were tossed, the closets were emptied onto the floors, boxes were turned upside down, all of Maria's belongings were strewn across the floor like a garage sale hit by a tornado.

Standing in the small master bedroom, Amber looked around and asked, "Did you notice anything missing?"

"Not yet."

"What about jewelry, did you have anything expensive?"

"Si, but here it is," Maria pointed to the open drawer of the night-stand next to the bed that had been taken out and dumped onto the pillow. There, plain as day, was a string of pearls, two gold rings and a diamond pendant.

"It makes no sense. Why would thieves leave these?" she asked, looking at Amber.

"Maybe they were after something else..." Amber suggested, letting that hang in the air.

"Si. I didn't want to believe it, but this happened the day after I gave you my son's military file." It sounded a bit like an accusation.

Amber had been thinking the same thing but hadn't wanted to alarm Maria. "I was thinking the same thing, Mrs. Lopez. Did you tell anyone about the file or that you gave it to me?"

"No, no. I have talked to no one about that." A silence hung between them for a moment as they slowly walked to the front door.

"I think you should call the police, Maria. They have resources to help. Maybe they'll see something we don't, or at least get some fingerprints."

"OK, I will call them. I just wanted to call you first."

Amber felt both touched that Maria had contacted her and angry that the break-in had happened the day after they'd met. "I'll come by after work and help you clean up."

"Oh no, it's OK. I've lost my son and my husband. It's time for me to get rid of some things. I've been meaning to clear out much of this for a while, now I have no excuse."

Amber knew how unwanted it would be to have a stranger wade through the detritus of your life. "I understand but let me know if I can help in any way. If the police find out anything, please let me know." Maria looked distraught as Amber returned to her truck.

Back at work, Amber let Nikita play in the snow behind the hospital before they went inside. Nikita built up so much energy on the long car ride to work that Amber had to let her get it out. Snow was nearly her favorite thing. She ran in circles, licking at the cool white powder every few feet. She plopped down on her back, rolling in the delightful white stuff, popping up and looking like she'd been frosted for Christmas. "Come on, girl, we've gotta get to work," Amber said, brushing the snow off Nikita's back and snapping on her leash.

They walked to the basement and Nikita crawled under Amber's desk to take a nap as Amber made a cup of coffee. She sat down, kicked off her shoes and massaged Nikita with her toes. She sipped the black coffee out of the cup and thought about what had happened to Maria's home. If, and it was a big IF, someone was searching for Sergeant Lopez's military records, why would they do it last night? The only logical answer she could come up with was that someone thought Mrs. Lopez still had them. Nobody knew she'd given the records to Amber. *Actually, that's not true,* she realized. She'd told Sergeant Garcia that Maria had given her Sergeant Lopez's last evaluation. She hadn't mentioned that she had the whole file. She'd also told Hannah last night at dinner. She picked up her phone.

Hannah answered after three rings. "Hey, Amber, what's up? I'm on patrol right now."

"I won't keep you, I just wanted to ask if you talked to anyone about our conversation last night."

"No, of course not. Why, what's up?," Hannah sounded a little nervous.

"Well, Sergeant Lopez's mother called me this morning on my way to work. Someone ransacked her house last night. She doesn't think they took anything, but I went over there and could tell someone was obviously looking for something."

"You think it could be those military records you told me about? But you said the mother gave them to you."

"She did, but no one knows that. Maybe someone thought she still had his file."

"Listen, Amber, it's probably just a break-in. It happens all the time in Grand Junkie. I've gotta run but let me know if you find anything else."

"Will do, thanks, Hannah."

Amber set her phone down. She needed to call Sergeant Isabella Garcia, but she paused to think about it first. Unlike her friend Hannah, Isabella might feel like Amber was accusing her of something. But she couldn't think of a way to sugarcoat it, so she made the call.

They had exchanged cell phone numbers, so Garcia knew it was Amber calling. "Hey Downing, what's up? Didn't think I would hear from you so soon."

"Yeah, me neither, but listen, Isabella I was wondering if you told anyone else about the conversation we had?"

There was that silence on the line again. Amber dreaded the idea that Garcia would be angry with her.

"As a matter of fact, I did mention it to Officer Holmes. He came by for some paperwork yesterday afternoon."

"What do you mean, *Officer* Holmes?" Amber asked, trying to hide her shock.

"Holmes is a Grand Junction police officer. He's a part-time soldier here with the National Guard. I told him you were doing this

VA suicide investigation thing on Lopez and Arnold. I knew he'd be interested because he deployed with those guys and knew them well."

"You didn't tell me he was a police officer." Amber tried not to sound accusatory, but she was stunned.

"Most of our soldiers are part-timers. Only a handful are full-time like me. I didn't think anything of it, since we were talking about what happened to Lopez and Arnold." Isabella was starting to sound defensive. "What does he have to do with this, anyway?"

"He doesn't have anything to do with my inquiry. I was just surprised to hear he was a police officer. Listen, I'm sorry, I didn't mean to make a big deal. It's all good."

"OK, but why did you call to ask me if I told someone? Has something happened?" Garcia asked.

Amber paused before answering. Holmes certainly had access and methods to break into Maria's home. If Holmes had tossed Maria's house, she didn't want him to know that Maria had told her about it. It would be logical to assume she knew nothing about the supposed burglary. Then again, she didn't want to lie to Isabella and lose her trust.

"I forgot to ask you yesterday to keep our conversation private. You know how it is with suicides and the news in a small town. We don't want to upset the families."

Another pause ensued, and Amber wasn't sure Garcia believed her lame answer. It was the truth, just not the whole truth.

"OK, I get it. I'll keep our conversation close hold."

"Thanks so much, Isabella."

"Hey, when you finish the report on our soldiers, can I look at it? Holmes wanted to see it too."

Amber threw out some privacy act mumbo jumbo to give her time and space to consider the request. "I'll talk to my boss, see what I can do."

"Got it, take care, Downing."

"Thanks, you too."

24

September 2008, Saladin Province, Iraq

Razor had lost the scent of his master and the other man who was with her. He'd sprinted after the truck when he emerged from the woods and saw Amber loaded into the back but couldn't catch it as it sped away from him. However, his nose was keen enough to pick up the smell of the tires in the soft brown dirt. The vehicle had run over a carcass recently and the odor of the dead animal was distinct and strong in the vehicle tracks. He was so completely locked on to finding his master that he didn't even feel the blood trickling down the fur on his left side from the wound on his back. Most of the blood had dried and congealed within the medicated patch, but now that he was running hard and pumping his iron heart, the blood started to seep out the edges of the bandage. Instinctively, he knew he couldn't catch the truck at a sprint, so he settled back into a long-distance trot, a pace that his ancestors had developed to chase animals for a 100 miles or more until the exhausted prey stopped and gave in to death. He looked like a lean wolf clipping across the tundra on the heels of an elk.

The rutted road ran parallel to several small weary farms and expanses of open fields. Rusted and dented 55 gallon drums, piles of tires and rocks delineated the property lines of the small farms. A low cloud of dark smoke hung over the horizon, permeating the air with the smell of burning crops and human waste. A young boy in dirty pants and a long Arab headdress looked up from shoveling out a drainage ditch by the road to see Razor fly past, his large tongue lolling to one side. In the early morning light, the black-nosed dog looked like a hound from hell on a mission from the devil. In the Arab world dogs are not known and treated as man's best friend.

◆

The colonel twisted in his uncomfortable seat. His lower back was killing him. *Too many parachute landings,* he thought. The lack of sleep, endless bad coffee and stress from trying to recover an American captive were beginning to get to him. Lieutenant Colonel Tinsdale suddenly appeared in the doorway. "Do we know which vehicle the dog is chasing yet?" the colonel yelled at his operations officer, immediately regretting his tone. He'd been in the young officer's shoes himself and had to deal with stressed out commanders demanding answers.

Tinsdale looked young for his age, with curly black hair and large eyes that were so blue they shone like sapphires. He stood in an ironed camouflage uniform at the entrance to his commander's office. As the point man for his boss, he too had been up for two days straight trying to coordinate all the details and assets to recover Downing. His commander was getting tired of excuses; he wanted results. If they didn't get Downing back shortly, all hell would break loose, and they might never rescue her. The president would be informed, a gaggle of senior officers across Iraq would descend on the task force, relegating him and the colonel to sitting in a corner and making coffee. Worst of all, it would immediately set back the effort to find Downing, as the larger task force would lack the situational awareness and agility that the small task force had developed.

"Sir, the UAV has a lock on three vehicles, each just ahead of the dog," Tinsdale spoke with a Boston accent as he briefed his boss. "We're convinced Downing must be in one of those three vehicles. We've labeled them Alpha One, Two and Three. Alpha One is a late model sedan, maybe brown or dark blue. It's the farthest from the dog, two miles ahead. It's moving slower than the other two, possibly due to the condition of the road and the low clearance of the car. Alpha Two is a small lorry, like they use to bring farm goods to market. It's a mile ahead of the dog. Alpha Three is a HiLux pickup truck, red or orange. It's about a half mile ahead of the dog.There are no other vehicles on the road right now that the dog could be chasing."

The colonel rubbed his gray stubble, considering his next course of action. Just then the red phone rang. He looked at his Ops Officer with the pained look that said, "Here we go." Tinsdale anxiously watched his boss pick up the line.

"Yes sir, I understand, sir. We'll be ready, sir." The colonel hung up the phone and looked back at his ops officer. "The general is on his way here." His boss was referring to the four-star Commander of all forces in Iraq, General Schwartz. Shit was starting to hit the fan.

"Launch that bird in Balad now," the colonel spat out to Tinsdale. "Put Parnell's team in low orbit five miles ahead of those three vehicles and await my orders."

"Yes sir," Tinsdale said, saluting sharply before he stepped out of the office, sweat beginning to bead on his forehead.

KAT picked up his mobile phone, dialing with one hand as he steered the truck in the early morning light down the bumpy road. He was heading northeast, and the red sun was peeking over the horizon, throwing orange light beams into his dark eyes. The phone rang twice before someone picked up. "Hello."

"I'm 10 minutes away."

"Inshalla sheik."

They hung up. KAT noted that the man had called him sheikh. No one had called him that before. It was a title of honor and respect. *They are finally beginning to see my dedication to the cause,* he thought with satisfaction. The capture of an American was the finest example of bravery for Al Qaeda. It would be like a Sioux warrior getting close enough to touch a monstrous bison before killing it. KAT sped on, full of pride now at what he had accomplished. He looked over his shoulder and saw the soldier lying on her back in the seat. Everything was good, he would have this infidel secure in less than an hour. Then everyone would come to know Sheik Khalid Al Thine, the mighty warrior of God.

A vehicle ahead of him was bouncing down the road at a slow pace. The early morning light streaming through the dust made it hard to see. KAT honked and the lorry moved to the right so he could pass. As he approached the big truck, he stomped on the gas pedal, intending to pass the lorry fast so the driver would not have time to look down into the back seat and see a soldier lying there. The swirling dust between the two vehicles made that just about impossible anyway.

Amber looked up from the seat and saw the top of the big lorry as KAT passed it. She had an idea. It was worth a try, nothing to lose but broken bones. As the small truck passed the lorry, Amber counted to 25, giving KAT room to get ahead of the big truck. She waited until KAT came to a sharp corner and had to decelerate. It was time—she reached the door handle with her bound hands and pulled it down, scrunching herself up at the same moment and vaulting out the back door headfirst into the dirt road. The truck was doing about fifteen miles an hour in the turn when Amber hit the road. She tumbled and rolled four or five times, landing on her face just off the side of the road. The dirt was softer than she'd expected, like brown flour. She pushed herself up to her knees and stood up, surprised that she hadn't broken any bones. Coming up right behind her, she saw the big lorry rumbling down the road. She ran toward it. At the same time, KAT was spinning the little truck in the middle of the road, pulling a U-turn as his tires spun and threw dirt everywhere. The road was too narrow, he couldn't spin the truck all the way around, so he had to make a three-point-turn. He stomped on the gas and flew back down the road, immediately seeing the headlights of the lorry that he'd passed.

The lorry driver stopped when he saw the woman standing in the road, and a big man stepped down out of the driver's seat. He was wearing loose pants, a faded blue shirt, sandals and a prayer cap. He looked Pakistani or maybe from Iran, Amber thought. She ran up to him, then looked back to see KAT making a U-turn and heading her way. All around her were low fields that had been recently cut. There was no cover or concealment anywhere if she took off running through the field. The big driver was her only hope.

"He's trying to capture me!" Amber yelled in English to the driver as she used her head to point at the truck now barreling back towards them. "I'm an American soldier. There is a large reward for me if you can get me to safety or an American base."

The driver clearly didn't speak English. He walked up to Downing, noticing the cuts and bruises on her face from the fall out of the truck. Her hair was disheveled, and her eyes were red. He looked stunned. He'd probably never seen an American female soldier. He looked up and saw the small pickup truck screaming to a halt. A tall Arab stepped out with a close-cropped beard and a hawkish nose. They greeted each other in typical Islamic fashion.

"Salaam alaikum."

"Alaikum salaam."

Amber moved behind the big man. KAT was keeping a close eye on her as he spoke to the driver. Amber could tell by the tone of voices that it wasn't going well. The big driver was probably asking questions about Amber and why she was tied up and injured. Suddenly KAT pulled a pistol from his belt inside the long robe he wore. The big lorry driver lunged forward, but KAT stepped back creating enough distance to get off a shot at close range. The 9mm bullet hit the driver in the neck, tearing through his windpipe and lodging in his spine. He fell to his knees, grabbed his throat then collapsed on his face in the dust.

KAT pointed the pistol at Amber. "Very stupid! You will pay for this." His face was a mask of rage and contempt. He walked over to

Amber and whacked her on the head with the pistol, knocking her to her knees.

25

April 2011, Grand Junction, Colorado

Sergeant Henry Lopez stepped out of Dr. Mankowski's office and noticed the small green buds forming on a tree in front of the medical building complex. It had been a long time since he'd noticed nature, or anything beautiful, for that matter. Everything in his life has been a shade of black and gray since Iraq. He'd just completed his sixth visit to the doctor and for the first time in a long while, he wasn't feeling overwhelmed by darkness. He jumped in his Subaru Forester and started to drive home. The air was crisp and clear, and he rolled his window down, even though it was 50 degrees outside. The cool air felt good on his face, made him feel alive, and blew away the cobwebs in his mind.

He pulled up to the curb at his parent's home and went inside. His father was still at work, but his mother was home cooking. He smelled the savory aroma of homemade tortillas coming from the kitchen.

"Hola, Momma," he greeted, walking into the small kitchen.

"Mijo, do you want to help me with these?" his mother asked, pointing to the large ball of tortilla paste she was kneading by hand.

"No, Momma, I can't do it as well as you," he said playfully, kissing her cheek.

"There's a letter for you from the post office, Mijo. Open it, I'm waiting to hear what they say."

Henry walked over to the coffee table and picked up the large brown envelope. He had applied for the U.S. Postal Service nearly four months ago. It had been a painful process. He ripped open the letter. *"Congratulations, Mr. Lopez, we would like to offer you a position as a mail carrier working in the Grand Junction area."*

"Hey, Momma, guess what, looks like I'll be working for the US Postal Service!"

Mrs. Lopez wiped her hands on a small kitchen towel, walked into the living room and gave Henry a big hug. "I'm so proud of you, Mijo."

Maybe, Henry thought, *just maybe, I can finally move past the demons of Iraq and start a new life. Maybe there's hope for me yet.*

The visits to the counselor had been making a difference and now this job opportunity came up after months of waiting. He decided to call Jerry, tell him the good news. The phone rang three times before Arnold picked up. "Hello."

"Hey, Jerry."

"Hi Henry," Arnold said, sounding down and out like he normally did.

"Hey, man, I just got hired at the post office," Henry said with enthusiasm.

"Good for you, Henry," said Jerry, but Lopez sensed he didn't really mean it. Both had been struggling since the mission in Iraq. They tried not to talk about it with each other, but it was a dark force that bound them together but also kept them emotionally apart.

"Listen, Jerry, I've gotta tell you something," Henry said to Arnold's silence. "I've been seeing a counselor about what happened. I was in a real bad place and I needed someone to talk to. He's good, a Vietnam vet."

"Wait a minute, Lopez," interrupted Arnold, reverting to Henry's surname as he'd done while they were in Iraq together. "We made a promise that we would never, ever tell anyone about what happened in Iraq. You remember that promise, don't you, Lopez? And you remember why we made that promise, right?" Arnold's voice was rising, the anger seeping through the phone.

"I know, I know what we promised, Jerry, and God knows I know why. But this is a counselor, man, there's that doctor confidentiality stuff. He can't say anything, and I really needed to talk to someone. I mean, the nightmares were getting worse. I'm having a hard time even getting out of bed, man," Lopez said, pleading his case to Arnold. "I thought maybe you might want to get some counseling too. I don't care what you say, Jerry, I know you're having a rough time like me. I'm just sayin' this would be good for you, bro. At least give it a try."

"Lopez, I can't believe you did that. After all the shit we went through together, and we made the pact. You're gonna get me thrown in the brig for the rest of my life!"

"No, man, that's not gonna happen, it's just a counselor," Henry said, trying to calm Arnold down.

"OK, then what did you tell him?" Arnold asked, his voice starting to crack.

"Calm down, Jerry. I didn't tell him anything. He just asked me questions, you know, and I tried to answer them."

"Yeah, like what kind of questions?"

"Just like what's bothering me and stuff like that."

"So what did you tell him, *specifically*, Lopez, about the mission, about you and me and those boys?" Arnold's voice was low now, almost menacing.

"I didn't tell him everything, man. I'm not stupid. Just that the boys died and it was our fault and I'm having a hard time living with it, that's all." Lopez was beginning to regret telling Arnold about the counseling.

"What do you mean telling him it was our fault? What exactly did you tell him?" Arnold was sounding hysterical. "Did you say we were forced to kill them? That they were only teenagers? That they were unarmed? What the fuck did you tell him, Lopez?" He was screaming now.

Lopez ended the call. "Shit!" he cursed under his breath. He couldn't have imagined it going any worse. He thought Jerry would understand that he had to get some help, and had to do something before the darkness swallowed him. But it hadn't gone that way. Jerry was still afraid that what they'd done, what he and Holmes had done, would come back to haunt them, would land them in jail, or worse. Henry shook his head, tossed the cell phone on his nightstand and lay down in the small bed in his mother's house. He wanted to forget it all now, forget the blood and brains on the wall, forget the look on Arnold's face after he'd shot those boys, forget the fact that he had watched it all happen, that he'd been powerless to stop it, that crazy Holmes had a gun to his head. He grabbed the pillow, pulled it over his face and tried to fall asleep.

An hour later, after he had calmed down, Jerry made a call.

"Hey," a voice answered, "What's up?"

"I need to talk to you."

"What's going on, Jerry?"

"Lopez is talking to someone about Iraq - a counselor."

There was silence on the other end, then, "Meet me at Sam's Tavern at four."

"OK," Jerry said, then hung up. As he put the phone in his pocket, he noticed his hand was trembling.

Jerry was filled with dark energy and fear that felt like a 1,000 monkeys running around in his head. He had an hour to kill before the meeting. He decided to drive up to the Colorado National Monument to take his mind off this shit. The massive rock cliffs towering above the west side of Grand Junction were a popular site. He enjoyed the long twisting road that wound through the park. It was like a vertical racetrack with miles of hairpin turns. He pushed his little Honda Civic through the curves, forcing his mind to think of nothing but steering, gas and brakes. For a few precious minutes, his mind was clear. At the bottom of the hill, he looked at his watch. He had 15 minutes to make the meeting.

John Holmes sat at the end of the long bar. He'd finished his shift, gone home and changed out of his police uniform into cargo pants and a windbreaker. He arrived early and picked a quiet seat near the back exit at the far end of the bar. The long, narrow building had barely enough room for the scratched and weathered bar top and a few dingy chairs and tables. Behind the bar was a tap, a large mirror and the typical selection of low to mid-grade liquor. There was no TV or jukebox, it was a varsity level drinking establishment, not a noisy sports bar. Two older vets sat at the other end of the bar, nursing bottles of Coors and chatting quietly. Holmes ordered a shot of cheap whiskey and took a sip, grimacing at the sharp bite as it burned going down. The front door opened, and Holmes turned to see Jerry Arnold step into the foyer, look around and nod at him. He was wearing blue jeans, army boots and a black pullover hoodie. Arnold saw Holmes at the end of the bar and felt his pulse quicken. Even though they had a pact, a blood promise, he couldn't shake the feeling that Holmes had put a gun to his head and would do it again if necessary. He passed the vets and took a seat on the bar stool next to Holmes.

"You wanna drink?" Holmes asked.

"Sure, whatever you're having," Arnold answered, pulling the hoodie off his head.

Holmes held up his glass and two fingers to the bartender and the gray-haired man with a huge jutting chin and a gash under his left eye poured two more shots of whiskey and set them on the bar in front of Holmes and Arnold. Holmes waited to speak until the guy moved back to the center of the bar and started wiping the bar top with a dirty rag.

"So tell me, Jerry, what exactly did Lopez tell you? Tell me everything."

Jerry took a sip of the cheap alcohol, and felt the burn in his throat. "First, he tells me he got a job at the post office. He hasn't started yet, he just got an offer or something."

Holmes nodded.

"Then he tells me he's been seein' a shrink and suggests I see one too. I can't believe the bastard broke our pact of silence," Jerry said, taking another slug of the dark whiskey.

"So tell me more about the shrink visit. What did he say?" Holmes asked, turning his stool to look straight at Arnold.

"You know Henry, he's always been weak that way. He said he's been having nightmares and shit, like the rest of us Iraq veterans are living with butterflies and rainbows."

Holmes nodded. "Go on."

"So I asked him what he's been telling the shrink, and at first, he says nothin', that the shrink is just asking him questions, you know like that Rorschach bullshit. Then I pressed him, and he admitted he told the guy about the mission in Iraq, said that two boys were killed, and it was our fault. I pushed hard again on what details he gave the guy, like did he tell him exactly how the kids died? Did he say how it went down? That's when he hung up on me."

"So you don't know if he meant you or me when he said it was *our fault*? Or if he told the guy exactly how the dirtbags died?"

"No, he clammed up and hung up on me, like I said."

Holmes tilted his head back and blew out a long breath, like he was letting the steam out of a motor before it blew up. The monster's anger was boiling below the surface. Arnold recognized the signs, he had seen it erupt too many times in Iraq.

Holmes drained the last of his whiskey and turned to Arnold. "It's good you brought this to me. We have to do something, I don't know what, but that mission in Iraq can't get out. No one would understand how those pieces of shit turned our buddies into goo, no one would understand how we saved the rest of our platoon from sniper fire."

Holmes balled up the drink napkin in his fist as he said, "This has to be buried once and for all."

26

Amber sat with her boots up on the desk, thinking about the new information she'd gleaned from Sergeant Garcia. Master Sergeant Holmes was a Grand Junction police officer, in addition to being a soldier. Garcia had told him about the evaluation report that Mrs. Lopez had given Amber, and the next day her house was ransacked. Holmes certainly had the means to do it, *but why*? she wondered. Something hit her, and she picked up the phone and called Lopez's mother.

"Hola," Mrs. Lopez answered.

"Hey Mrs. Lopez, it's Amber. I just wanted to check and see how you were doing with the mess after the break-in?"

"Si, thank you, Amber. I've been slowly cleaning, boxing things up and getting rid of a bunch of stuff. Maybe I'll take some to Goodwill, you know?"

"That sounds like a good idea." She paused for a moment, then said, "Hey, Maria, can I ask you a couple of things?"

"OK..." answered Mrs. Lopez, sounding hesitant.

"Did you find any other papers ... you know like letters, correspondence or other kinds of documents that belonged to Henry when you were cleaning up?" Amber held her breath as she waited for Maria to answer.

"Well yes, since you mentioned it. Inside a book in his closet, I found four or five medical statements tucked away that looked like receipts to me."

Her son was dead, and Amber didn't want to intrude on her privacy or her son's memory, but she needed to ask, "Do the statements have any information? I'm asking because I'm trying to figure out what happened to your son."

There was a pause. Amber heard Maria shuffling through some papers. "Here they are," she said. "All they say is that TRICARE military insurance paid the bills for Henry's visit to a Dr. Mankowski. It doesn't say what the service was for or anything. I didn't know Henry was seeing a doctor, he never told me anything about that."

Amber had a gut feeling about what Dr. Mankowski's specialty was and why Lopez wouldn't want to tell his mother about it. "OK, thank you, Maria. Just one last question. Did you call the police after I came over?"

"Si, I called after you left. They came right away, took pictures and fingerprints and told me there had been some break-ins in the neighborhood lately. I told them nothing was missing, but it didn't seem to matter to them. They said maybe the burglar was looking for something like a gun or big screen TV."

"Did you get the names of the officers you spoke with?"

"Let me see, one of them left me a card in case I needed to contact them." Maria shuffled into the kitchen and found the card on the counter. "Here it is, Officer John Holmes."

"And the other officer?"

"I don't remember. Officer Holmes was the only one to leave me a card," said Maria.

Amber's heart hit her throat. "OK, thank you so much. And please let me know if you need any help over there."

After she hung up, Amber put her hands over her face. *What is going on? Holmes, the guy with a direct connection to Lopez, had visited the scene of the crime the next day. Was he trying to find something? Maybe those medical receipts? Or the military files? Did he break into the house the day before and come back to clean up the scene?*

This is getting crazy, she thought. She put the leash on Nikita and walked her outside for a break. Another late spring snow was floating down from a slate sky, covering everything with tiny white flakes. Nikita licked the snow sticking to the grass blades and bounded around in circles, snapping at her own tail, excited to be in the cool snow once again.

Amber walked back and forth in the small patch of grass adjacent to the VA Medical Center, lost in thought. Wet snowflakes landed on her face and melted. She felt a tingle of fear creeping up her spine as she thought of Officer Holmes at Maria's home. That anxiety opened the dungeon door to her Iraq captivity. She tried not to think about it, but she saw a scene so vividly—KAT shooting the poor lorry driver in the neck. All the blood pooling down his shirt as he reached for his throat. The lorry driver had turned and looked at Amber before he fell on his face, as if to say, *See what you have done to me by bringing me into this mess?* The next thing she remembered was KAT whacking her over the head with that pistol, and then blackness.

Nikita sensed that Amber was off task, not doing well. Instinctively she ran to her master and poked her head through Amber's legs, looking up at her with those radiant eyes. "OK, girl, I get it, thank you. I'm back now, thank you, girl," Amber said, bending down and rubbing Nikita's ears. She stood up and knew what she had to do next. She would visit Dr. Mankowski and see what, if anything, he could tell her about Lopez.

Back in the office, Amber looked up Dr. Mankowski in Grand Junction on the internet. Dr. Stanley Mankowski was a psychiatrist specializing in depression, anxiety and PTSD. Bingo. She would have bet money on it. Lopez had been seeing a doctor to get help with PTSD after his tour to Iraq. She dialed the phone number listed for Mankowski's office.

"Doctor Mankowski's office, may I help you?" an overly eager female voice said.

"Hello, my name is Amber Downing and I work at the Grand Junction VA Medical Center. I'd like to set up an appointment with Dr. Mankowski."

"May I ask the nature of the appointment? Is it personal or business?" The woman sounded leary after hearing Amber was from the VA.

Amber knew she would never get an appointment to discuss a patient, even a dead one. "I can't talk about it over the phone, but it concerns a study that the VA is conducting on the suicide of veterans in this area."

More silence, then, "Well, we did have a cancellation for tomorrow at 9 in the morning. Will that work for you?"

"That will be perfect, thanks. You've been very helpful." Amber knew how much the gatekeeper could help or hurt her chances of getting into the big office. She always treated secretaries, administrative assistants, or whatever they were called, with respect.

It had been a productive day. She was beginning to feel like her work mattered, like she was doing something important. At least it kept her busy and tamped down the dark thoughts that were ever just below the surface of her consciousness, like black sharks. This Lopez, Arnold and Holmes business was starting to look like a puzzle. Fortunately, Amber was good at puzzles. She thought again of Lopez and Arnold's mothers. She had to get this right. They deserved her best efforts.

At nine a.m. sharp the next day she arrived at Dr. Mankowski's office. He worked out of a nondescript building in a U-shaped strip mall off Patterson Road. The neighboring vendors were a pottery shop, a dry cleaner, an insurance agent and a few more medical offices.

Inside, the place looked larger than it appeared from the outside. The furniture in the lobby was all shiny oak that was fashionable 20 years ago. An older woman stood up from behind a tall counter with crazy cat eyeglasses from the '70s. "How may I help you?"

Amber recognized the voice from her call yesterday. Nikita sniffed the air and turned her head to Amber as if to say, *What the heck is this place?*

"Hi, I have a 9 o'clock appointment with Dr. Mankowski," Amber answered, wondering why the woman hadn't assumed that already.

"Ms. Downing?" Amber nodded. "Please follow me," said the woman as she opened a side door and walked Amber down a narrow hallway to a back office. The door was ajar, and the woman peered inside and spoke to the doctor, "Your 9 o'clock is here, Ms. Amber Downing from the VA."

"Send her in, Mrs. Anderson." The woman pushed the door all the way open and Amber stepped inside the office. There was a small desk against one wall with a chair in front of it and two comfortable-looking chairs near a large window overlooking the back of the strip mall where a single pine tree stood amid a tiny patch of grass. It was like a mini Zen garden.

The doctor stood, looked at Nikita, then back to Amber and motioned for Amber to take the seat across the glass and chrome desk from him. *I guess we don't get the comfy chairs with a view,* she thought. The doctor knew she was here for business, not counseling.

Amber sat and looked across the empty desk at the man, trying to size him up. Nikita lay down on the floor, her tail under the doctor's desk. Amber put him in his early 70's. He had short, gray, cropped hair, silver eyes and thin glasses perched on the end of his red nose. She scanned the wall behind him and among the typical certificates hanging she spotted a purple heart citation from the U.S. Army. That was her in.

"I see you were in the Army," she said.

He twisted a pencil in his hand. "Yes, that's right, I was in Vietnam, 1st Cavalry Division. And you?" He'd guessed she was prior military. Amber knew a little about the 1st Cav in Vietnam, popularized by the movie, "We Were Soldiers." They'd had some terrible battles with hardened North Vietnamese Army troops.

"I was an MP and a military working dog handler in Iraq," she said, unconsciously looking down at Nikita and thinking of her running mate and savior, Razor.

"Both wars have brought me a lot of clients I'm afraid. But now you work for the VA, I understand?" He said, driving her to the point of her visit.

"Yes, I work in the dungeon and crank out statistics."

He smiled at her self-deprecating humor. "So what statistics have brought you to my office today Ms. Downing?" he asked, leaning back in his chair.

Amber paused, thinking how best to express why she was there. This doctor seemed friendly, so she decided to shoot straight. "Well, Dr. Mankowski, I'm working on a project to better understand the suicides of veterans in this area over the last five years. I collect data on the veterans, their suicide, potential motives, methods, things like that. I hated this project at first, but I've come to hope that some of my work may somehow be used to prevent future suicides."

"That sounds like a difficult project with a lot of unknowns," he observed, scratching at the gray stubble on his chin. "I imagine you've first-hand experience with suicide if you spent time in the Army?"

He'd hit that on the head. "Yes," she responded, trying to look nonchalant and hoping he wouldn't dig deeper and learn about Chris. "Unfortunately, I have."

He nodded sympathetically. "Well, what exactly can I do for you, Ms. Downing?"

"It concerns a patient of yours, Henry Lopez, a soldier who was stationed here at the National Guard unit."

"You must know I can't talk about any of my patients or their treatment."

"Yes, but what about when they're dead and the family is destroyed, and the mother pleads with me to find out what happened?" She worried she'd gone too far, but needed some lever to break the doctor out of his comfortable confidentiality shell.

She saw Mankowski lose his cool demeanor for the first time, as a cloud of anger swept over his face. "Henry Lopez, about five-nine, 175 pounds, lived with his parents on the north side of town?" he asked, raising his voice slightly and leaning forward in his chair.

"Yes, Sergeant Henry Lopez."

The doctor bent his head, closed his eyes and shook his head. He took his glasses off and pinched his tired eyes. *Lord knows how many suicides of patients this guy has experienced.*

The doctor put his hands over his face as if to hide his grief, then said, "Screw the rules, I'm about to retire, he's dead, I'm tired of seeing veterans kill themselves. I'll tell you what I can."

Amber felt a rush of relief knowing the doctor was on her team now. "Well, I've talked to his mother, and she had no indication that Lopez was at risk for suicide. She knew he'd had a rough tour in Iraq, but she said he had been improving and had just been hired at the post office. I also talked to a female soldier, a Sergeant Garcia at the National Guard unit. She told me that Lopez and another soldier named Jerry Arnold were in the same platoon in Iraq and apparently the two of them and a soldier named John Holmes were caught in a bad ambush."

Mankowski sat back, maybe reconsidering how much he was willing to tell Amber. Then he spoke in a low voice, "Henry first came to see me about nine months ago. He was suffering from what I diagnosed as acute PTSD based on severe moral injury." *There was that term moral injury again,* thought Amber. "He experienced a traumatic event in Iraq that left him with deep-seated mental and emotional problems. I treated those problems and saw Henry make some real progress. After five or six sessions, he stopped coming. I had the sense he was feeling much better about himself and had the tools to start to deal with PTSD. I would have liked him to continue in treatment, but he said he wanted to take time to use the new strategies he had learned first." He sat back, looking like he had said all he could. But none of this was news to Amber; she needed more detail. She played her ace cards.

"I was a captive of Al Qaeda in Iraq for a time. I understand the nature of PTSD." He nodded but let her continue. "Sergeant Garcia told me about the ambush in Iraq, but she didn't have the details of what really happened. That's what I'm trying to decipher here, Doc. And there's something else, something I shouldn't tell you, but I think you need to know. Some very strange things have happened that are causing me to question the nature of Lopez's suicide." Amber knew she was being vague, but she was taking a big risk with his confidence. If her boss found out about her extra-curricular work on this case, he would forbid it, or maybe even fire her.

Dr. Mankowski stood up slowly like he was bearing the weight of all veterans he had treated unsuccessfully, walked to the window, and stared out at the gray sky with his hands clasped behind his back. Amber thought he was about to usher her out of the office. He turned from the window and looked straight at her. "Henry's case was one of the most egregious examples of moral injury I had ever seen, and believe me, Ms. Downing, I have seen a lot in my 30 years of practice."

He paused then started again, "All I know is what Henry told me about the incident. Sometimes a patient has a skewed view of an event, especially if they feel guilty about their role in the trauma and moral injury." Amber nodded but didn't interrupt.

"Henry told me that his platoon ran into an IED ambush and that three soldiers in the vehicle ahead of him were killed. He and another soldier named Arnold were directed by their Master Sergeant to enter a building and suppress enemy sniper fire." Mankowski paused again and looked at Amber to gauge her reaction.

"Upon entering a second story room, Henry said they came across an old man and two teenage boys. There was a rusty rifle by the window, but the three were unarmed." The doctor looked down at his shoes before starting again. "The master sergeant shot the old man, then forced Lopez and Arnold at gunpoint to shoot the teenage boys. Henry said he refused but that Arnold shot them both as the master sergeant held a gun on Lopez."

Amber's head was spinning, her gut wrenching. She had to fight the dark images of Iraq, bile bubbling up into her own consciousness. She finally understood what moral injury was. Instantly she knew that she was also dealing with it. She hadn't been able to put a name to it before or get a handle on it, but now it clicked. Her mind raced, *What would have happened if I had not gone after Razor? Would all of those people still be alive? Would Razor still be alive?* She clenched her jaw and forced her mind back to the present.

"Can I ask you, Dr. Mankowski," she said, trying to hide the dread in her face, but following up on the hunch she'd just had, "How exactly were the old man and the boys shot? Did Henry tell you?"

Mankowski turned and looked out the window for a while. Amber was sure he was through answering questions. Then, without turning, he said softly, "Arnold and Holmes stuck a pistol in their mouths and blew out the back of their heads."

27

Amber was supposed to be back at work that afternoon, but she called in sick after the meeting with Dr. Mankowski. The story he'd told her had shaken her to the core, and she felt dizzy. It wasn't even lunch yet, but she stopped at the first bar she could find that was open. It was a drab tavern off Main Street that catered to locals. The neon sign in the window buzzed and crackled as it spewed out a pitiful welcome to drinkers.

The place was nearly empty, with one old guy at the bar sipping cheap whiskey who had long stringy hair, a beard and a pot belly the size of a basketball. The bartender was a plump woman with short, purple hair, an armful of tattoos and a bunch of hardware in her face. Amber took a seat at the far back of the bar and Nikita curled up under the bar stool.

"What'll it be, honey?" the bartender asked in a Texas drawl. Amber was always surprised at how many Texans she met in Colorado. You'd think half the state had moved to Grand Junction. They both shared the same love of ranches, wide open spaces, Mexican food and guns, she guessed.

"I'll take a shot of Tres Generacions," she said, barely pronouncing her favorite tequila.

"I'm sorry, honey, we don't carry that brand."

"Okay, whatever you have is fine."

The bartender pulled a tall bottle from the shelf behind the bar and gave Amber a long pour into a short, fat glass. No limes in this joint. Amber threw it down like it was cold water after a hot hike in the desert. After the roar in her throat, she felt the warmth hit her stomach. She nodded to the bartender, motioning her to bring the bottle over.

"You better slow down on those, honey, or you'll end up on my floor."

Amber glanced down at the area under her bar stool where Nikita lay and realized it wouldn't be a good place for a nap, even for a dog. It looked like spilled sticky drinks, peanut shells, grime and mud had been spread with a thin putty knife. She nodded at the bartender and the woman poured another tall shot. When Amber took a small sip of the drink, the woman walked back to her station where she resumed her work on a crossword puzzle.

Amber finally let herself think about what Dr. Mankowski had told her. She had suppressed it as soon as she heard it come out of his mouth. She used this technique in the Army to carry on when things all around her were going to shit. You had to keep moving forward or you'd drown in the muck.

But now it played out in her head. Her mind took the words that the psych doctor had told her and spun them into a 3D horror movie. She knew Iraq well; the smells, the sounds, the screams, the dirty roads, the ambush points, all of it. The scene played out in her mind.

Lopez, Arnold and Holmes had witnessed an IED attack that would have shredded their friends in the vehicle in front of them. Shooting unarmed civilians was murder. Civilians were shot in Iraq by accident all the time, that was part of the fog of war. Wrong place, wrong time. But to murder an old man and two teens in cold blood ... that was different. Yeah, they might have been taking some pot shots at the soldiers, but that didn't justify murder. And then there was the pistol in the mouth method of killing. That was beyond obscene. Amber's gut wrenched, something rose in her throat, and she felt like she might throw up as her mind replayed the killing of the boys. She envisioned their terror as the pistol was shoved into their mouth.

What had the doctor said? Arnold shot them both? Because Holmes held a gun to their heads? What kind of craziness is that? She'd seen and heard her share of bad stuff in Iraq, but this took the cake.

Her deep dive into the vengeful acts of Arnold, Lopez and Holmes opened the door to her own mental horror show. She saw the knife going into Razor, felt the chains on her wrists in the dark basement, saw the bloody lorry driver drop to his knees, felt the terror of her captivity. If she stayed in that mental hell hole for one more minute, she'd go crazy. She threw down the rest of the tequila, tossed a wad of cash on the bar and headed toward the door, Nikita in tow. Suddenly she stopped. A thought popped into her head. She remembered what KAT had told her when he'd first captured her - that U.S. soldiers had killed Iraqi prisoners. She'd scoffed at this as propaganda, something to get her to doubt herself, her fellow soldiers and their mission in Iraq. Now she realized, for the first time, that it was possible. Under the right circumstances with poor leadership and revenge in their hearts, her fellow soldiers could commit atrocities.

What she also realized, at the same moment, is that the act of putting a pistol in someone's mouth, pulling the trigger and splattering brains all over the wall, would be beyond terrible. It could easily be the catalyst for moral injury, suicide or even murder. She knew what she had to do next, but she dreaded it. She had to interview Holmes, the only person still alive from that operation.

This day was turning out to be a gut kick for Amber, vomiting out a bleak view of humanity. The depressing knowledge that man was capable of such inhuman barbarity plunged her even deeper into darkness and depression. She was buzzed before lunch and felt like she was in a deep hole with no way out. She pulled her phone out and called Tony. He answered after three rings.

"Hey, Amber, what's up? I'm teaching class right now," he spoke quickly.

Damn, she forgot he was a teacher during the day and worked at the bar at night. "I'm sorry, Tony, I didn't mean to call you at school."

"Hey, is everything OK? I'm glad you called," he said, clearly trying to soothe what he recognized as anxiety.

"I just ... was wondering—"

"How about if I come over to your place tonight?" It was like he was reading her mind.

"Yeah, that would be nice. Six o'clock?"

"Perfect."

She gave him her address and said, "See you then."

She put her phone in her pocket and started walking down the street. *Did I just make an ass of myself?* The alcohol was making her head fuzzy and she wanted to burn it off before getting behind the wheel. She spotted a small green patch of grass two blocks ahead and

Nikita led the way. It was a city park stuffed into a residential neigh-borhood, but the place was empty except for a homeless guy sitting on a park bench at the far end beside a shopping cart overflowing with stuff. Amber unclipped Nikita from her leash and her service dog took off running around the grass, chasing a flock of blackbirds that were pecking in the dirt. Nikita treed a squirrel, did her business then trotted up to Amber and nudged her with a wet nose. "I know, girl, I'm not doing well today. But we'll get through it together, right?" Amber sat on an empty park bench and stared up at the tall pine trees as Nikita lay down at her feet, somehow knowing that she needed to be close to her master at this moment.

28

Amber fussed around the house, folding the blanket on the couch and putting last night's dirty dishes in the dishwasher. She was nervous about having Tony over. She'd been tipsy on cheap tequila when she'd called him and was beginning to have second thoughts. *Should I call him and say I have a headache?* It was a real emotional risk for her to have him over. She hadn't had a man in her house since she bought the place, except for a couple of contractors. She reached for her phone, intending to cancel the date, but couldn't do it. She decided she would just let it happen. *God knows I need some company tonight.*

At 6 o'clock, Nikita let out a bark and ran to the windows overlooking the deck. Tony's silver Jeep rolled up her long dirt driveway, coming to a stop in front of the garage. When he opened the car door and got out, she saw he was wearing blue jeans and a black fleece top. It was warm in town today, but up in the woods where she lived, it was always a little cooler. In his hands he held a bundle of flowers and a bottle of wine. She opened the sliding glass door on her deck and stood at the rail as he walked to the front door below her. He stopped and waved at her. She was wearing black tights and a white pullover sweater. Nikita wagged her tail and barked in anticipation, obviously remembering Tony from Phelanies.

"Come on up," she said, so he didn't have to knock and she wouldn't have to go downstairs to let him in. She wasn't in love with the basement entrance, but the spacious deck and big windows above it more than made up for the narrow doorway that opened directly into a stairwell and the living space above. It was not a good ADA design.

She waited at the top of the stairs while he took his shoes off. *How considerate.* She appreciated that, although with Nikita tracking in endless dirt from the woods, it wasn't necessary.

At the top of the stairs, he handed her a bouquet of daisies and a bottle of wine.

"Thank you," she said, smiling and taking them in both hands, smelling the sweet fragrance. "Please sit down," she said, taking the flowers and wine to the kitchen. He pulled a leather dog chew from his back pocket and gave it to Nikita as he took a seat on the couch. She sniffed it for a few moments, then gingerly took it from his hand, trotted over to the window, lay down in her sphinx pose and started to gnaw on it.

"You have a beautiful view," he said as Amber put the daisies in a vase.

"Yeah, that's why I bought the place," she explained, returning to join him on the couch. "I fell in love with the large windows and the view of the trees." Nikita trotted over to Tony with a ragged red bear in her mouth. He grabbed it and started a game of tug of war.

"You'll never win that game," Amber smirked, then command-ed, "Nikita, down," and Nikita lay down at her feet, looking up at Amber with eyes that said, "I guess the fun is over."

"Do you have a dog Tony?"

"No, I don't really have the time for one, it wouldn't be fair with my schedule," he said, sipping his wine.

Amber stood up to check on dinner in the oven. "Hope you like lasagna," she said, moving to the kitchen and pulling the dish out and setting it on her small kitchen counter.

"One of my favorites. Does it have meat in it?"

Dang, what if he's a vegetarian? I didn't think of that.

"Yeah, it's got ground beef. I didn't ask, I'm sorry."

"Aw, it's not a big deal, I'm not a purist. I just generally don't eat meat, but it doesn't bother me. Don't even worry about it."

Strike one, she thought. They sat at her small table off the kitchen, and she served up the meal with salad and garlic bread. Nikita came and lay down under the table between them, chewing on a toy. "I think she's always trying to get between me and you," Tony noted, looking under the table.

"Yeah, that's her nature and training. Very protective. Would you mind opening the bottle? You're the expert," she said, hand-ing him the wine.

He efficiently opened the bottle and poured a small amount in her glass then swirled it like a pro. "Ma'am, please enjoy this vin-tage 2020 wine. It has elements of Peruvian blackberries, Arizona sage, aged pine nuts and Spanish licorice."

She giggled, "Wow, that's fancy: red or black licorice? I hate black."

"It's red, ma'am," he smiled, now pouring himself a glass. He raised his glass for a sip just as Nikita dropped a big rope tug in his lap, causing him to jerk back in surprise and spill a drop down his chin. Amber smiled to herself, pleased to see Nikita liked him.

They ate in silence for a few bites.

"It's really delicious," Tony complimented, taking another sip of wine.

"Thanks, it's my friend Hannah's recipe." Amber went on to tell Tony how she and Hannah had met in the Army as MP's and had been stationed together in Iraq at the same time. Eventually, Tony looked directly at her and asked, "So how was your day?" He'd obviously suspected she'd asked him to come over after a hard day.

Amber took a sip of wine as she considered how much she should share with Tony. Not that she didn't trust him. She didn't trust herself not to go too far, to revert to her captivity in Iraq, to let the emotions spill out that she was carefully keeping locked up deep within herself. She'd already told Tony about Chris's suicide, they had that in common, but she hadn't spoken of her experience in Iraq. She wasn't ready to talk about that yet.

"Remember I told you about that project I'm working on for the VA? The suicide data collection project?" He nodded, looking like he knew whatever was bothering her had to be related to that horrible task. "Well, a couple of cases caught my attention because of some strange coincidences."

He didn't interject with questions, just let her talk it out, sipping his wine and listening attentively.

"After peeling back the onion a bit and talking to a few people, I found out something terrible happened in Iraq that's related to two of the cases." She paused, not sure how to proceed, then sighed, looked down at Nikita, patted her for her own comfort before telling him the whole story of Lopez and Arnold.

She finished the story, "The junior soldier killed both of the teens, probably so his friend wouldn't have to kill the second kid like the master sergeant wanted him to." She paused, feeling her stomach turn. "And here's the thing: both of those guys ended up committing suicide in Grand Junction with a pistol in the mouth." Tony's eyes widened as the horror of the act hit him.

Tony stood up and walked around the room for a minute to process what he'd just heard. "You mean they shot all three captives? Murdered them?" She nodded.

"How did you find this out?" he asked, still standing as Amber drained her glass and began to clear the table. "I found out that one of the soldiers had been seeing a psychiatrist. I went to the doctor to see what I could find out about the soldier. He didn't know his patient had killed himself. I think that shocked him. He thought about it, then told me what the soldier had shared with him in counseling, breaking a bunch of confidentiality rules, but I think he knew I was only looking for reasons for the suicide, not to start a witch hunt."

"But isn't that like a war crime or something?" Tony asked.

"Yeah, but two of the soldiers are dead and the doctor told me this story in confidence. And here's the kicker: the third one, the senior enlisted soldier, is a Grand Junction police officer."

Tony's mouth fell open in disbelief. "How is that possible?"

"He's in the Army National Guard, part-time soldier, full-time cop."

"You mean he's still in the Army?"

"Yep, and I've got to interview him."

"Amber, are you sure that's smart?" asked Tony, helping her load the dishes into the dishwasher.

"I don't really have a choice. I promised the mothers of those soldiers that I would find out what happened to their sons. I'm not going to back down."

The revelation cast a dark pall over the evening. Amber finished cleaning up the kitchen as Tony moved to the couch with his wine, where he sat scratching Nikita's ears and pondering her story.

Amber came into the living room carrying the bottle of wine, poured herself another glass and sat at the other end of the couch. Nikita stood between them, her head up on the couch as they both scratched her back and ears. Tony moved his hand from petting Nikita to rest it on Amber's hand. She didn't move her hand, just looked into Tony's eyes. It seemed like an hour passed, but it was only a few seconds. He slid over next to her, keeping his hand on top of hers. He reached up tenderly and brushed the hair above her eyes, saying softly, "I'm really sorry, Amber. This is a horrible thing for you to have to deal with." Just then Nikita nudged her nose between them, knocking Tony's arm away from Amber. She was not going to let anyone get too close to her master.

"It's OK, girl," Amber said, smiling. "Go to your bed." She pointed to a fluffy brown dog bed by the window and Nikita slowly walked there with a look of reluctance and lay down, like she was being put in the penalty box.

Amber's heart was racing. She was fond of Tony. He was very considerate and they had a lot in common. She turned to look at him and he moved in slowly for a kiss. She didn't budge and let him kiss her on the lips. It was gentle, his lips warm. She slowly closed her eyes and he drew closer, giving her a more intense kiss. He turned and held her in his arms, putting his hand on her neck. It was like a glacier melted inside Amber. All the shit she had been holding in from Iraq, Chris's suicide, this horrible case she was embroiled in, all of it burst to the surface like lava finding a fissure in the earth. She started to sob into his shoulder.

He leaned back, held her head up and wiped away her tears. "What is it, Amber? You can talk to me. Is it about these two soldiers?"

She knew that Lopez, Arnold and Holmes' actions in Iraq and the subsequent suicides of two of them was a tipping point for her. But the underlying weight on her soul was her captivity in Iraq, Razor and the loss of Chris. She hadn't been able to get over those yet, despite all her efforts.

She pulled back and looked at Tony's thoughtful eyes. "There are many things about me you don't know. When I was in Iraq, I was a military working dog handler. My dog's name was Razor…"

29

Lieutenant Colonel Tinsdale, the operations officer, ran into the colonel's office. He didn't wait for his boss's approval to enter, he burst in, out of breath.

"Spit it out, Tinsdale, what is it?"

"Sir, the UAV reported that two of the three vehicles we're tracking stopped near each other and there may have been gunfire. The red truck kept going after the firefight and the lorry remained in the road. The UAV pilot was able to focus in and see a dead body in the road."

"Can he tell anything about the body? Male, female, dress?"

"He says it looks like a local, a big man maybe, lying face down in the road."

"Get that Air Force Major in here ASAP."

"Yes, sir," Tinsdale responded, running out of the commander's office. He returned in two minutes with Major Archuleta in tow.

"Get in here, you two," the colonel ordered. "Pull up the UAV." Major Archuleta stepped behind the colonel's desk, logged in and brought up a view of the UAV cameras.

"Can we still see the dog?"

"Yes, sir, it's running down that same road 1000 meters behind the red truck," she said, pointing to the screen.

"What is the red truck doing now?" the colonel asked, standing behind his computer as Archuleta worked the screen.

"Sir, the truck just turned off the main road and entered a large covered storage shed. We can't see what's going on inside."

The colonel turned to his operations officer. "How far out is Parnell's assault team?"

"Sir, they can be in that building in 10 minutes or less."

"Make it happen, tell them what you know and order them to assault that shed. Send them everything you can get on the entrances, exits and surrounding area."

"Yes sir," said Tinsdale hustling out of the colonel's office to the Joint Operations Center floor where his team was communicating with the helicopter crew and assault team.

The colonel turned to Major Archuleta. Her dark hair was tucked in a tight bun. She had olive skin, high cheekbones and dark eyes. She was calm and cool, considering how much pressure they were all under to rescue this soldier. She was the first one from her family back in New Mexico to go to college and join the military as an officer. She had thought about what it would be like for Amber, a female soldier, to be held captive by Al Qaeda. She was going to get Amber back, whatever it took.

"What's happening in that shed?" the colonel thought out loud.

"Sir, look at this!" Archuleta pointed at the screen. The colonel bent forward to get a better look. "What the hell!" They both saw three nearly identical red trucks drive out of the shed, all heading in different directions down separate roads.

"Can we track all three?"

"We have another platform almost there, but we can only follow one closely right now."

"Damn it!" the colonel yelled, pounding his fist on the desk. "They know we're watching them and they brought in the other two trucks to throw us off. Which one of the trucks is heading towards Baghdad?" he asked. If he could only follow one, he'd take the vehicle headed to a major city. They would quickly lose that truck in the traffic. The UAV's could more easily follow the other trucks in the country. Archuleta pointed to a small moving dot on her screen.

"Put the UAV on that one. Have the incoming UAV track the other two with a wide angle or something," the colonel ordered pointing at the screen.

"Yes, sir," said Archuleta, not wanting to argue with the colonel about the ability of the other UAV to track two vehicles at once. She typed in the commander's order to the UAV pilot over a secure network and the big aircraft detached its focus from the shed and began tracking the truck heading south toward Baghdad.

The headset in Master Sergeant Parnell's ear squawked and came alive. The pilot of the helicopter relayed the information he'd received about the order to assault the shed. Parnell felt the Blackhawk bank and turn east. The sun was coming up now and he could see the orange glow above the horizon out the window of the helicopter. The second Blackhawk turned and followed the leader.

Parnell pushed his radio mic to talk to his team. They'd heard the orders that Parnell had received over the radio, but were silent, waiting for the master sergeant to give them directions. "OK guys, you heard the order. We're going to land in a field, right next to this barn. The other helo will remain aloft for fire support and to chase any squirters. Thompson, you and Johnson split up, run around opposite sides to the back of the structure and link up. Keep your eyes open as you patrol around the building. Pino and I will wait for a count of 10, then enter the front. You guys cover down on anyone coming out the back. This place looks like one big shed, not the typical maze we usually have to deal with. If Pino and I need backup, you guys come in the back door, guns blazing. Got it?" They all responded with an affirmative. "We're going in to take back one of our own, let's be quick and deadly." He looked at them, making sure everyone was mentally ready and each man nodded with resolve. The team had been up for over 36 hours, but this is what they lived for. They were ready.

In five minutes, the lead helo began to bank hard and drop altitude. Warrant Officer Hockley, the pilot, had more flight time than any other pilot in the regiment. As a warrant officer, he'd been able to specialize in flying and avoid the management time his regular officer pilot counterparts had to deal with. Hockley came in low, banked hard, dropped the big helo quickly, then pulled up at the last second for a soft landing 50 yards from the target. The other helo hovered around the back of the building to watch for any escapees. Thompson and Johnson were the first out, since they had the farthest to go. After they exited the side door, Parnell and Pino jumped to the ground and ran to the front of the structure. The building's large sliding barn doors were open in both the front and the back. It looked like it was used to house farm equipment, although there were no vehicles inside as Parnell and Pino ran into the large opening. They immediately spread out and searched through the barrels, farm tools and bags of feed and fertilizer. The place was empty.

Parnell jumped on the radio net for his team. "Nothing here, anything out back?"

"Negative," came the response from Thompson.

"Wait a minute," said Johnson over the net, "I've got something coming down the road toward us."

"What is it?" Parnell asked.

"It's a dog running. I'll be damned, it's that working dog, Razor. He chased Downing all the way here!"

"Grab that dog, Johnson!" shouted Parnell.

"I'm trying, Sarge, but he just swerved past me."

Pino, listening in to all this, ran out in front of the building, kneeled and called the dog to him as the black-faced creature raced around the corner. Razor stopped at the front opening, saw Pino and trotted over to him, panting.

Pino grabbed Razor's collar. "Here, boy," he said, calming the dog. Pino pulled out his water bottle and poured some in the lid for Razor. The dog lapped up the water as Pino checked on his wound. The bandage they had put on him was soaked in blood and dripping down his side into the dirt.

Parnell suddenly appeared at the dog's side. He changed channels on his satellite radio and contacted the colonel.

"Jackal, this is Honcho."

"Go, Honcho."

"Sir, the place is a dry hole. No sign of the package. But the soldier's working dog just showed up. Looks like he's been tracking her. I bet she was here just a few minutes ago." The colonel hadn't had time to brief Parnell on everything he knew about the canine following Downing and the three-truck diversion fiasco.

"Roger, Honcho. We've been tracking the dog intermittently, figuring he was on the scent of his master." The colonel gave Parnell a quick idea of what happened at the shed, as Downing was undoubtedly brought there and ferried off in one of the three identical trucks.

"The dog is bleeding pretty bad, sir. We'll grab him and bring him on the helo with us."

"Wait one," the colonel said, looking up at Sergeant Major Brown, who was standing on the other side of the desk, listening to the conversation on the speaker phone. It was an awful decision to make, but that's why he was the colonel. The big square-jawed sergeant major who had been to hell and back with his commander nodded to his boss. The colonel nodded back, nothing needed to be said.

"Honcho, this is Jackal. Let the dog go. It has the scent of our soldier and has followed her accurately so far. We need him on the ground."

Parnell paused for a moment. He knew this was a possible death sentence for the loyal Army animal. He wanted to argue with the colonel and take the wounded dog with him, but he understood the logic. To trade a dog soldier's life for a human soldier's life was a rational decision, even though it felt wrong to Parnell. It went against his instincts to take care of his team at all costs. *Who were they to decide who lives and dies?*

"Let him go, Pino," he said quietly.

Pino looked up at Parnell, shocked at the order.

"Let him go, he's our best chance of finding Downing." Parnell didn't say, "The colonel told me to let him go." He made the order sound as if it was his decision. That's how he'd earned the respect of his men and superiors alike. The buck stopped with him.

Pino gave Razor more water, scratched his ears one last time, tightened up the bandage as best he could and let him go. The amazingly athletic and loyal member of the US Army sniffed around the front of the structure, then took off at a trot down the dirt road heading south.

30

JUNE 2012, GRAND JUNCTION, COLORADO

Amber entered the lobby of the VA Medical Center and headed to the stairwell leading to her basement office. "Amber, do you have a second?" She turned to see her boss, John, walking across the lobby with a cup of coffee in a paper cup from the cafe.

"Sure, John, what's up?" she asked, hoping he hadn't received any calls or complaints about her deep dive into the deaths of Lopez and Arnold.

"I just wanted to see how you're doing on the project?" John was shorter than Amber and had his hair slicked to the side with some sort of greasy product. She always felt uncomfortable around him.

"It's going fine," she offered, not wanting to give him any more information than he asked for.

"So you're doing OK, you know, with all the suicide details?" *What a stupid question,* she thought. *Yeah, it's like pickin' flowers and watching the sunset,* she wanted to say. "I'm fine, John, it's just a paperwork drill. No bullets are flying over my head." She figured the best defense is a good offense. "The heat seems to be not working well in my office, though. Is there anything the facilities guys can do?" It never worked well, but it was a nice diversion.

"That basement area is always cold, but I'll have the technician take a look."

"Thanks, John. I've got a phone appointment, so gotta run." She didn't give him time to respond but turned and headed down the stairs. John stood sipping his coffee and watching her walk downstairs a lot longer than would be considered polite.

Amber sat at her desk and stared at her phone. She knew she needed to contact Officer Holmes, but she dreaded the call and the possible meeting with him. *Is this guy a murderer or does he have a different story?* Nikita was scratching under one of the bookcases as if a mouse was hiding there. She made the call.

"Grand Junction Police Station, may I help you?" a woman answered.

"Yes, hello, my name is Amber Downing. I work at the Grand Junction VA Medical Center and I'm trying to get in touch with one of your officers, John Holmes."

"Let me see." There was a pause for a few moments while the woman checked her computer. "He's working a day shift right now, but I'll pass him your phone number if you want to give that to me." Amber gave the woman her phone number and hung up.

She planned to knock a few more cases off her project list, but thoughts of last night with Tony barged in. She hadn't planned to tell him about Iraq, her captivity and Razor, but it all boiled over after she'd told him about the Lopez and Arnold cases. As much as she didn't want to admit it, she knew her ordeal in Iraq was always just below the surface veneer of her life and ready to bubble up anytime, like a latent volcano.

Tony had been amazing. He'd sensed the dark currents she was fighting and gave her space to talk it out. He listened intently as she told him the gruesome tale of the murder of the teenage boys. When she followed up with her own heartbreaking story, he was nearly speechless. He'd come over to her house figuring she'd had a bad day at work, having no idea the depth of pain and darkness she was drowning in.

After she told him what had happened to her in Iraq, she sobbed into his shoulder for a long time. He'd held her, fighting off two competing urges common to men, to take her to bed or to run out of there like the place was on fire. In the end, his better half won out. They sat together on the couch and he held her for what seemed like hours. At some point, he felt her breath deepen as she fell asleep. When Nikita scratched at the door to go out, he quietly let her out to do her business, let her back in, then pulled the blanket off the top of the couch and laid it over Amber before driving home.

I told him too much. He's going to look at me like I'm a broken butterfly now. Why didn't I keep my mouth shut? But then again, it was good to talk to someone about Iraq. He wasn't a veteran himself, but he was a compassionate listener. She remembered how she'd woken up on the couch with a blanket over her and wishing she was still in his arms. She knew she would have to call him later to apologize for falling asleep and gauge his reaction to the whole evening.

Her reverie was interrupted by her cell phone. "Unknown caller," flashed on her screen. "Hello?"

"Is this Amber Downing?"

"Yes."

"This is Officer Holmes with the Grand Junction Police Department. What can I do for you?"

Amber figured he knew exactly what she was looking into after Sergeant Garcia had filled him in. He was playing coy.

She feigned ignorance as well, "Oh, thanks for calling me back, Officer Holmes. I work for the VA Medical Center and I'm conducting an analysis of the suicides of veterans in our geographic area for the last five years. I wonder if I could meet with you to discuss a couple of cases."

"Sure, ma'am, I'd be happy to help." She noted that he didn't ask questions about which cases she was working on. *He knew.* "I get off shift at five today. I can meet you then."

"Great, how about I meet you at the Coffee Trader at 5:30?" she proposed. "I'll be the one with the service dog."

"OK, see you then." He hung up.

Amber was able to work through two more cases on her project list before the end of the day. At 5 o'clock, she left the office and took Nikita out for a walk around the building. There was a golf course next to the VA and the greens were busy with the early spring warm weather. She checked her watch and they made their way to the coffee shop to meet Holmes.

When she walked in, a tall man with reddish hair cut into a flat top, a pale face and freckles waved at her from a small, private table by the window. Amber walked over to meet him and Nikita's hair rose unexpectedly on her back. This confirmed her bad feeling about the guy; evil comes in all shapes and sizes. He was still wearing his police uniform and held out his hand quickly and confidently. His eyes were dark green, almost black.

"Amber, I'm Officer John Holmes," he said, standing. Nikita growled, very low, almost silent.

She looked down and tightened the leash, whispering, "No," to Nikita.

Amber shook his hand - it was cold. "Nice to meet you," she said, sitting down and making Nikita sit under the table.

"So how can I help you?" he said with his confident, friendly community police voice. *I guess we're going to play the game,* she thought. "You said you have some questions about a suicide project you're working on for the VA?"

"Yes, that's right." She decided to dive right in, get it over with. "Two of my cases are Sergeant Henry Lopez and Corporal Jerry Arnold. I found out they served in the same unit and even the same platoon in Iraq." She paused, searching his eyes. He already knew she had all this information. "Sergeant Garcia told me you were in the same unit with them."

"That's right, we were deployed together. I was the First Sergeant for the platoon."

"Garcia told me that the three of you were in the same HUMVEE when your convoy was attacked and three of your soldiers were killed." She left it there, kind of a question, but open-ended.

He cocked his head and looked at her like she had no idea what kind of crap happened in Iraq. "That's right, it was a total soup sandwich. But what does that have to do with their suicides?" *He's trying to figure out what I know,* she thought. *I can't let him know that I've talked to Dr. Mankowski.*

"Well, it seems like a traumatic event like that could have a profound effect on a soldier and part of my job is to try to find a cause for each suicide. Could you tell me what happened?"

He smiled at her like she was the village idiot. He proceeded to tell her the story of the ambush of their convoy in the dusty Baghdad alley. Finally he got to the part she was waiting for, "We entered the building, found a set of stairs by the door and moved to the second floor where the shooting was coming from. When we entered the flat, we found three armed insurgents by the window. I took out one and Arnold was able to get the drop on the other two. After that we returned downstairs and provided security as our soldiers were evacuated." He stopped talking, waiting for Amber's reaction.

She couldn't give away the fact that she knew the insurgents were an old man and two teenage boys or that there was only one rusty AK-47 or that they had all been executed. She didn't want to show her cards, but she needed to get Holmes out of his comfort zone, provoke him a little bit, see how he reacted.

"Garcia told me that Arnold and Lopez were close, even best friends. I'm trying to understand how they could both commit suicide within a few months of each other. That just seems strange to me. You'd think two close friends would be talking to each other, supporting each other. What do you think?"

There was that BS smile again, hiding a flash of anger. Holmes was used to being on the other side of an investigation. "As you must know, veterans have come back from wars in Iraq and Afghanistan with high rates of PTSD and traumatic brain injury. Their rates of suicide are far higher than the general population. It's a damn shame, but I assume Arnold and Lopez both succumbed to their demons."

Succumbed to their demons, she thought. *That's probably more accurate than he intended.* "Of course. It's just the timing of the two suicides that has me confused. Two soldiers from the same unit, two months apart. It's just strange, don't you think?"

Those greenish black eyes stared back at her. "Those men were my friends and fellow soldiers," he said, shifting to righteous indignation. "I don't know what you expect to find by digging into their deaths, but you're picking at a wound that this whole community and the National Guard unit suffered." There it was, the implied warning.

She stared back at him for a few moments, trying to get a read. "I understand, Officer Holmes. One last question. I believe there are police reports for each of their suicides. Do you know how I could get a copy of them?"

That hit a nerve. He tried to hide it, but a vein was bulging in his neck. "Those are confidential records, Ms. Downing. Other than for legal purposes, they would remain secured at police headquarters."

"All right, I understand," she nodded. "Well, thank you for your time, Officer Holmes." She stood up quickly, making sure he knew that she was in charge of this conversation. She held out her hand and he reached for it, much slower than before.

As she walked out of the coffee shop and headed to her car, Holmes dialed a number on his cell phone.

"What is it?" a voice answered, clearly coming from a moving vehicle.

"We've got a problem."

"Tell me about it."

31

June 2012, Montrose, Colorado

Amber called Hannah to see if she was available for dinner or drinks tonight. It would be good to catch up.

"Hey, Amber," Hannah answered quickly.

"What's up, Hannah?"

"You know, normal small town police work. I arrested a guy who stole a case of beer from a gas station and another guy who walked out of Home Depot with a 60-pound air compressor and tried to hoof it down the street. I guess he wasn't used to carrying a 60-pound box."

"Sounds like small town police work."

"You got that right, girl. Just how I like it, nice and easy."

Amber laughed and said, "I was wondering if you wanted to grab a bite or a drink tonight?"

"Sure, how about drinks at that new Blue Corn candle factory bar place?" A new venue had recently opened in Montrose. Half of the building was a beeswax candle factory and the other half sold coffee, cocktails, light food and was also a retail store for the candles.

"That sounds great, 7 o'clock?"

"Perfect, see you then."

She knew Tony was working tonight at the speakeasy. She wanted to see him but didn't want to bother him at work. She settled for a text message, "I really enjoyed last night. Sorry I fell asleep, it was a tough day. Are you available this Friday for dinner?" She hoped he'd respond right away but decided to put it out of her mind for the moment.

At a little after 7, Amber walked into the coffee shop bar with Nikita and scanned the place. Hannah was sitting in a corner next to the window. One interior wall of the place was a huge glass window where you could see the candle makers at work in the factory as you sipped cappuccino with your feet up and admired their hard-working diligence. Nikita greeted Hannah, sniffing her hands. Hannah had already ordered two glasses of white wine. She'd changed out of her police uniform and was wearing faded jeans and a blouse, with her long black hair tied up. Amber hadn't changed but was wearing slacks and a sweater.

"So what's up with you, anyway? Anything new?" Hannah asked.

"Well, I did have kind of a date."

"Oh, please do tell," Hannah cooed, leaning in expectantly. "Anyone I know?"

"Since you're a cop, I hope you don't know him." They both laughed. "Remember last week when we went to the speakeasy?"

"Of course."

"Remember the guy who brought our drinks?"

"Yeah, I think so. Tall, dark and handsome?"

Amber smiled, "That's him. I went back to the bar another night and we kind of hit it off. I found out later that his wife committed suicide, so we have some things in common."

Hannah sipped her wine, not sure how to respond to that. *Maybe having unimaginable loss is not something you want to have in common with a new boyfriend,* she thought. "Tell me more about him."

"For starters, he's an English teacher at the high school, he just moonlights at the bar."

"So he's hardworking and can spell correctly," Hannah quipped. "Or he's in debt," she joked.

"You've got to be hardworking to teach English to high school students who mostly play on their cell phones and don't want to learn. My mother was a history teacher. All those papers to grade at night and on the weekends. They don't pay teachers enough."

"Agreed. But tell me about the date itself," Hannah prodded.

Amber didn't want to talk about how she'd sobbed into his shoulder after letting her ordeal in Iraq creep into the conversation. Hannah would frown on her first date manners. She already thought Amber was a little off her rocker.

"He came to my place for dinner, we had a nice time talking. He brought flowers and wine. Real sweet."

"And?" Hannah asked with anticipation.

"No, he didn't spend the night, if that's what you're referring to." Of course she was. "Actually, I fell asleep on the couch, and he let himself out." She regretted telling Hannah that as soon as she'd said it.

"Are you serious, Amber? What if he had raped you or something? You don't know him that well. Did you have too much wine or something?" Hannah wasn't known for her tact.

"No, just a long day. I did tell him about my experience in Iraq, though. He's a nice guy and a good listener. Plus, Nikita was there, protecting me. The last time we met I told him about Chris's suicide. Maybe he's thinking I'm too much of a basket case?" Amber wondered out loud.

Hannah winced at the mention of Chris. Amber had learned over time that Hannah didn't like to talk about Chris's suicide, though she could never understand why.

"Yeah, maybe you're dropping a little too much in his lap this early in the relationship. Gonna see him again?"

"I hope so." He still hadn't responded to her text from several hours ago. Maybe he'd had his fill of her tragedy.

"Anything new on that project of yours?" Hannah changed the subject.

"Yeah, I interviewed a Grand Junction police officer today."

"What was that about?" Hannah exclaimed with surprise.

"It turns out he's a part-time soldier in the National Guard. He knew Arnold and Lopez, the two suicides I told you about that seemed weird to me. Anyway, they were on this mission in Iraq together and after an ambush, they ended up killing an old man and two teenagers. At least I think that's what happened."

"How in the world did you find that out?" Hannah asked, astonished.

Amber didn't want to reveal Dr. Mankowski as her source. He'd gone out on a limb and broken doctor-patient confidentiality to tell her about Lopez's confession. She'd keep her word and protect the doctor. "I can't say how I found this out, but I think it's legit. I asked the police officer about the incident, and I sensed he was hiding something, or at least not telling me the whole truth."

"What's his name?" Hannah asked, with some anxiety in her voice. Amber remembered that Hannah's boyfriend Brian was a Grand Junction police officer. Surely he would know the guy.

"Holmes, John Holmes. He's a Master Sergeant in the National Guard too." Hannah made a funny face, like she'd bitten into something rotten.

Suddenly Amber remembered something from Iraq she'd wanted to ask Hannah about. "Do you remember when I was rescued, and you were working security in the Green Zone?"

Hannah nodded, "Yeah, of course."

"After they let me go from the debriefings and hospital, Chris seemed very strange, almost distant. I know my captivity must have been hard for him, but he was really distraught, like something was wrong. Did you ever see him while I was gone, notice how he was doing?"

For a second, Hannah looked uncertain about the question, clearly not expecting it. "No, of course not. We were on two different schedules, remember? I saw him in the dining facility a few times and we talked about the latest news about your captivity. I mean, it was the main topic for the whole base. But that's about it. He did tell me about a mission gone wrong with his platoon and felt he should have been there, felt maybe he could have saved a kid from the IED blast. He hinted that there was another mission that was really bothering him, but he didn't provide any details."

Amber nodded, but somewhere in the back of her mind she had a feeling that Hannah wasn't telling her the whole truth.

On the way home, Hannah called Brian. "You're not gonna believe what Amber told me tonight," she said. She hadn't told Amber that Brian and John Holmes were good friends, figuring Amber would think less of Brian than she already did. She'd never said it outright, but Hannah could tell Amber didn't like her boyfriend.

"What?" asked Brian, sitting on the couch at Hannah's place, sipping a beer and waiting for her to come home.

"She said she interviewed John today, and told me he was on a mission that went south with those two soldiers who killed themselves recently, that some civilians were killed too. She didn't mention it, but I had the feeling that she thinks the mission had something to do with their suicides."

Brian was quiet for a moment before finally speaking. It came out with a torrent of rage. "That's bullshit. She's chasing ghosts. I mean, who does she think she is, accusing a police officer and a decorated soldier? She's full of shit. She's just dredging up crap from the past to make a name for herself." He hung up.

Hannah wasn't surprised. Brian was prone to fits of anger and she just hoped he wasn't in one of his moods when she got home.

32

Colonel Harrison and Sergeant Major Brown stood outside the Joint Special Operations Task Force headquarters north of Baghdad. A Blackhawk helicopter was landing 100 yards in front of them on the makeshift cement pad that had been constructed when the Army built this impromptu base in the middle of nowhere. They both looked away as the helo kicked up a swirl of dust and small rocks around the compound. The helicopter touched down and General Schwartz stepped off with a small day pack over his shoulder. He was tall and lean, like a point guard. He'd spent years of his life in Iraq and Afghanistan, leading missions and trying to hold fragile coalitions together. Equally comfortable negotiating with Iraqi government officials or leading troops into combat, in the Army he was known as a general's general. Following quickly behind the four-star commander of all forces in Iraq were his aide and other close staff officers he'd brought on this initial flight.

Colonel Harrison and Master Sergeant Brown stood at attention and rendered sharp salutes as the Commander United States Forces Iraq approached them with his entourage. The general returned the salutes, then said, "At ease men," before reaching out and shaking both their hands.

"Sir, please follow me this way," Harrison said, leading the general and his staff into the Special Operations Joint Operations Center. As they walked, the Blackhawk lifted off and headed back toward Baghdad.

"What's the latest, Jim?" the general asked, turning toward Colonel Harrison as they walked.

"Sir, I think we may have a bead on our soldier." The colonel began to tell General Schwartz all the latest developments, starting with the red truck carrying Downing and the confrontation with a lorry in the middle of the road. By the time they reached the Joint Operations Center he'd brought the general up to date.

Colonel Harrison took the general to his office, "Sir, you can utilize my office, I'll be manning a station on the Joint Operations Center (JOC) floor."

The general nodded and set his backpack in the corner of the colonel's office. His aide was hovering outside the door, waiting for directions from the general. "Captain Symonds, please find me a cup of coffee and a place to sleep," he ordered.

"Sir, we already have you and your staff set up in huts out back behind the JOC," said Colonel Harrision. The Army had contracted for hundreds of portable rooms and shower stations throughout Iraq. They could be picked up with a forklift, airlifted and set down just about anywhere. They were plug and play and allowed the Allies to set up a base in a matter of days instead of months.

"That will be fine," said General Schwartz and nodded to his aide to get busy. When the aide left, the general turned and closed the office door. "Have a seat, Jim," he said. The colonel sat on the other side of the desk as the general settled into what was usually the colonel's seat.

Harrison knew what was coming. He was either going to be fired and sent home for letting one of his troopers be captured, or he was going to get an ass-chewing and be put in charge of counting brooms and mops.

"Jim," the general began, pausing, "I've known you a long time and followed your career. You're an excellent officer and leader. What I want you to know is that every senior leader in the military faces adversity, at least one big challenge that defines him or her, one massive kick in the groin. You understand, Jim?"

"Yes, sir," responded Colonel Harrison, sitting a little straighter in the chair.

"What defines an officer and leader is how he handles adversity, not the fact that he got himself into a mess. Do you see my point?"

"Yes, sir," nodded Harrison.

"You've got a mess on your hands here. We haven't had a soldier captured in Iraq since Jessica Lynch and we recovered her. Nobody, and I mean *NOBODY*, wants to see one of our soldiers hauled in front of a camera and decapitated for propaganda."

There was a knock at the door and the young aide entered with a paper cup of steaming coffee for the general. He handed it to his boss and left the room, closing the door softly behind him.

"Here's the bottom line, Jim—I want you to continue running this operation to get our soldier back. I trust you. You know this task force and your men and their capabilities. You run your big decisions by me, but I'll be here to get you the support you need and keep the

Secretary of Defense and the President up to date on the situation. Understand?"

"Absolutely, sir," Colonel Harrison said, feeling a great weight lift off him, knowing he wasn't going to be fired in disgrace.

"What do you need right now, Jim?" asked Schwartz.

"Sir, I need more eyes in the sky. We need to follow three potential vehicles closely and try to track our military working dog."

"Consider it done," the general said, sipping his coffee. Like Harrison, he hadn't been able to sleep for 48 hours. He'd been constantly giving updates to the Secretary of Defense and fielding questions from the National Security Council. The eight-hour time difference between Iraq and DC didn't help either. He'd been up at all hours answering the red phone or sitting in on high level video teleconferences. The coffee gave him a needed short-term burst.

"Now," he said, leaning back in the colonel's chair, "Tell me about this dog."

High above the smoke-filled skies of Iraq, two large Predator UAVs turned west and left their mission of tracking Iranian arms smuggling on the eastern border of Iraq and checked in with the Special Operations Task Force for a new mission. Major Archuleta answered the radio call from the UAV pilots from her desk on the JOC floor. The crazy thing was that the pilots were sitting in an air-conditioned room in Arizona flying the missions over Iraq. The three red trucks had all dispersed in different directions, making it hard for the task force to track Downing and her captor. Now that she had three Predator drones in her quiver, Archuleta put her plan into play.

She assigned one UAV to each vehicle. As of now, one was heading north, in the general direction of the Special Operations Task Force near Balad, one was headed east, toward the Iranian border and one was headed south toward Baghdad. With three Predators in play, she was able to drill down and get much better detail on each vehicle instead of performing a wide area search.

She was watching the cameras of the three big drones on her screen when Colonel Harrison walked up behind her. "What's the latest, Major?" he asked.

"Sir, we were just assigned two more Predators; I've got them tracking each of the three trucks," she replied pointing to her screen.

"Good, General Schwartz just pulled some strings and got us those. Have you been able to track the working dog?"

"No, sir, we had him for a while, but he's so nimble, dashing through forests and neighborhoods that we lost him on visual."

"What about the GPS collar?"

"We get an intermittent signal. The battery is probably going dead after 48 hours," she replied.

"Can you tell which direction he was headed?" the colonel asked, knowing Razor was his best chance to narrow down Downing's location.

"All I can say is that he wasn't heading north. He could be following the eastbound or the southbound vehicle at this point."

"OK, keep looking and find that dog for us."

"Yes, sir, "said Major Archuleta as the colonel walked over to the operations officer's desk.

Lieutenant Colonel Tinsdale stood up. He was a West Point graduate and, like many of them, he was meticulous with his military bearing.

"Sit down, sit down," the colonel said. "Listen, I want you to spin up one more assault team. Put them in orbit on the northbound vehicle. We'll keep Parnell's team up in the air to cover both the southbound and eastbound vehicles. They're not that far apart currently. The helo could be on top of either vehicle in less than 10 minutes. If the trucks get more than 10 minutes apart by helo, then prepare a third team."

"Sir, I'm on it," Tinsdale said, picking up a secure phone to relay the orders.

Colonel Harrison was walking back to his desk on the JOC floor when he saw Sergeant Major Brown hustling toward him. Something was up.

"Sir, we've got a situation. Major Archuleta needs you." Together they walked quickly to her desk and stood behind her. She wore a headset and was talking to the UAV pilots. She turned in her seat to the colonel, pointing at the screen simultaneously.

"Sir, look, the trucks have stopped at three different locations almost simultaneously, just two minutes apart from each other. Look here," she said, pointing out the locations on her screen.

"Damn it," the colonel spat. "They know they're still being followed. This is their way of throwing us off, making it hard to pin them down, spreading our resources too thin. I've gotta brief the general. Sergeant Major, tell Ops to get that assault package moving asap."

The big man nodded and hurried down the JOC floor. Colonel Harrison motioned for his UAV officer to follow him and they headed to General Schwartz's office. They stood outside his door as the general spoke on the phone. The general saw them waiting and gave a "wait one" signal. In a few minutes he hung up and waved the entourage in.

Amber awoke in the back of the pickup truck, her head throbbing like a pinata at a 12-year-old's birthday party. She reached up to check the wound where KAT had whacked her and found that her hands were bound again with zip ties. Raising both hands together, she felt blood oozing down her forehead. At least it wasn't a gusher. She pushed gingerly on her skull to see if it was fractured. The pain was intense, but everything seemed to be intact. A nasty swollen lump was growing over the wound area.

The truck was still rumbling down a bumpy dirt road. Amber sat up slightly in the backseat and saw that KAT was driving. She didn't want him to know she was conscious, so she quietly lay back down. *Alright, what's my next move?* she pondered, with equal parts fear and determination.

The truck bounced on as Amber racked her brain for plan B. She felt under the seat for a tire iron or something she could use. Nothing. After about 15 minutes, KAT slowed the truck down, took a turn to the left and drove down a long dirt driveway. He stopped the truck under a big covered awning attached to a house, got out, then opened the rear door, holding the pistol on Amber. She looked up at him, squinting as the afternoon sun shone through the open sides of the covered parking area directly into her eyes. He reached into the truck, grabbed her under her arm and lifted her outside the truck. She stood there for a moment taking in the scene. It looked like another remote farmhouse. All she saw were date palms all around, with the small brick building next to her set in the middle of a dirt clearing. KAT shoved the pistol into her back and pushed her toward the brick building. The place reminded her of a 1950's brick rambler back in the States. With one hand, KAT opened a door between the covered parking area and the house and pushed Amber into the small entry-way. She heard movement in a back room and another Arab stepped into the entryway wearing the traditional red and white headscarf and white robe. He spoke to KAT in Arabic. She didn't understand any of it, but she did hear the man call KAT sheikh on several occasions.

KAT stopped talking with the man and pushed Amber from the entryway down a long hallway lined with several doors. The first door they passed was partially open. Amber glanced in as KAT continued pushing her down the hallway. What she saw in that room made her legs wobble and almost give out. It was a propaganda room. The black Al Qaeda flag was pinned to the back wall and a camera with a tripod was set up in front of the room, facing the flag. *This is where it happens,* the thought ran through her head like lightning. *This is where prisoners are decapitated in front of the camera for all the world to see.* On the heels of the almost immobilizing fear, she felt a new resolve. Dying was one thing, but she would never let them cut her up in front of that camera for her friends, family and fellow American citizens to see. She would fight like the third monkey on Noah's ramp. She would go out as a warrior, fighting for her life.

At the end of the hallway, KAT stopped and opened the door to the last room on the right. There was a window, but the glass had been removed and replaced with plywood that had been nailed from the outside. In the corner was a bucket, a small mat and blanket sat along the right wall. KAT cut off the zip ties on her wrists and shoved her into the room and closed the door. She heard a large deadbolt engage in the hallway. She was trapped again.

33

SEPTEMBER 2008, SALADIN PROVINCE, IRAQ

"What's your plan, Jim?" General Schwartz asked as Colonel Harrison and his operations officer stood in front of the general at his desk. Colonel Harrison had just informed him that all three of the vehicles they were tracking had stopped at the same time under different awnings or covers to prevent the drones from seeing who was in each truck or what was happening.

"Sir, we have two assault teams ready now now. The team that has been up for a while could hit either the southern or eastern target within 10 minutes. The new team we spun up could hit the northern target within 15 minutes. I could put a third team up, but that would take another 30 minutes." Harrison was kicking himself right now for not activating the third assault team earlier.

"Why don't we have three teams already in the air?" the general asked, obviously frustrated at the turn of events.

"Sir, that was my call. I planned to spin up the third team when the eastern and southern vehicles separated beyond 10 minutes from each other. I didn't anticipate that all three vehicles would stop at the same time."

The general looked like he wanted to chew some ass, but there was no time for that. "What about the working dog? Have we got a bead on him?"

"No, sir. We know he headed either south or east, but we lost his visual track and his GPS beacon is not functioning, probably dead battery."

"Damn it!" the general exclaimed, slapping the table. "If we knew where that dog was, we'd have a good chance of narrowing down our target sets."

"There's a lot of things that could go wrong with the dog," Colonel Harrison said. "He might lose the scent, go off the trail, get lost or run into some hostile forces. He's also injured and could succumb to his wounds along the way."

"All right, Jim, use your best judgment. Have the northern assault team hit the building as soon as they're able. Decide if you want the other assault team to hit the eastern or southern compound first. Let's execute this. And get that damn third team up and running."

"Yes, sir," Colonel Harrison saluted and stepped out of the general's office. Once he and his operations officer were in the hallway, he faced Lieutenant Colonel Tinsdale. "You heard the general, let's make it happen."

"Got it, sir. Which house do you want Parnell's team to hit?"

The colonel thought for a moment. "Have them hit the eastern house first, that's closer to Iran. We don't want Downing ending up over there somehow."

"I'm on it, sir," Tinsdale said, rushing down the hallway to pull the trigger on the rescue operations.

Parnell's headset squawked and Lieutenant Colonel Tinsdale came up on the radio net with that perfect West Point command voice. Parnell and the pilot listened carefully as Tinsdale gave them the mission to hit the eastern house. He fed them all the useful intelligence the Task Force had about the structure, along with the exact coordinates. Parnell and the pilot both acknowledged the order as Warrant Officer Hockley turned the helicopter east. The second fire support helicopter behind them turned also and took a position off their right flank.

Parnell grabbed an electronic tablet from his pack, turned it on and pulled up a picture of the target house taken from the UAV that was hovering overhead, out of sight. He studied the aerial view of the structure for a few minutes, then took a stylus and marked where he wanted his assault team to position themselves before they entered the building. He passed the tablet to the other members of the team. Johnson, Thompson and Pino huddled around the screen nodding and pointing to each other.

"Got any questions?" Parnell asked over the radio. "We've got five minutes till we're on the X." The soldiers all shook their heads. Parnell looked at his team, then spoke to them over the radio. "I'm damn lucky to be here with you guys. Let's kick some ass and get Downing back." The boys nodded and began to check their weapons.

Parnell was usually calm once on site, but he was always nervous when they were one minute out from the target. It was the landing of these damn helicopters. He'd never get used to it. Two of his buddies from his first unit had been mangled when a Blackhawk dropped out of the sky 50 feet off the ground before the landing. Parnell hated the feeling of being at the mercy of all those spinning mechanical parts. One nut comes loose, BAM, you're splattered all over the ground.

Hockley set the first helo down quickly, as they had planned, 50 yards in front of the house in a fallow field of brown and decaying crops. The second Blackhawk took position in orbit around the back of the house with one of the air crew soldiers manning a machine gun out the side door.

Parnell leaped out of the helo as soon as it touched ground, followed by Pino, Thompson and Johnson. As planned, Parnell and Pino took positions on each side of the front door of the house. Johnson stepped between them, placed a small breaching charge near the door handle and stepped back. Everyone nodded and turned their heads as Johnson pushed the remote detonator and blew the door in. Pino charged into the room, followed on his heels by Parnell. The room was dark and eerily quiet. And then Parnell saw it: wires on the floor led to a block of orange SEMTEX plastic explosives taped to the wall. Parnell yelled "IED!,"into his mic, warning his team, as the fireball blasted through the front of the house like a runaway freight train driving through a tunnel.

The lead Blackhawk was still on the ground, waiting for Parnell to report, when the pilot, Warrant Officer Hockley, saw the blast flames shoot out the front windows, throwing shards of glass and wood against the side of the Blackhawk. Before Hockley could give the order, his aircrew sergeant leaped out of the side door and raced towards the house.

Johnson lay underneath a jumbled pile of cracked lumber and bricks where the front of the house had been blown out. Someone was pulling debris off his legs.

"Hey man, are you all right?" It was the aircrew sergeant. He'd grabbed Johnson by his body armor and dragged him out of the pile. Johnson saw his lips move but couldn't hear the guy's voice.

"I'm OK," Johnson yelled loudly, his ears bleeding. Thompson was already standing up and tearing through rubble, looking for Parnell and Pino. The blast had tossed him onto a pile of old tires near the front of the house, cushioning him from the blast. He was covered in dust and looked like he'd just stepped out of a flour factory. Johnson stood up on wobbly legs. Reaching up to his face, he felt a piece of glass embedded between his left eye and his nose, shooting pain through his head like a screwdriver being driven into his face. He walked over to Thompson, who was lifting a piece of the front door off a large pile of bricks.

"Hey man, pull this out," Johnson said, pointing to the shard in his face.

"Geeez!" said Thompson as he reached for the Leatherman pliers on his belt. "That son of a bitch just missed your eye." Thompson carefully grasped the piece of glass with his pliers, nodded to his buddy and yanked hard. The glass tore a bigger hole on the way out, followed by a gush of blood. Thompson shoved Johnson's hand over the wound as he reached for a bandage in his waist pack. Fumbling to open the pack with his teeth, he freed the bandage from the wrapping and stuck it into the hole in Johnson's face. Johnson had been quiet this whole time, but now he let out a howl as his teammate stuffed the medicated gauze into the hole in his face.

"Hey, I've found a soldier," the aircrew sergeant yelled out as Thompson placed a strip of white tape over the bandage. He'd been digging while the other two were dealing with Johnson's facial injury. The two Special Forces soldiers hustled over to the pile and helped the aircrew sergeant pull out Pino by his feet.

"Shit!" Thompson exclaimed, looking away before vomiting. Pino was completely crushed, as if he'd been run over by a Mack truck. He was literally flat, his face a mass of blood and bone fragments. The aircrew sergeant jumped on his radio to let the pilot know they had one friendly KIA and were looking for one last soldier.

Thompson rallied back after seeing what was left of his brother in arms. "Let's find Parnell, guys!" With that the three soldiers left Pino where he was and started digging out the rest of the debris around the front of the house. The rubble was still smoking and smelled of fire, burnt wood and that sharp, pungent odor of high explosives.

Five minutes later, Johnson yelled out, "I've got 'im!" Parnell was still inside what used to be the perimeter of the house. Plaster, wood beams and bricks covered his body, but he opened his eyes when Johnson tapped on his cheek. "Jimmy, are you OK?"

Parnell nodded but didn't speak. He winced in a whirl of pain. The three soldiers carefully removed the remaining blast debris from Parnell, checking for wounds as they went. After clearing all the broken remnants of the front of the house off their buddy and leader, they performed an assessment on the master sergeant. The only obvious wound they found was a broken leg, although there were undoubtedly some internal injuries. The aircrew sergeant started running to the helo to grab the litter board.

The operations officer at the Task Force took the radio call from Warrant Officer Hockley. "Jackal, we've got one friendly KIA, and three wounded. Honcho is coming back on a litter board. We'll be airborne in five mikes."

"Copy all, Blue Dog, we'll have MEDEVAC on standby."

Tinsdale set the radio handset down. Normally an ultra-composed officer, he punched the plywood that made up his makeshift office, leaving a crack in the wall. His job was to keep all the plates spinning in this big circus, which he was damn good at. But occasionally, he hated his job, like right now when his soldiers were hurt or killed. He knew all four of the soldiers. When Tinsdale was a young buck captain, Parnell had been his platoon sergeant. He'd learned a lot from the tall, easy-going Texan. Their wives had become friends and kept in touch. He also knew Pino well. They had both worked together as instructors at the Special Forces Q course, training new Green Berets. He stood up and ran out of the office to inform the colonel.

Colonel Harrison knew what had happened before Tinsdale reached his desk. He'd been monitoring the radio at his desk while working through contingency plans. As soon as Tinsdale reached his desk, Colonel Harrison started delivering his orders. There was no time for emotion now, that would come later. What they needed now was clear direction and he was the one to give it.

"Launch that second assault team ASAP against the southern target. Let them know about the IED ambush at the eastern house," he directed calmly. "Get a MEDEVAC bird to take Parnell and his men to the hospital in Baghdad." The Task Force had its own medical staff, but anything that required serious surgery or specialists would be handled at the hospital in Baghdad before the soldier was sent to Ramstein and on to the U.S.

"Got it, sir," Tinsdale said, expecting both of those orders from his commander.

"And Ops," the colonel added, "Drop a fucking bomb on that house and flatten it, wouldya?"

"With pleasure, sir," Tinsdale said, turning back to nod at the colonel.

⁂

Colonel Harrison stepped outside the operations center for a moment to clear his head. The death or injury of any of his troops was the worst part of his job. He thought of the calls he had to make to the States to start the process of informing the families. One of his men along with a chaplain would be knocking on the family's doors at all hours of the day or night and informing them of the death or injury. It was a terrible task. He'd had to do it several times himself, knocking on some young wife's door with a five-year-old tugging at her mother's skirt. "Ma'am, I'm sorry to inform you..." Then came the wailing. He always felt like his heart was being torn out of his chest. Any death or injury also sent shockwaves through all the other families of his troops. They would rally around the stricken families, but in their beds at night, they would thank God that the knock on the door had not been at their house.

He noticed one of the Navy Seabees assigned to his unit leaning against the wall 10 yards away, taking a smoke break. The colonel had given up smoking 15 years ago but he walked over to the sailor, who popped tall and saluted when he realized it was the colonel.

"Mind if I bum a smoke?" he asked. The sailor pulled a pack of Marlboros from his shirt pocket and handed the colonel a cigarette and lighter.

"Thank you," Colonel Harrison said, noticing that the sailor looked like he was no older than 17. *It's always the young who pay the costs of war,* he thought. *We get ourselves into this shit and kids pay the price.*

"Where are you from, son?" The colonel asked, taking a drag on the cigarette.

"Fort Worth, Sir," said the nervous sailor. The colonel immediately thought of "CowTown," the stockyards, the great food and friendly people. *I wish I was there right now,* a thought bubbled to the surface. *No, this is where I belong,* he immediately squelched any thoughts of home. *This is where my duty is, where I'm needed the most.* The young sailor stubbed out his cigarette and turned to the colonel and said, "By your leave, Sir." Harrison was always amused at the strange customs and language of the U.S. Navy, but he understood that the sailor was asking permission to get back to work. The colonel had long ago learned that the Seabees were the best at getting things built quickly, as long as you didn't ask too many questions.

"Have a good day sailor."

Back at his desk, Tinsdale called the commander of the third assault team, which happened to be a U.S. Navy SEAL lieutenant aptly named Butcher.

"Lieutenant Butcher, this is the Task Force Operations Officer."

"Yes, sir."

"When can your team be ready?"

"Sir, we were ready 20 minutes ago. My men are on the helo right now, just waiting for orders."

Tinsdale was taken aback. He'd only given the warning order 30 minutes ago to spin up an additional assault team. He was a Special Forces officer through and through, and as such, he always wanted his Green Berets to come out on top. But these goddamn SEALs were always leaning forward, itching to get in the fight; he admired that, reluctantly.

"OK, Lieutenant Butcher, you're cleared to launch. Be advised that the team on the eastern target ran into an IED ambush inside the main door of the house. That could be waiting for you too. Be ready. This is an American soldier we're trying to get back. Give us your best, lieutenant."

"Sir," Butcher replied, "That's all you're ever going to get from a Navy SEAL." "Cocky bastard", Tinsdale mumbled to himself as he hung up the phone.

Butcher ran out from the small tactical operation center his team used to prep for this mission and headed toward the two blacked-out helicopters on the tarmac. When he reached the helos, Butcher gathered his squad of SEALs, along with the two aircrews, and relayed the information he'd received from Lieutenant Colonel Tinsdale. Everyone nodded and jumped into action. In two minutes, the two Blackhawks lifted off and set their sights on the southern target.

———◄○►———

Amber stood facing the plywood that covered the opening where a window had once existed. It was a small window, maybe 2-feet by 2-feet, but plenty of room for her to escape if she could just find a way to get past the plywood. The wood had been fastened to the outside wall of the house so she couldn't tell how it was secured. She felt all the corners of the plywood, searching for any weak or rotten spots. There were none. If she just had something strong, like a screwdriver, she might be able to wedge it between the wall and the plywood and pry out a section.

Suddenly she heard the door unlock from the outside and KAT stepped into the room holding the pistol on her. This time he was dressed in all black, like one of those nut jobs who cut off some poor sap's head in front of a camera. He looked at her with his dead eyes.

"Follow me, we have to move quickly," he said, motioning with the pistol for Amber to step into the hallway. *What did that mean we have to move? Where? Why now?* If this was the stage call for Amber's big TV show, she was going to go full ape on this guy, pistol or no pistol. He followed her down the hallway but he passed the propaganda room of horrors on the right. The door was closed. He led her into a big open room near the kitchen, like a living room, but it was filled with weapons and RPG's stacked like cord wood against the walls. *It's more a dying room than a living room,* she thought morbidly.

"Stay put," he commanded, moving in front of her and securing her wrists with zip ties. He reached down to the ground and dragged a six-foot prayer rug off the floor in front of them, revealing a small wooden hatch door in the floor. Holding the pistol on Amber, he reached down and opened the hatch.

This must be the first door to hell, thought Amber. "You go down there," he pointed the pistol towards the hole. Amber's heart raced. *Is he going to throw me down in this dark pit and leave me to die or rot?* He shoved her when she froze. She carefully sat down on the edge of the opening and stepped in. The hole was about five feet deep and in the dim light she could see that it led to a tunnel. Keeping the pistol at the ready, KAT stepped into the hole behind her, then reached up and pulled the hatch and carpet over the opening. The tunnel was illuminated with a string of small dim lights dangling from the rafters. It was about four feet high and reinforced with railroad ties every six feet. Crouching down, KAT ordered, "Go."

The tunnel looked freshly dug to Amber. She tried to walk, bent over at the waist, but she kept whacking her head and back on the beams. Finally, she plopped to her knees and looked back at KAT. He was on his knees with the pistol in one hand on the ground.

"I have to crawl; you need to cut my hands loose," she said. In the dark shadows of the tunnel he looked like a demon with his black dress, sharp beard and dark eyes blazing in the dim light. After a few moments of hesitation, KAT pulled a knife from his waist and cut the zip ties holding Amber's hands together. She put her hands into the moist dirt in front of her and started crawling in front of him. She had been counting her steps and crawls, trying to get an estimate of the length of the tunnel. She figured each step had been about 18 inches and each crawl was about a foot. After what seemed like an hour, but was probably a lot less, they came to a fork. She stopped and looked back at KAT. He pointed with his pistol to the right and Amber moved on, calculating about 85 yards to this first turn. *If I have to come back this way, I need to memorize all these turns,* she thought to herself.

They crawled for another 15 minutes until the tunnel came to an end. Amber stopped and noticed the wooden hatch above her head. *It must connect to another house,* she thought. KAT stepped forward, grabbed her arms roughly and snapped another set of zip ties on her wrists. He then reached up, pushed up on the door and slid it to the side, letting light into the tunnel. He scurried out of the hole, then reached down, grabbed Amber under her arms and lifted her out.

She looked around furtively. Sure enough it was another house. The room she was in looked like a bomb-making lab. There were steel drums, tools all over the floor and bags of chemicals leaning against the walls, some of them open and spilling out onto the dirty wood floor. The room had brown brick walls, a low-slung ceiling and no windows. It looked about the size of a large bedroom.

KAT pushed her across the room to another hallway that contained several doors, with a similar design to the previous house. He led her to the end of the hallway and opened the last door on the left. The stench hit her in the face like a slap. It was a putrid, queasy, greasy smell. KAT opened the door, shoved her into the room and latched the deadbolt behind her. Flies were hovering around a metal bucket in the corner. Amber cautiously walked over to the bucket and looked inside. A man's head stared back at her, eyes open, tongue hanging out, organs spilling out of the neck into the bottom of the bucket. She turned and threw up in the corner.

The two blacked-out MH-60 helicopters were heading southeast toward the southern target. Butcher had three SEALs with him in the lead bird; Lone Wolf, the point man, Gonzo, the sniper and Spartacus, the radioman and explosive breacher. The other four were in the second bird; Denny, the Platoon Chief, Black Heart, Jonesy, and Hulk.

Butcher knew his boys were ready for this. They were on their fifth month in Iraq and had already knocked out a host of direct action missions on AQI targets. This mission, however, was the peak, the Mount Everest of missions, a hostage rescue of an American soldier. To him and his men, there was nothing more important. It was one thing to take a bunch of bad actors off the board, it was another thing altogether to rescue an American. It took a level of precision, teamwork and savvy that very few Special Ops units could achieve. The boys had a plan based on the intel they'd been given right before the launch. But in his gut, Butcher knew it would all come down to improvising on the target. Nothing ever went according to plan in the chaotic world of military special operations in Iraq. He and his team had nearly seen it all: being dropped at the wrong target house, more terrorists on the target than were expected, civilians and kids in the line of fire, IED's, hazardous bomb-making chemical labs, torture rooms, enemy snipers in hiding, and every imaginable weapon being used against them.

The objective of this mission was clear: rescue the American soldier. But the unspoken mission was always the hard part: don't get your own guys killed, don't kill any innocent bystanders. That's where precision and teamwork came in. Anyone could shoot up a building and everyone in it. It was mind-bendingly difficult to be micro-precise and aggressive at the same time. His team needed to balance poise and caution with aggressive lethality.

Butcher looked out the small window in the side of the helicopter. It was dark and a sliver of moon was rising in the east. He could see scattered lights below from farms and villages they were passing over. A thought of his family back home crossed his mind, but he immediately shut it out: this was no time to think warm, happy thoughts. He tightened up the chinstrap on his helmet. Time to focus on controlled violence for a good cause. To a lot of people, that was an oxymoron, but to Butcher it made sense, he lived it. In his world, really bad men had to be taken out by semi-good men. There was no way around it, otherwise the bad men would take over everything. The trick was to stay on the decent side of killing, not give in to murder, torture, indiscriminate killings. Do your job, shoot them in the face, go home to your kids, but don't become like the evil men. It was not always that easy, he knew.

After his first deployment to Iraq, he and his boys were redeployed back to their families within two days. Turns out that was not a great idea. You can't go from splattering someone's brains against the wall to coaching your daughter's soccer team within the same week. The higher-ups got smart when the operators were getting into trouble right after redeployment. They realized the boys needed some time and expertise to decompress from a violent deployment. They started to send special operators to a stop in Germany on the way home, providing them with counselors, specialists, medical experts and shrinks, preparing them for a better reintegration with their families and society. Butcher knew it didn't always go well when the boys finally got home, even after the sessions. He'd dealt with a bunch of problems: suicide, domestic violence, alcohol abuse and general PTSD symptoms. The decompression stop was a good idea, but he knew it was not a cure-all. There was no easy antidote to the daily bloody violence they experienced.

He felt the helo bank as the pilot came up on his headset. "Five minutes out," he relayed.

"Copy all," Butcher responded, then gave his boys a five-minute hand signal. His men each peered at him, probably unconsciously. They were looking for confidence and resolve from their leader and they got it in spades. Whatever his emotions were, they would spill out and affect them. He was calm, but a river of anger flowed beneath the surface—an American soldier had been captured. That anger would keep him and his boys in the fight as long as it took.

The pitch of the big engine over their heads changed as the MH-60 banked again and made a rapid descent towards an improvised landing field 30 yards away from the house. The two helos landed simultaneously as the seven SEALs rushed out the doors and sprinted for the house in two teams. Butcher and his team took the front entry door. Chief Denny would lead the second element to the back door.

As Butcher and his team reached the front door, Spartacus set the small breaching charge on the hinges and lock and waited for Butcher's signal. Butcher knew there was a good chance they'd encounter another IED, but he and his men were prepared. Once Butcher heard that Chief and his team were in place at the back door, he gave the signal. The charges blew the door off the hinges and the men rushed through the doorway as Chief's team flooded in from the back. In the eerie smoke and dust, Butcher had a bad feeling. It was a dry hole: the boys met no resistance. The two teams methodically searched the entire house, clearing every room.

"Take a look at this!" Chief Denny called out in the hallway over the radio. Butcher joined the chief and stepped into the propaganda room, scanning the black Al Qaeda flag, the camera and lighting.

The two men turned to look at each other, each thinking the same thing, I *hope to God Downing didn't get turned into a horror film here.*

When the men finished clearing the building, they went about checking for clues that might point to Downing having been there: a backpack, water bottle, helmet, uniform top, anything. Suddenly, Gonzo came over the radio net. "I'm in the last room on the right, I've got something."

Lieutenant Butcher and Chief Denny hurried down the hall while the rest of the men continued their search. Gonzo was squatting in the corner when they opened the door. "Check this out," he said, pointing to the floor in the corner of the room. It took a minute and then they both saw it, the word DOWNING was written in the dust in the corner. It looked like she'd written it with her finger. Butcher and his chief looked at each other and nodded. *She'd been here recently.*

Bucher stepped outside the house so he could get a clear satellite call to the Special Operations Task Force. "Jackal, this is Red Bird, over."

"Go ahead, Red Bird," Colonel Harrison spoke over the radio. A small crowd stood around him at his desk, hoping for good news from the SEALs on the target.

"Jackal, we've got a dry hole here, but we think the package was here recently."

"Explain, Red Bird," the colonel ordered.

"We found her name written in the dust in the corner of a room. It looks like she was held in that room for some time. The place is empty now. We need to get an exploitation team here, see what they can find."

"Copy all, Red Bird," Colonel Harrison responded, thinking about his next move. He was nearly out of options.

Butcher scanned the fields with his night vision while waiting for an answer from the colonel. *Wait, what the hell?* Suddenly he saw a dog sprinting out of the darkness across the field toward him. It was a speck at first but within a few seconds it was nearly at the house. The dog stopped near Butcher, looked at him and trotted through the front opening where the door used to be.

"Jackal, a military working dog just ran out of the field and into the house," Butcher reported to the commander. Butcher had read all the reports on Amber and her dog Razor and knew that Razor had been injured but was also seen at the last site by the Army ODA team. He knew that the dog had been following Amber down a road before the Task Force lost sight of him from the UAVs and that his GPS collar had gone dead. Yet here he was on this site, further confirming that Downing had just been here.

"Copy all, Red Bird, what's the dog doing now? Check his injuries and give us an assessment."

Butcher stepped into the house and stopped in amazement. His men were all standing around in a circle in what looked like the former living room. Razor was running and sniffing all through the room. He let out a high-pitched whine, like he knew he was close as he sniffed everything. Suddenly he started to paw at a dirty rug near the middle of the floor. Chief Denny stepped forward and lifted the rug by the corner. He rolled the rug back, revealing a hidden door cut into the floor. While his men pointed their weapons at the hatch, Butcher reached down and pulled the trap door open, revealing a dimly-lit tunnel below the house. "Everyone hold right here," Butcher said to his men over the inter-squad radio as he rushed outside to contact the task force.

"Jackal, this is Red Bird, the dog found a hidden door in a room that leads to a tunnel. I intend to explore it. It's our best lead on the location of the package."

There was quiet on the other end of the line for a few seconds. Colonel Harrison was talking to his Sergeant Major. "The other team already ran into one ambush," Sergeant Major Brown said, always keeping the safety of his men paramount. A tunnel would be simple to booby trap and one insurgent at the other end could easily fire on the men as they crept down the dark tunnel. Only the first man could shoot - the rest were sitting ducks."

Colonel Harrison nodded to his Sergeant Major, then spoke, "The team is poised to rescue an American soldier, a soldier who might end up being killed on live TV if they didn't get her back." The Sergeant Major nodded.

Colonel Harrison cued the mic, "OK, Red Bird, what's your plan?"

34

Lopez thought about the new job he would be starting at the post office in two weeks, hoping he could become a letter carrier. The thought of being able to drive and walk around by himself and deliver mail to people made him smile inside. *Heck, all I have to do is avoid a few dogs*, he thought. *This will be a cakewalk compared to Iraq.* Plus, it would give him more time to work on the stuff Dr. Mankowski taught him in those sessions. He thought kindly of the doctor. In the Army, Lopez, like most soldiers, had avoided talking to the psych doctor out of fear of what his superiors and other soldiers would think. He'd seen several soldiers quietly pulled from their units and given less stressful jobs after talking to the shrink. He didn't want that. He wanted to stay with his unit, his team, his band of brothers. Nothing worse than to be cast out to some menial job and have everyone think you're batshit crazy. But speaking with Dr. Mankowski had been a good decision. He'd been a soldier in Vietnam and understood, first-hand, what Henry was struggling with. He didn't ask him to spill his guts, he already knew what was wrong. Best of all, he gave Henry some effective methods to combat the PTSD symptoms when they flooded in like a rising dark tide. He'd been practicing them since he left the doctor's

212

office two weeks ago and found them very helpful. He was good at putting things to work that he learned. That was one of the reasons he had been such a good soldier.

Later that evening, when the brief warm weather had been replaced by a gentle cool wind, he told his mother he was heading out for a few hours. He didn't tell her he was going to watch the Broncos game at a local tavern—she hated bars and alcohol, having seen her father and brother become useless drunks. "Okay, Mijo, be careful." His father and mother had started living apart about a year ago. They were not divorced, just separated for some reason. Deep down, Henry figured it was because of his father's drinking.

"I will, Momma," he promised, before walking out into the dark night. There was no moon and the stars were hidden by the ambient light of the dull yellow streetlights. The local tavern, Jimmy's Place, was only two blocks past the Dollar General. Jimmy's had three TVs screwed into the wall behind the bar. The place was dingy, with sketchy hardcore local drinkers usually hanging around, day or night, but it was close to home and they would have the game on. Henry could walk home after a few beers and not worry about having to drive.

He chose a seat at the weathered bar down on the left side, in front of a small TV on the wall. He ordered a Modelo from Jimmy, the owner and bartender, and looked around the place before the game started. He knew a few more folks would show up to watch the Broncos when kickoff started in 20 minutes. There was only one other customer at the bar, a guy wearing one of those Day-Glo yellow safety vests, like he was a road construction worker who'd just finished his shift. Henry flipped through his phone as another customer walked in. It was a tall, lean man, with a high-top haircut and Ray-Bans. He wore a black leather jacket and sat at the opposite end of the bar from Lopez. Just as the game started, a group of five rowdy friends showed up wearing their Broncos T-shirts and hats. They sat at one of the tables by the window near the street and ordered a bucket of PBR's from Jimmy.

On the Raider's opening drive, the Broncos linebacker picked off a pass and ran it 40 yards into the end zone for a touchdown. The road worker raised his arms in the sign for a touchdown, the rowdy five went berserk, high-fiving each other, standing up and doing chest bumps. Henry noticed that the tall guy at the other end of the bar didn't seem to care. The guy spun his drink around on the table and glanced at his phone periodically.

With four minutes left in the game, the Broncos were down by 17 points. The game was lost. Henry didn't feel like watching the inevitable defeat of his team. He paid up his tab, walked out and headed home. He stopped at an intersection, waited for the light to turn, then continued walking down the dark sidewalk. There were no cars on this narrow back street shortcut home. After two blocks, a dog started barking as he heard an engine wind up behind him and he turned to see a brown panel van pull up next to him with a screech of tires. The guy in the passenger seat was the same tall guy Lopez had seen at the other end of the bar at Jimmy's.

Lopez froze. He was about to run when the guy pushed a taser gun out the window and shot him in the chest. Lopez went down hard on the sidewalk, his eyes fluttering and his arms and legs bouncing off the pavement as the high voltage surged through his body. The two men in the van jumped out and ran to him. The tall guy who had tasered him pulled a roll of duct tape from his pocket, tore off a piece and slapped it on Lopez's mouth. The driver, who wore a black hoodie and had bandages on his face, pulled out another roll of duct tape and secured Henry's arms and legs. Lopez was conscious as the two picked him up and quickly tossed him into the back of the panel van. He looked at the man in the hoodie suddenly recognizing him, screaming into the duct tape. Although he looked different, Henry could never forget that face. The men closed the door and sped away down the dark street.

They drove to a seldom-used park, overgrown with weeds, about two miles away. The park had become a hangout for drug dealing and homeless encampments so most people avoided it. The van drove into the parking lot of the park, then took a left down a short dirt road that led to an abandoned maintenance shed. The two men jumped out, shutting the doors quietly, walked to the back of the van and opened the rear doors. Lopez lifted his head off the floor and tried to yell, but the duct tape over his mouth muffled the sound. He looked at the man he recognized and shook his head, but the man ignored his pleas.

They pulled him roughly out the back and set him down next to a large willow tree just off the road. The tall man took a U.S. Army issued Beretta pistol from under his belt at his back. He was wearing gloves now. He looked over at the other man with the hoodie and handed him the pistol.

The man with the hoodie took the pistol, but looked confused, "We're going to scare him, remember? Make sure he doesn't talk anymore," he said with a frantic whisper.

"Plans have changed," said the other man. "The risk is too high." Lopez looked back and forth between the men then screamed into the tape over his mouth, but nothing came out.

"I'm not going to kill him," said the man in the hoodie. "This is insane!"

"Give me the fucking gun," said the tall man. The man in the hoodie slowly passed the pistol to the tall man.

With one clean motion, the tall guy ripped off the tape from Lopez and shoved the 9mm pistol in his mouth. Lopez tried to scream but the barrel was choking him. The guy in the hoodie turned away, averting his eyes. *This can't be happening,* Lopez thought. *They're trying to rob me or scare me.* The shot went off, the bullet traveled through Henry's brain and exited out the top of his head. Henry's life fluid poured out into the moist dirt.

The tall man cut the tape from Henry's lifeless body and propped him against the tree into a lifelike sitting position, then put the pistol in Henry's hand. The man in the hoodie was walking in circles, talking to himself and crying. "Let's go," said the tall man. He walked over, took the man in the hoodie by the arm and led him to the truck. They walked quickly back to the van where the tall man made a call. The phone rang after two rings. "It's done," he said, and hung up.

35

JUNE 2012, GRAND JUNCTION AND MONTROSE,
COLORADO

Amber sat at her desk contemplating her next move. Nikita was asleep under the desk with her paws on Amber's feet. She thought about the meeting with Holmes—he'd definitely been ruffled when she asked about access to the police reports of Lopez and Arnold's deaths. She was sure they wouldn't give her access to the files, but it was worth a shot. At least she might find out what kind of legal request or form she would need to see them.

"Let's go girl, road trip," she said, looking under her desk. Nikita sprung up at the word *road trip;* always up for adventure.

Police records were held at the downtown station. Amber hated going downtown because it was always a pain to find parking. It was Friday and there was some kind of outdoor art fair spread across the street where she liked to park. She drove around the block looking for a parking spot and pulled in behind a dingy strip mall. The place was full but she found a spot next to a big green dumpster. As she was opening the car door for Nikita, a man stepped out from behind the dumpster. She could tell immediately that he was high on something as he staggered over to her. He was wearing filthy jeans, had two mismatched shoes and wore an Army fatigue jacket from the Vietnam era.

"How about you gimme your wallet, lady?" he said, reaching into his pocket, maybe for a gun, a knife or who knows what. Amber already had her hand on the back door—she pulled the door handle and Nikita shot out like a fur missile. The German Shepherd had watched the encounter with her master and the strange man from the back seat and had started growling, knowing instinctively that the man was a threat. Once outside, she took two large strides and leapt at the man, biting his forearm, where he held a small pocket knife. The guy screamed as Nikita shook her powerful jaw, tearing into the man's wrist. He dropped the knife and yelled at Amber, "Call it off! Help!"

Amber yelled, "RELEASE!" and Nikita let go of the man, stepping back to Amber's side and growling. The guy turned and ran down the alley behind the dumpster. Nikita was primed and ready to take him down from behind, but Amber calmly said, "DOWN." Nikita slowly and reluctantly lay down, looking up at Amber as if to say, "Are you kidding me? I get a chance to take down slow running prey from behind and you call me off?"

Amber leaned against the car for a moment, letting her heart rate slow. She breathed in and out deeply. "OK, time to go," she said aloud. *I'll let the police know about this guy,* she thought as she walked to police headquarters.

At the front desk, Amber reported the man with the knife to the officer manning the desk. When she finished filing her report, she asked him where the records office was located. He directed her to a door in the corner of the lobby. She quietly stepped into the office, Nikita at her side, and a young woman with fake blonde hair, big eyelashes and tight jeans looked up from a computer screen and said, "May I help you?"

"Yes, I work for the VA Hospital here in Grand Junction," Amber began, while pulling her VA identification from her pocket and showing it to the woman. "I'm conducting an analysis of the suicides of veterans in this area and I was hoping I could check out the police reports for two veterans who committed suicide, Henry Lopez and Jerry Arnold."

"Well, for one thing, we don't give out police reports to the public. They have to be requested by a judge or a Freedom of Information Act request approved by headquarters," the woman explained, standing up and walking over to the counter where Amber stood. "And for another thing, we don't have those reports here anymore. A police officer from Montrose PD checked them out yesterday."

Amber was stunned. *Who had checked out the reports yesterday? And from Montrose? Why would the police in Montrose have anything to do with the cases of Lopez and Arnold?*

"Would you be able to tell me who from the Montrose Police Department checked them out?" Amber asked, figuring it was worth a try.

"No, I'm sorry, we're not allowed to reveal that, and the officer from Montrose cautioned me not to discuss anything about those files. She said someone might come looking for them."

"She?" Amber said, unable to hide her shock. "Was it a female officer?"

"I'm sorry, I'm not allowed to reveal any details," the woman said, returning to her desk, embarrassed and realizing she'd already screwed up by saying too much. She stared at her computer, clearly hoping

Amber would take the hint and leave without pestering her for further information.

Amber nodded and walked back to her car, Nikita tight at her side, sniffing all around for any signs of the bad man who'd confronted her master. They both jumped in the truck and headed back to the VA Medical Center. *I only know one female police officer in Montrose,* Amber thought, *but why the hell would Hannah check out those reports, if it even was her?*

Back at the office, she went through her Friday afternoon routine, cleaning up, emptying the trash, deleting junk emails and preparing for the weekend. Suddenly, the landline phone rang. Only people in the VA system used that number, so she knew it had to be official VA business.

"Hello?" she answered.

"Hello, is this Amber Downing?" a male voice asked.

"Yes."

"Hi, my name is Dane Hutchinson. I work at the VA Hospital in San Diego. I've been tasked with conducting an analysis of suicides of veterans in our area." The guy droned on as Amber's mind raced ahead. She knew deep down that this call would come someday, she just didn't think it would happen so soon.

"Are you still there?" the guy asked.

"Yes, yes, I'm sorry."

"As I was saying, one of my cases is an Army soldier named Chris Hawkins." He paused, and Amber's heart beat like a drum. "His mother told me you were his fiancé." He paused again, as if waiting for confirmation.

"Yes, that's right."

"I'm very sorry for your loss," he said solemnly. "I'm calling because his mother shared copies of some emails Chris had on his phone and I thought you might want to see them."

Amber was confused. She and Chris always spoke over the phone or occasionally used texts, but never emails. *What were these?*

"I can email them to you if you'd like?"

"Yes, thank you, I'd appreciate that," Amber said, giving him her work email address.

"I don't need anything from you," he assured her. "I just thought you might want to see these emails."

She thanked him again and hung up, wondering what could be in these emails that pertained to her. She stared at her computer, as if it was an oracle, waiting for the email to come through. She sat there for what felt like hours, though it was only minutes. She grabbed a rag and started to dust off her desk and keyboard when she heard the ding indicating a new email had arrived.

Dane's email had one attachment. She opened the file to see it was a short email exchange that had been copied and pasted into the document. She read it and almost fell out of her seat. She slammed her fist on the table and cursed out loud. Nikita popped out from under the desk in alarm, knowing that something was wrong. Amber paced around the room. "How could I have been so stupid!" she yelled to herself. Finally, she sat down in a corner on the floor, put her head in her hands and began to sob. Nikita rushed to her side. Once the tears started flowing, she couldn't hold them back. It was like a dam breaking—big tears came followed by sobbing and she couldn't stop them. The unfairness of it all came crashing down: ruthless KAT, her captivity, beautiful Razor, Chris's suicide and now this. *When am I going to get a break? What did I do to deserve all this? Why am I such a shit magnet?*

Her face still in her hands, she felt Nikita licking her ear. She looked up and saw those golden soulful eyes looking back at her with concern. Nikita lay down at Amber's side and put her paw on her leg. The touch was enough to snap Amber out of her dark mood. She reached down and scratched Nikita's ears. "I'm OK girl, thank you," she assured her, bending over and giving her best friend a kiss on the top of her furry head. She printed a copy of the email and left for the day.

In the parking lot, her phone dinged in her pocket. She reached for it and saw a text from Tony. "So sorry I didn't get back to you sooner. I'm available tonight if you want to get together. How about dinner at my place - 7?" It was the best thing that had happened today. She was surprised at how happy the text made her feel; it was like a lifeline to pull her out of the depths of despair. She tried to suppress it. She couldn't be hurt again. But a thought bubbled up that she needed to be with Tony tonight, needed him badly.

Tony lived two blocks off Main Street in downtown Montrose, in a modest two-bedroom house built in the 1950's. It was the kind of place someone could afford on a teacher's salary. The yard was simple, with a well-kept lawn surrounding a brick walkway from the street to the front door. Amber checked herself in the rearview mirror before opening the car door. *I'm ready for this,* she thought, as she got out of the car. She wore a blue knee length dress and black heels. Before heading to meet Tony, she had put on slacks and a blouse and stared at the mirror, but realized she looked too professional, like she was going to an interview. She put on her blue dress, looked in the mirror again, and saw that figure of hers highlighted. *Is it too much?* she thought, but in the end she went with it. She let Nikita out the back door and realized her dress was half covered in dog hair. *Oh well, that's dog life.*

She knocked, and within seconds Tony opened the door with a big smile. He was wearing a long sleeve white button down shirt, jeans and loafers.

"Wow, you look amazing," he complimented. It was the first time she'd really dressed up for him and worn makeup. He reached down to pet Nikita, but kept his gaze on Amber. She smiled and handed him the bottle of wine she'd picked up on the way. He leaned over to give her a peck on the cheek and she turned her head at the last second and kissed him on the lips. It was a short kiss and he pulled back out of respect, but he knew what she was telling him.

"Come in, please," he said, standing aside and welcoming her into his home. It was tidy and cute, she thought. A hallway to the left led to the two bedrooms and the entryway led to a small kitchen with a breakfast bar that could fit two people, and an adjacent living room with a small leather couch, a slim recliner and a small table beside a sliding glass door that led out to the back yard. Scenes from Paris hung on the walls of the living room. There was a large photograph of the Eiffel Tower taken at night, a black and white sketch of a Paris cafe scene and a painting of a colorful Paris street.

Amber walked over and admired the artwork. She turned back to Tony as he opened the bottle of wine in his tiny kitchen. "You must like Paris, have you been there?" she asked.

"No," he said, "Angelica—my wife and I always wanted to visit. She picked up the artwork to remind us that we planned to go someday."

Amber thought instantly of the email she'd received earlier that day. She clenched her fist and felt her heartbeat blast away. She needed to talk to somebody about it. Tony would be wonderful, but she didn't want to drop another heavy load on him, make him think that she was just a magnet for trauma and bad luck. She'd think about it.

"I've never been there either," she offered. "Closest I got was Ramstein, Germany, but that was just a U.S. Air Force base I stopped at on the way home from Iraq. Not a real European vacation."

Tony brought two glasses of the red wine and handed one to Amber as they both sat on the couch where Nikita had already curled up on the floor.

Amber took a long sip. It was merlot, her favorite.

Tony asked, "So how is that suicide case going?"

Geez, where do I start, she thought. She brought him up to speed on everything she had learned since she'd told him about the cases on their last date. "Here's the crazy part," she said, finishing her story. "I went to the Grand Junction Police Department to ask for a copy of the police reports on Lopez and Arnold's deaths. I didn't really expect they would give me anything, but it was worth a shot. The desk attendant let it slip that a police officer - a woman - from the Montrose PD checked out the records yesterday."

"What? Who? And more importantly, why is someone checking out reports of two suicides that you just happen to be investigating?" Tony asked, looking at her with concern.

"Yeah, I know, weird, right? I asked Officer Holmes about the reports, he looked nervous and the next day an officer checked them out. I'm thinking someone doesn't want me seeing those reports."

"What's your theory on what they're hiding?" he asked.

"Well, I can only guess, but there's something fishy about both suicides. They're connected, but I just can't pin it down. I hate to even think it, but it's possible they weren't suicides."

"You mean they were murdered?" Tony looked shocked.

"I don't have any evidence of that," she said, "But it's a possible conclusion I can draw based on the facts at hand."

"That's nuts, Amber, you should take this to the police," he said.

"I know, but which police can I trust at this point? And what am I gonna say? I have a few bits of circumstantial evidence and I want you to reopen two suicide cases? Pull the scab off the wounds of the families and community … on my hunch?"

Tony frowned and nodded. "Good point," he admitted. "So what *are* you going to do?"

"I don't know. I think I'm at a dead end here unless I can come up with another idea."

Tony stood. "Let me check on dinner," he said. "I'll be right back. I hope you like seafood?" he asked as he moved to the kitchen and pulled a tray out of the oven.

"Actually, I'm on a seafood diet," Amber quipped. "If I see food, I eat it."

"Ha Ha," he said.

"All right, dinner is served," he announced.

They sat at the small two person table by the sliding glass window in the living room. Tony served up plates of Chilean sea bass, asparagus and homemade bread sticks.

"Wow, you can really cook. I'm kind of used to Army chow. This is delicious," Amber remarked effusively, taking another bite of the flaky white fish. Tony beamed at being able to please her.

After dinner, they both cleared the table and Tony brought two small slices of cheesecake to the couch.

"Boy, you know how to get to a woman's heart," she joked, taking a bite and rolling her eyes at the creamy, sweet taste.

He grinned and poured the last of the bottle of wine into their glasses.

Amber set her dessert plate down. The email she'd received earlier popped into her head again. She couldn't continue pretending it wasn't bothering her. It was too exhausting to always pretend that everything was OK, that she is doing well, that life is clicking along like one of those Hallmark movies. She had to tell him.

"I got a call today from a VA rep in San Diego," she shared. "He'd been tasked with doing the same suicide project as me for his own area which is where Chris died. Anyway, he told me he had an email he thought I should see. Apparently, Chris's mother gave it to him." She reached into her purse and handed a folded up piece of paper to Tony.

He looked at her as he took it slowly, unfolded it and read it aloud.

"Chris, you and I are meant for each other. What we had in Baghdad was real. I know you feel guilty about it, but it was a connection we both felt deeply, a touch of pure happiness in that shitty place.

You know me, Chris, I'm strong, I'm sexy and I love you. We have that rare bond that people yearn for. Amber is my friend, too, but she's not for you. She's too wrapped up in herself, you two won't make it. I've known her longer than you, trust me. I'll tell Amber about us if you want me to.

Do the right thing, Chris, call it off with Amber and come to me. I will be with you always and will make your dreams come true.

Love always,

Hannah

"Hannah, the night we had while Amber was in captivity was a mistake, in fact the biggest mistake of my life. I don't know how I let you cross the line when I was so weak and vulnerable. I regret it every minute of every day. Amber was captured, in harm's way, a flicker away from death and you and I were having sex. As I look back on this, I'm disgusted with myself. You are her best friend, how could you do that and live with yourself?

I am so angry with myself over this that I don't know if I want to live anymore. It's like a giant demon in my life. I betrayed my fiancé at a time when she needed me to be strong. No one can make me happy after what we did.

Please do not contact me anymore.

Chris

Tony paused and looked at Amber with shock and sadness in his eyes. She looked at him and then nodded at the paper, indicating that she wanted him to finish.

"Chris, you're weak. We had something special, and you want to throw it away because your little conscience doesn't approve? How does your conscience like all the shit we saw in Iraq? The children used as suicide bombs, the beheadings, the shitheads leaving IED's to kill our soldiers and friends, the torture houses? We both thought Amber wasn't coming back. We did what we had to do to survive.

If you can't stand up for yourself and see that you have to live life and not let your puny conscience drive your life for you, then I feel sorry for you. You probably are right to wonder if you belong in this world. You lack spine.

Hannah

Breathless, Tony looked up at Amber. She was silently crying. "I don't know what to say," he said, reaching across the couch and squeezing her hand. He moved closer and took her in his arms. "Who is this Hannah?' he asked with disgust.

"She was that woman I was with at Phelanie's when we first met. She came in with her boyfriend, remember?"

"Oh my God, yeah, of course I remember. To be honest, I thought she was kinda rude. So what are you gonna do?" he asked, pulling back from their embrace and looking into her eyes.

She didn't answer for quite a while, then said, "Well I've lost my fiancé and now the person I thought was my best friend, too." She didn't mean it to sound like she was seeking pity, but she realized that's what it sounded like. "I guess I'll have to confront her about it. Geez, what a mess. I feel like a blind idiot. You think you know someone, right? Why the hell was Chris so weak that he let her take advantage of him?"

Tony spoke in a quiet voice. "I haven't told you this, Amber, but before my wife committed suicide, I found out she'd been having an affair. I guess I was embarrassed about it ... still am. That she needed someone else besides me? That I wasn't good enough for her?"

Amber sat up, reached behind his neck with both her arms, leaned in and gave him a deep kiss. She came up for air after a few moments, her heart racing. "You're good enough for me, Tony," she whispered into his ear. At that moment, she let it all go, the pain, the embarrassment, the shame, the hurt ... let it all melt away, at least for now. He reached for her face and began kissing her beautiful eyes, her nose, her gorgeous lips. She leaned back slowly and lay back on the small couch, looking up at him with eyes of blue glass. He gently lay on top of her, kissing her neck.

It's been so long, she thought, *I hope I can do this.* "Let me sit up," she whispered to him after a minute.

He pushed off the couch, like he'd gone too far, that she wasn't ready. But when she sat up, she gestured for Nikita to move a discreet distance away, then slowly removed her dress. She reached behind her back with both hands and unclasped her bra.

Amber looked up at Tony and wondered if he was ready for this too, this coming together in an intimate way, this sharing of vulnerable bodies and wounded souls. He lay gently on top of her and somewhere in the night they both lost themselves completely in the love of another, a shared love. Amber felt the pain in her life seep slowly away like a drain opening up and letting the muck flow out. She knew the darkness would eventually creep back into her life, but for now the tender affection was the best thing in the world, the only thing in the world.

36

Butcher keyed the mic on his chest to inform the colonel of his plan, "I'm going to lead one team down the tunnel with the dog, the other team will stand by as a quick reaction force once we find out where the tunnel is heading."

Colonel Harrison answered back, "OK, Red Bird, keep us informed. We'll have fire support in the air if you need it."

"Roger all," Butcher replied then turned to his men. "Fire Team One, we're going down the tunnel. Chief, standby with Fire Team Two behind the house. I'm not sure if our radios will transmit from underground, but if they do, we'll give you a bearing on our location and you can follow us above ground. If you come across any more than one or two tangos, use the fire support and drop holy hell on them. No sense getting into a firefight when we have all this high priority air support up there." Butcher stood in the middle of the room, and his men circled around him and nodded in acknowledgement. Razor was standing at the edge of the tunnel, pawing at the corners and whining. His bandage was soaked in blood. Butcher wished he had time to work on the wound, but they had to move fast. Downing had already been relocated a couple of times. The enemy was smart. They kept their

230

hostage on the run, making it harder for the Task Force to locate and rescue her.

Butcher jumped in the hole first. Lone Wolf would normally go first as the point man, but Butcher was not about to make one of his men lead the way into an ambush—he would take point. The men had fashioned a six-foot leash out of a piece of rope they'd found at the house. Butcher would lead with Razor out front on the leash, following Downing's scent. Lone Wolf, Gonzo and Spartacus would follow close behind him. The men had not practiced fighting in a tunnel, but it was not unlike any other channelized area that they had trained for, like a narrow hallway.

The tunnel was lit with dim lights hung on wires from the shaky rafters. Razor tugged at the rope, straining to go faster as Butcher crawled behind as fast as he could. He heard his men right behind him, clanging along. He thought they were losing noise discipline until he realized how much the tunnel amplified sound. The thought of those three warriors behind him filled Butcher's heart with confidence There was no one in the world he would rather be with in this dark tunnel, headed, he was sure, to a gunfight.

⎯⎯◆⎯⎯

Amber curled up in the far corner, away from the dreadful bucket holding the severed head. She tried not to think of that face, eyes open, tongue hanging out, but the stench was unbearable. *He's just trying to get to me, weaken me,* she thought to herself of KAT. She closed her eyes and tried to imagine something peaceful. A thought of her partner Razor came to mind. Six weeks ago, Chris had come out to the kennels when he was off duty to watch her work with Razor for attack training. Chris had volunteered to put on the protective suit, a big padded jumpsuit that would protect the wearer from dog bites when the military working dog was set loose on a simulated target. Chris thought Razor would just leap up and grab his arm; he'd never seen a Malinios charge at full speed and hit the target like a linebacker with a full head of steam. He stood there arms at his side as Amber gave the signal and pointed at Chris. Suddenly there was a black and brown flash as Razor sprinted and hit Chris in the chest, knocking him flat on his ass. Before he could even roll over, Razor had grabbed his padded arm and jerked it like he was trying to yank it out of the socket. Chris had yelled, "STOP!" and Amber called Razor off. She'd laughed and laughed at dinner that night in the chow hall as Chris told everyone at their table how he had been mowed down by a furry linebacker.

The door to Amber's prison room banged open and KAT stood in the doorway with the pistol in his hand and a fold of black cloth draped over his other arm. "Put this on," he said, tossing the black abaya at Amber. It was the head to toe garment that some women wore in the Middle East.

"To hell with that," Amber snarled, standing up. She figured he was going to dress her up for a propaganda film. "You're not going to get me into that thing!"

"Very well," KAT said, closing the door. In about two minutes he returned, this time with a terrified young girl, about 12-year-old, who was crying. KAT had her by the neck with one hand and put the pistol to her head. "Your choice," he said. "Put on the abaya, or this girl dies, right here, right now." The girl screamed and tried to fall to the ground, but KAT lifted her up, put his arm around her neck, choked her and held the pistol to her temple. "I'm going to count to five," he said. "One, two, three…"

"OK, I'll put it on. Let her go!" Amber yelled. KAT tossed the girl aside like she was a piece of trash.

"Good, good, you're beginning to see how this is going to work," he said with a disgusting grin, backing out the doorway and locking the deadbolt with a thunk.

Amber pulled the black robe-like dress over her uniform. It fell all the way to the ground, hiding her boots, making her look like a raven Red Riding Hood. She was feeling the garment when she noticed something hard near the waist, on the inside seam. She felt around and poked her finger on it. It was a sewing needle, a big one, maybe two inches long. Someone mending the garment had left it there. With the needle in her hand, Amber walked to the corner. She dared not look in the bucket again, but she grabbed what she had seen earlier on the ground—a small piece of wood, maybe the size of her thumb. She stuck the blunt side of the needle into a small crack in the wood, then gently tapped the sharp point against the wall until the needle was stuck deep in the wood. She thought about where to hide her homemade shiv and finally settled on slipping it up her right sleeve. *If they try to make me a propaganda star, I'll make sure KAT gets a few holes in his head before the curtain call,* she thought, holding the improvised weapon in her sleeve.

***

Butcher and his team came to a fork in the tunnel. He could hear his men breathing heavily as he kept up a fast-paced crawl. He took his UHF radio out of the pouch and tried to contact his other fire team. He calculated that they had traveled about 140 yards underground at a heading of 275 degrees from the last house. The radio couldn't penetrate through the earth above them. *We might have to close this one out by ourselves. No problem,* Butcher thought. *Surprise and initiative were worth several additional men.*

Spartacus was six-foot-four, 230 pounds of muscle. He'd gained his name because he looked like a model: perfect body, tall, tanned, blonde hair, chiseled chin. The girls swooned over him. In truth, he was an introvert who spent his spare time reading history, but he was a hell of an operator. He could carry so much belted ammunition that he was able to continuously fire the heavy machine gun he carried while everyone else was out of ammunition and changing magazines. It was a fearsome sight to see this giant standing and unleashing fire and destruction at a target. Butcher saw him lying on the ground behind him for a moment, trying to stretch out his back. *The tunnel must be hell on the big man,* Butcher thought.

Gonzo and Lone Wolf were both leaning against the tunnel wall, drinking out of their Nalgene bottles. Gonzales, or Gonzo, was the first one in his Mexican American family to join the military. He tried out for the SEALs and was almost dropped because he swam like an anvil. But he was tough as nails, and learned to swim in the ocean with the help of his roommate, who was a college swimmer. Butcher had been in the same SEAL training class called BUD/S with Lone Wolf. The wiry Lone Wolf had been a self-described *Turd Chaser* on Navy ships before he decided to try out for the SEALs. He came in the Navy as a hull technician, but found out that a lot of his job was sorting out plumbing problems on big Navy ships. The energetic Lone Wolf was a natural in the field. He could track animals and men and had the sixth sense of a wolf which is how he earned his nickname.

The air in the tunnel was stale. The confined space reminded Butcher of SERE training: survival, evasion, resistance and escape. At one point, his instructors had put him in a small metal box and left him there for hours to simulate a form of torture. He laughed to himself as he remembered singing inside that dark, stuffy box, which only pissed off the SERE instructors.

Razor ignored the turn to the left and tugged Butcher towards the tunnel on the right, scratching at the ground and sniffing the moist dirt while the men rested for a minute. Butcher looked back at his operators, gave a thumbs up, received one in return from everybody and started a fast crawl down the new tunnel. In 10 minutes, the tunnel terminated, leading the men into a small hole about the size of a big garbage can. There was a piece of plywood over their heads that looked like it opened into a room above. It was dark in the little cave at the end of the tunnel, as the lights had been disabled for the last 50 yards. Butcher and his men had been crawling in pitch dark, except for the occasional beam of a red lens flashlight.

In the back of his mind, Butcher figured this tunnel would lead to another house like the one behind them. It was a way for the AQI terrorists to clandestinely move men, equipment and hostages between locations.

The other three guys crawled up tight next to Butcher to discuss the plan. He turned on his red lens flashlight, illuminating the ground between them which made his men look like red-faced devils. "All right, here's what I'm thinking," he whispered while holding Razor tight against him and squeezing the dog's muzzle to keep him from growling. He knew the dog was trained to be quiet on the target until he received a signal, but Butcher wasn't taking any chances. As he held the dog, he felt the blood from Razor's wound seep into the side of his uniform.

❖

KAT shoved open the door, again holding the young girl at gunpoint. Amber looked in her eyes, and saw absolute terror. The girl thought she was going to die. It was too hard to look at. Amber looked up at KAT. If he wanted to see her weak and fearful, she wasn't going to give him that. She stared back at him with narrowed eyes of steel.

"Come," he ordered, waving the pistol while holding the girl. "Or I shoot her right here, then you."

She had no choice. She was not going to see that girl killed in front of her. She walked toward the door and slowly down the hallway. At the second door on the left, KAT stopped and knocked. A large man, his face completely covered in a black scarf except his large, cruel eyes, opened the door. "Aw, hell no," Amber whispered to herself as KAT shoved her and the girl into the room. KAT said something menacing to the girl and she walked over, sat down in the corner and pulled her legs up, burying her face in her knobby knees and sobbing.

Amber saw there was a third man in the room besides the beast who had opened the door. He was fiddling with a camera on a tripod. On the opposite wall hung the black Al Qaeda flag. In front of the flag was a table with a nasty-looking short sword. Her heart pounded so fiercely it felt like it might leap from her chest. But then, slowly, something came over her, a spark of iron resolve, a remembrance of who she was, an American soldier, never out of the fight. *Well, if I'm dying here,*

I'm taking one of you assholes with me, she thought, reaching for that shiv in her sleeve.

⸻⸻◆⸻⸻

Butcher reached up and felt the heavy plywood hatch over their head; it was loose. He nodded at the men crouching behind him and slowly slid the hatch to one side. He poked his head up and looked around, aiming his gun in all directions before seeing the dimly lit room was empty. Lone Wolf was holding Razor back behind Butcher. The dog was squirming and paddling the air as the wiry point man held on to the little fur rocket with all his strength.

Butcher nodded back down to his men then cautiously pulled himself up out of the hole. Swiftly, he took cover behind a crate, aiming his weapon at the front entrance, as the other men quietly emerged from the hole. He heard voices down the hallway speaking in Arabic. Gonzo had climbed out of the tunnel and Spartacus stood in the hole, half his large body already in the room. Gonzo had taken up a position covering down on the back door. Lone Wolf was handing Razor up to Spartacus when the back door opened and two black-robed terrorists stepped into the room carrying AK-47's. Before the AQI members could lift their rifles and get off a shot, Gonzo dropped them both with two quick headshots.

Suddenly there was shouting in the room down the hall. Butcher knew they'd lost the element of surprise, but he had a backup plan. He nodded at Spartacus and Lone Wolf, they would follow him down the hall. Gonzo would remain and cover their backs while they assaulted the next room. When they turned the corner of the hallway, Spartacus let Razor go as they had planned. Razor would lead them straight to the room where his master was held captive, preventing the terrorists from killing their hostage or escaping with her while Butcher and his men searched the wrong rooms, losing precious time.

***

KAT stood proudly in front of the camera next to Amber, AQI operatives from his cell standing behind him in front of the Al Qaeda flag and holding their AK-47's. This would be KAT's big moment. The moment he would become a legend in the worldwide movement of Al Qaeda. He hadn't sought permission from his seniors for this propaganda film. He planned to do it by himself, the first time a female American soldier would be executed in front of the camera. This was his captive. He would be immortal after this. The true brothers would shout his name with glory as he shed the blood of the infidel female soldier, broadcasting it across the internet.

One of the men stepped down from behind him to turn on the camera, and that's when KAT heard the shots fired. He knew it could only mean one thing—the Americans were here. They had found him somehow.

***

KAT was yelling at the men behind him, directing them to take cover, when Razor rounded the doorway at Mach 2, his paws seeking traction on the dirty tile floor. KAT had just enough time to raise his pistol and fire a shot at the dog leaping at him in the air. Simultaneously

Amber thrust the needle in her sleeve into KAT's left eye, tearing it sideways to maximize the damage. The bullet hit Razor in the shoulder, but he was already in the air, jaws open, teeth bared. He hit KAT with so much force he knocked the black-clad terrorist right off his feet and onto his back.

Immediately behind Razor, Butcher, Lone Wolf and Spartacus stormed the room, weapons at the ready. As smooth as butter, Lone Wolf moved down the right wall while firing at the terrorist crouched in the corner behind a small table. He shot the man in the top of his forehead, the only part visible above the table.

The other terrorist had hit the deck in the opposite corner of the room, seeking cover behind a stack of ammunition boxes. Spartacus slung his rifle, pulled a long, nasty black hatchet off his belt, took two big steps then leaped over the boxes, landing on top of the black-clad man and burying the hatchet in the back of his head.

Butcher ran straight for KAT as he was the target closest to the hostage. KAT managed to fire one shot, but was now on his back, pinned beneath the dog. Razor's powerful jaws were clamped on KAT's throat, ripping into his jugular vein, spewing blood everywhere. Butcher saw Amber on her knees, repeatedly jamming something into KAT's eye. When Butcher reached the melee, he pulled the dog off by its collar. The terrorist was no longer a threat. If he could be saved, he could be interrogated and maybe a new network could be exploited, but Butcher saw it was too late. As he pulled Razor off, the injured dog took a chunk of KAT's throat with him. The man was lifeless as massive amounts of blood flowed out from his neck, down his chest and onto the floor.

Amber sat back and dropped the shiv onto the bloody floor.

"I'm Lieutenant Butcher from the Special Operations Task Force. I'm here to take you home," he said, kneeling in front of her. "Are you hurt?"

She looked up at him and shook her head, then she looked at Razor. The dog was lying on the ground at her feet, bleeding where KAT had shot him in the shoulder. She crawled on her knees over to him and put her face right into his, looking at him eye-to-eye and gently petting his head, "I love you, boy," she said softly. "You saved me." Razor looked up at his master with dark brown eyes full of pain, but also loyalty and love. He'd found his master. He closed his eyes and nodded off. Amber fell on top of her loyal partner, suddenly crying uncontrollably. Butcher gave her a minute then reached down and lifted her off Razor. He set her in the corner. "Lone Wolf, watch her," he said, pointing at her with his chin. He grabbed the mic of his radio and made the call to the Task Force, "Jackal, we have the package, I need a MEDEVAC for a wounded canine soldier ASAP."

37

June 2012, Grand Junction and Montrose, Colorado

It was Monday and Amber was back in her office. She dove into two more fairly straightforward suicide cases as a way to not think about Hannah and Chris. But she knew she had to deal with it, and couldn't let it go. Finally she sat back and let her mind think about the options. She couldn't pretend it never happened and continue hanging out with Hannah. She couldn't just ghost her and ignore all her phone calls and texts - Montrose was too small a town for that. She'd have to confront her, there was no other way. Deep down Amber knew that, but she dreaded the confrontation. It made her stomach turn. She'd had enough confrontation in this life and didn't need any more, but there was no way out. She made the call. Hannah picked up on the second ring.

"Hey, Hannah, what are you doing?"

"Unfortunately, I'm adding to the stereotype of police officers by having a donut and coffee with my partner, what's up?"

"I was wondering if you wanted to come over after dinner tonight, have a drink with me and chat."

Hannah hesitated a moment before answering, "Sure, that sounds nice, what time?"

"Let's make it 7," Amber said.

"Sounds good, see you then."

Hannah hung up and stared at her coffee while her partner checked his phone. There was something different in Amber's tone, a reserve, a coldness even.

"Hey, I need to make a quick call," she said to her police partner, who was still deep in social media scrolling. She stepped out of the coffee shop and into the parking lot, where she dialed a number from her contacts. A male voice answered.

"What's up, Hannah?" he asked.

"I think we might have a problem," she answered.

"Tell me about it."

"Amber invited me to her home tonight, but she sounded a little cold over the phone. Maybe she discovered that I picked up those reports for you," Hannah spoke into her cell phone as her partner climbed into their police car.

"I'm sure it's nothing, just hear what she has to say. You haven't done anything wrong. Call me if you have any problems," the man said.

"OK, will do."

⬧

Amber and Nikita strolled down to the cafe for a late lunch. She hadn't talked to Sheri in a while and she wanted to see her friend, catch up a bit. Plus Nikita always loved to see Sheri. The cafe was quiet except for a table where two elderly VA volunteers were having lunch. They did a great service helping 7 new to the VA figure out how to get signed in and find their way through the big hospital. They wore bright red, white and blue hats, marking them as volunteers.

Thankfully, Sheri was working today as Amber stepped up to the counter. "Well, look who we have here! My favorite girl in this hospital," Sheri joked, as she reached over the counter and handed Nikita a big biscuit. Nikita took it softly from Sheri, her tail wagging as she crunched right into it and scarfed up all the crumbs.

"Hey, Sheri, sorry I haven't been up here in a while, work's been crazy lately."

"Are you still deep in that project you told me about?" Sheri asked with barely hidden concern.

"Yeah, it's gotten a little weird lately," Amber confessed. After Amber ordered a sandwich, Sheri stepped away from the counter to sit with her for a few minutes. She wanted to be there for Amber, whatever she needed.

"So what's the latest, my friend?" Sheri asked as Amber finished up her lunch. Not for the first time, Amber wondered where to start. The news about Chris and Hannah was too raw, too embarrassing. She'd told Tony about it, but that was after a few glasses of wine. She'd loved their evening together, but had been second-guessing her decision to tell him about Chris and Hannah. It all seemed so nutty and seedy, like an episode of *Jerry Springer*. But Sheri was probably the least judgmental person she knew and Amber really needed to tell her friend about it, so she shared the whole, sordid story.

Sheri listened with her eyes, never saying anything or asking questions as Amber spilled out the tale of the emails leading up to Chris's suicide. When she finished, Amber felt better. The crazy monkey in her gut calmed down just a little as she laid out her story of betrayal. There was something in just the telling of it that helped her get a grip on her future, even if only for a minute.

Sheri didn't say anything, which was a little disconcerting to Amber. "So what do you really think?" Amber asked her after a long moment of silence.

Sheri looked down for a moment before speaking. Amber needed to hear the truth - at least Sheri's view of the truth. "This may be hard to stomach right now, Amber, but in some way you've been blessed here." Amber tightened her face and clenched her jaw. She hadn't expected to hear this from Sheri.

"What I mean is that if Chris couldn't be there for you, in your time of deepest need, *during* your captivity, of all things, then he wasn't the right one for you. Maybe there was some hidden fault line in his psyche that came undone with stress, maybe it saved you a lot of heartache and a divorce later. I know you think Chris was the victim here, and to some extent he was, but it takes two to tango, you know what I mean?"

Amber didn't like what she heard as it came out of Sheri's mouth, but deep down she knew there were nuggets of truth there, that Chris had not been faithful during her darkest hour, that he had allowed himself to be seduced by her best friend. She hadn't really thought about it that way. She'd been so focused on Hannah's betrayal and Chris's suicide that she had mentally excused him from fault, especially after reading his email. But Sheri had struck a chord. Chris's suicide was like a knife wound to her soul, but Sheri was right, he had thrown away their chances of being happy together. Even if he had not committed suicide, he probably would have felt so guilty about his betrayal that their relationship would not have survived, or their life together would have been built on a lie. It didn't lift the burden she felt, but it did open a door to the possibility of getting over this whole mess someday. Amber nodded, hugged her friend and told her she'd think about what she'd said, then left Sheri to finish up in the cafe.

On the way home from work, Amber thought about the meeting she would have with Hannah tonight. Her stomach churned as she anticipated confronting the person who, until yesterday, she'd considered her best friend. She tried to plan out what she would say as she drove, but it all sounded stupid to her. She decided to just say what she felt when the time was right.

When she arrived home, Amber let Nikita out of the truck and she shot out the door, nose to the ground, on alert for any animals in her domain. She raised her head at the smell of some deer in the distance then trotted off to patrol her territory.

Amber popped an Asian noodle meal into the microwave and attempted to eat it, but her stomach felt queasy at the thought of the upcoming confrontation with Hannah. She thought about changing clothes, but decided it didn't matter. She wasn't aiming to impress Hannah. Her jeans and sweatshirt would do.

At 10 after 7, Nikita barked a warning as Hannah rolled up the driveway in her Audi. Nikita met her at the door with a big wet nose.

Amber tried her best to be nonchalant, "Hey, Hannah, come on in."

Hannah looked a little wary, throwing kind of a fake smile back at Amber. Amber picked up on that and thought, *she knows something is up.* Hannah handed her a bottle of pinot noir.

"Oh, thanks, I'll get us a couple of glasses. There's a cheese board on the coffee table." Most cheese boards at the level of a dog's head would not survive the night, but Nikita knew what was hers and what was off limits.

Amber returned to the living room with two glasses of the wine. Hannah was seated in the chair across from the couch, so Amber took the couch. Amber thought it would be a little weird, if not dishonest, to spend time chatting about life before springing the emails on Hannah. She decided to rip off the band-aid, get right to the point.

She had the emails printed out, but folded on the table. She reached for the papers and slid them across the table to Hannah without a word. Hannah looked at her for a few moments. *She knows,* thought Amber. *I can see it in her eyes.*

Hannah picked up the pages and read each one then dropped them on the coffee table. "You never deserved him," she said nastily. "You were only thinking of yourself and that crazy dog. You were gone, captured by Al Qaeda, you don't come back from that."

"But I did," said Amber calmly. "I was captured, not dead."

"Chris was a mess," Hannah said, angry at being ambushed. "You never deserved him. I comforted him when he was out of his mind worrying about you."

"I'd say you gave him more than comfort," said Amber, surprised at her own sarcasm.

"Oh, fuck you, Miss high and mighty," blurted Hannah. "You're dumb enough to leave the target area and get captured, and yet you get all the glory and expect us to walk on tiptoes around you." Amber flinched at the underlying truth in the statement. *It was like a whole different Hannah had come to the surface,* thought Amber, horrified.

"I live with my actions every single day. I might have been able to understand my best friend sleeping with my fiancé, but when he was feeling regret about it, you made him feel like shit, like he was weak and worthless, even said he didn't deserve to live. How could you?" Amber asked, moving to the edge of her seat and feeling increasingly angry.

"I never said he should kill himself," said Hannah defensively.

"No, but the message was clear, wasn't it? He was looking for some kind of remorse from you, too. But all he got from you was contempt. Shortly after that he killed himself."

"Like I said, he was weak."

"Who are you, Hannah? Our friend, a fellow soldier, my fiancé, killed himself and all you can say is that he was weak?" Amber was boiling now, her rage framing every word. Hannah had nothing to say.

"Did you know what was really eating him up? The things he saw on a mission in Baghdad?" Hannah asked angrily. Amber looked confused. "Of course not, you were too busy all the time with that dog, too busy with yourself!" Hannah hissed.

Amber hadn't planned to mention it, but her rage got the best of her. "When I went to the Grand Junction police station to ask about the reports on Lopez and Arnold, the attendant told me a female police officer from Montrose had just checked them out. She probably wasn't supposed to reveal that, but she let it slip. I found that incredibly coincidental, since I'd just told you the day before about my suspicions that something was off with their suicides. So I'm guessing it was you who grabbed those files, Hannah, but I can't figure out why."

Hannah sat forward, she spoke defensively, "Brian asked me to check those out, he was over in Denver for some training and said he wanted to review those two cases." Hannah stood up and pointed at Amber, "You invite me to your home then ambush me with all this crap, and you don't even have your facts together, don't even know what's really going on! I'm outta here," Hannah said in disgust as she stood up and walked down the stairs, slammed the door and drove off.

Amber remained seated and watched her friend leave. She put her head in her hands, the confrontation had taken the steam out of her, she felt like the room was spinning. Nikita stood up and put her wet nose in Amber's lap. Amber spoke to Nikita, thinking out loud, "I know I was right about Chris and Hannah, but maybe Hannah had nothing to do with this Lopez and Arnold mess. Maybe she was telling the truth?" *And what was this mission in Baghdad Hannah alluded to? Chris had never spoken of that. Why would he hide something from me?*

Amber sat there for an hour or so then dozed off—it had been a long week. Nikita curled up on the couch next to her and fell fast asleep. The moon shone through the large windows gently illuminating the room. Amber was jolted out of her slumber by Nikita's frantic bark. Then she heard footsteps coming up the stairs from the ground floor. She realized that she had not gone downstairs to lock the door for the night after Hannah left. Nikita moved to her side and began to growl and bark. Suddenly, a man wearing a hooded sweatshirt reached the top of the stairs and stepped into the room holding a pistol.

Nikita stood, hair up on her back, ready to charge at Amber's command. She let out a low, menacing growl. It was the growl of her wolf ancestors protecting their pack, and it struck fear in the heart of any animal in North America.

"Get her in that bathroom now, or I'll shoot her!" the man said, backing away from Nikita, aiming his pistol at her. Amber had a feeling she knew this man, just couldn't place him. The man waved the pistol again, "I'll do it!" he yelled, "You better get her out of here."

Amber knew Nikita could get to the man in a flash, but the man would have time to get off at least one shot. Amber couldn't let her best friend take a bullet for her—not again. She had no choice. "Nikita, heel!" she commanded, and Nikita walked to her left side as if glued to her leg. Amber walked her to the guest bathroom near the kitchen and made her go in before shutting the door behind her. Nikita knew something was wrong and began barking loudly and scratching the door.

The man stood with the pistol trained on Amber.

"What happens now?" asked Amber.

"Well, if you weren't such a snoopy idiot and had stayed in your lane, nothing would have happened. But you couldn't just do your job, could you? You had to become a suicide detective. You had to ask *why* when there is no *why* to suicide. Some people just kill themselves. That's it, end of story. You just couldn't see that, could you?"

"Oh, I saw something all right," said Amber. "I saw two soldier suicides that made no sense, that had too many coincidences, that were suspicious. I just can't figure out who you are and how you're wrapped up in all this."

The man pulled the hood back and Amber nearly fell back. He looked strange with a beard, and maybe something was different about his nose, as if it had undergone plastic surgery, but she recognized the face from the pictures in her file. It was Corporal Jerry Arnold.

38

Jerry motioned for Amber to sit on the couch as he took a seat in the chair across from her. She was trying to process how it was that she could be staring at a dead man.

"We've never met," Jerry said, holding the pistol on her. "But I've been following your work at the VA. Too bad you couldn't just leave things be."

"I've met your mother, Jerry. She's heartbroken over your death. How could you do that to her?" Amber asked, trying to appeal to his feelings for his mom.

He paused for a moment. Amber had hit a nerve. "I had no choice," he said. "Lopez wouldn't stop talking about Iraq. I tried everything, but he kept telling people about what happened over there, saying it was part of his healing process, whatever that is. No one would understand what happened, nobody saw three of our friends chopped up like butcher meat. Lopez had the idea that we were the bad guys, like we were guilty." Disdain rose in Jerry's voice as he spoke of his former friend. "Spilling his guts to that shrink was the last straw. He was going to get us all put in jail for doing our jobs."

"I don't think killing teenagers and old men was your job, Jerry, especially when they were your captives," Amber said with contempt.

"I heard you were a self-righteous bitch, now I see it," Jerry said, shaking his head. "I thought you, of all people, would know that we were dealing with animals over there that needed to be put down before they killed more of us or launched another 9/11 attack."

"Is Hannah mixed up in this?" Amber asked. Jerry looked at her for a long moment, clearly debating how much to tell her.

"I told John Holmes about Henry talking too much. He went to his best friend, Brian - you know, Hannah's boyfriend, another Grand Junction cop, for help. Brian agreed to help us. He used Hannah to gather some information a few times, but she doesn't know what's going on."

Amber hoped that was the truth; it was one thing to have your friend sleep with your fiancé, it was another to have her plot your murder.

"Why would Brian agree to be involved in this murder plot?" she asked.

"There's a lot you don't understand. John Holmes rescued Brian from a firefight that erupted when a domestic violence arrest went bad. Holmes ran through a hail of bullets, grabbed Brian, who was shot up, and carried him to safety. You could say they are brothers now, blood brothers."

Amber shook her head in disbelief. "So how did you fake your own suicide?" she asked, anxious to understand.

"It wasn't that hard. John found some homeless druggie stiff who overdosed and was about my size, and they shot him in the face so he was hard to identify. John and Brian were on the inside so they were able to swap the fingerprints and DNA tests to make it look like me." Nikita was barking and tearing at the door like crazy. Jerry turned to look at the bathroom for a moment before turning back to Amber.

"But why, Jerry? Why fake your own death? What kind of life do you have now?" Amber was beginning to sense that maybe Jerry hadn't thought this all the way through.

"It's a good plan," he said proudly, "Better than life in the slammer. If it was just Lopez, someone might have looked harder. Things were going so well for him that people might not have believed he'd kill himself. But when it became two guys who'd been in the same shit together, everyone figured it was because of Iraq and the crap we had to go through." But Amber had pursued the case precisely for that reason; two suicides in the same unit a few months apart seemed suspicious. She didn't want to shoot holes in Jerry's logic right now, but wasn't sure why he thought that made sense. "It took suspicion off John," he went on. "Plus I was ready to get the hell out of here, start a new life anyway. John and Brian are sending me to Belize. I'll start over down there on white sandy beaches and forget all this shit."

"So you killed Henry? Your friend and battle buddy in Iraq? So Brian and John wouldn't have to be involved?"

"That was not the plan," Jerry glared back at her defiantly. "Things got out of control. I thought we were going to scare him." For the first time, Amber saw some remorse in his voice.

It suddenly hit Amber. Jerry was a huge loose end in this crazy scheme. He was gullible and easily influenced by others, she could see that now. " Jerry, you need to think about this. John and Brian aren't going to let you waltz down to Belize and start over. You're the one person who can put them away for life. Do you think they're going to take the chance that you never talk?"

"That's bullshit," Jerry snarled.

But Amber could see a little doubt starting to creep in on his face. "Do you have new identity papers, Jerry, a new passport?"

"Not yet. John and Brian are working on it." He was looking visibly worried now.

"That's not gonna happen, Jerry. They just want you to take care of me, then they'll be done with you, don't you see? You're being used one last time." Amber was stretching her guess, but at least Jerry was hearing her out, giving her more time.

Suddenly, a dark figure stepped out from the stairwell. A shot rang out and Jerry fell to the floor as the bullet passed through his brain. Amber screamed and turned to see Brian in his police uniform pointing his service 9mm Glock at her. He must have parked down the driveway, walked up quietly and waited for this moment.

"I got a call about a disturbance," he said with a dry smile. "I rushed in here and shot Jerry right after he shot you. That cleans up things nicely, don't you think, Amber? Two of my problems taken care of at the same time."

Brian had black gloves on, Amber noticed. He walked toward her, reached down to the floor next to Arnold and picked up the .38 revolver, careful to keep his other pistol trained on her.

Nikita had heard another stranger enter her master's house and went wild. She pawed and jumped on the door and this time the bathroom door handle flipped open. Tucking her head, and pinning her ears back, she roared and sprinted to the living room, her instinct to protect driving her forward.

Brian heard the bathroom door fly open, followed by a primal growl and the flash of brown and black fur behind white fangs. He turned his head to see Nikita leaping at him with single-minded ferocity. As his arm swung from aiming at Amber to fire at the dog, Amber jumped across the coffee table, knocking him off balance. Brian saw Amber out of the corner of his eye and fired the .38 in his left hand at her, but he was too focused on the crazed dog leaping at him. Both his shots missed in the melee. Amber grabbed his left arm with the .38 pistol as Nikita clamped on to his right arm that held the 9mm Glock. Brian let out a shriek as Nikita shook her powerful jaws and tore into his arm with over 250 pounds per square inch of bite force. Her teeth, which were designed for ripping and tearing, sawed through the skin, muscles, tendons and hit bone. Brian yelped and screamed as Nikita ripped deeper in violent shaking motions. He dropped the Glock.

Amber held his other wrist that was holding the .38 and had been bending it backward until she felt a snap, the wrist broke and he dropped the revolver. Brian lay on the floor on his back as Amber kicked the Glock away, grabbed the .38, quickly stood up and aimed it at him. He was writhing and screaming and trying to kick Nikita who was still latched onto his right arm. His left hand was useless.

Nikita now began to yank Brian's arm backward over his head, as if she was playing tug of war or trying to yank a carcass across the tundra. Amber held the gun on Brian as he screamed. Blood was pouring out of his right arm all over the wood floor, and yet he was still a dangerous man. He swung his leg off the ground and kicked Nikita hard in the ribs, enough for her to yelp and let go.

That's when Amber fired. She put a round through his thigh, not wanting to kill him. It nicked his femur, spun, tore flesh and landed near his hamstring. He howled, sat up for a moment and bent his other leg. That's when Amber saw it. He had a small backup pistol in a holster on his ankle. He reached for the weapon and Amber shot him in the chest.

39

JUNE 2012, MONTROSE, COLORADO

I t was after 8 p.m. when she called 911 and the sheriff's deputy arrived at Amber's home. Nikita barked as two Montrose County Sheriff SUV's rolled up her driveway, alerting Amber of their arrival. After the attack on her master, Amber wasn't sure how Nikita would react to the police taking Amber into custody. She put Nikita in the back seat of her truck and closed the door. Four officers entered her home, surveyed the scene, arrested her and took her to the Montrose County Jail. When an officer is found dead on scene, the arriving police are not in a mood to hear your story. Amber was booked for murder. She called Tony with the one phone call they allowed her.

The phone rang several times and Amber thought it would go to voicemail, but then he picked up. It was late at night, and he sounded tired. He'd probably worked a shift at the bar after school that day.

"Hello?" he answered, half asleep.

"Tony, it's Amber ... I'm in trouble. Can you please go to my house, pick up Nikita and bring her to your house for the night? She's in my truck."

"What's going on, Amber?" Now he was wide awake.

She dreaded telling him about the shootings, Jerry Arnold and the dead police officer in her living room. It all sounded so crazy. It was too much to explain. "Please, Tony, just do this for me. I'll fill you in as soon as I can. Her food is in the pantry in a bin. There's a spare key underneath the big cactus pot out front."

"Uh, OK, sure, not a problem. Where are you?"

She couldn't lie to him. "In the Montrose County Jail."

"'Why? What's going on?" He was starting to sound a little frantic.

"Tony, I'll fill you in later, I promise. I know this is a lot to ask, but please trust me. Just take care of Nikita. I shouldn't be here too long. It's a crime scene, but they should let you take Nikita from my truck. The police just have to check out a few things. I've done nothing wrong."

The morning after Amber's arrest, Detective Hackberry from the Montrose County Sheriff's Department came to interview her. He wore a blue suit that looked like it had come off the rack at the Salvation Army, wrinkled and with some kind of mustard stains on the lapel. He had a crew cut above a huge nose in the middle of his pink wrinkled face. He sat across from Amber and offered her coffee and the option to call a lawyer. She knew she should have a lawyer present, but she was anxious to get the process over with so she could get back to Nikita. She turned down the lawyer and the coffee.

"So, Ms. Downing, please walk me through the events of the evening, with special emphasis on how two dead bodies ended up in your living room, one of which was a decorated officer from the Grand Junction Police Department." Despite his sloppy attire, Amber quickly sized up the man and realized he was sharp as a tack. His eyes didn't miss a thing.

"How far do you want me to go back?" she asked, moving uncomfortably on the metal chair in the small interview room.

Hackberry, crossed his thick arms, stared back across the small wood table at her. "As far back as you need to go to explain how those men died in your house."

Amber nodded and began with the story of the project given to her by VA leadership to gather facts on veteran suicides within the last five years. It took her nearly 30 minutes to bring Hackberry up to the present. He listened attentively, scribbling short notes on a yellow notepad. When she laid out the facts that led her to conclude that Lopez and Arnold might have been murdered instead of committing suicide, Hackberry interrupted her.

"But why not come to the police with your theory at that point?"

"For starters, I didn't have conclusive proof of anything and I know the police department wouldn't reopen the cases of two suicides and put the families through that if they didn't have evidence. But I was getting close. Also I didn't trust the police. I mean, Holmes is one of you, right?" Hackberry looked up from his notes and stared at Amber, grimacing like he'd just bitten into a rotten apple.

She continued, "As I said, I suspected Officer Holmes of being involved. He was the first to arrive on the scene when Mrs. Lopez's house was ransacked. That was too much of a coincidence for me." She paused, waiting for his reaction. The only thing cops hate worse than losing one of their own is finding out one of their own is dirty. Hackberry didn't show any emotion. She went on, "I did confide in my friend, Hannah Livingston, an officer with the Montrose Police Department. I invited her over last night for a drink and confronted her about a personal matter and then told her I suspected her of checking out the police reports on Lopez and Arnold so I wouldn't be able to see them. You may not know it yet, but she's Officer Brian Dixon's girlfriend, and she's been helping him in some way. I don't know if she's involved in this murder plot, but you can check her story. Her boyfriend, Brian Dixon planned to kill me and make it look like the other dead person at my house had shot me. Then Dixon would make it look like he shot the other guy. Dixon is a close friend of Officer Holmes. "

Hackberry leaned back in his seat, sighed heavily and put his pencil down. "So now you're accusing a third police officer of being complicit in murder?" He looked incredulous.

"No, I just said to check out her story. She's been passing information to Brian Dixon from our conversations, I don't know how deep she was involved, or what she knew," Amber replied.

Hackberry went on. "You said the other person killed last night is Jerry Arnold, but you just told me he was one of the suicides you were investigating. Would you care to explain that?"

"Yes," Amber nodded. "He was a dead man."

"Meaning?" he prompted.

"I found out last night that he, John Holmes and Brian Dixon faked his death after they killed Lopez and staged it to look like suicide. Arnold told me they used a dead homeless guy and made it look like Arnold with swapped DNA and fingerprints so he could start a new life in Belize. Except I figured that Holmes and Dixon never planned to let Arnold get away. Arnold was a loose end. That's why Brian killed him last night. If it wasn't for my service dog, Officer Dixon would have killed me, too."

Hackberry shook his head and ran his hand over his chin, incredulous. It was almost too much to take in — this story, when it gets out, will make national news.

"Arnold told me everything because he was planning to kill or kidnap me, but I started to convince him that Holmes and Dixon would never let him just walk away. It was a guess, but it seemed plausible. That's when Dixon stepped into the room and shot Arnold. A few minutes later, Nikita, my service dog, escaped from the bathroom where Arnold forced me to put her and we both jumped Dixon. We struggled and I shot him defending myself."

Hackberry looked skeptical. "And how did he get shot in the leg and also the chest?"

Amber knew that wouldn't look good. "I shot him in the leg as he and Nikita were fighting. I didn't want to kill him. But then he reached for a pistol hidden on his ankle, and I shot him in the chest."

Hackberry considered her story. It lined up with the forensics at the crime scene, but he looked skeptical. He changed tactics. "I looked into your military record, it turns out you were a captive of Al Qaeda and came home with acute PTSD." He let that sit like it was an accusation.

Amber was furious. She glared at him and clenched her jaw. "That has nothing to do with what happened last night!"

"But people with PTSD are prone to fits of violence at times, right? Maybe experiencing a flashback or something like that? Maybe you snapped when Officer Dixon showed up at your home? We have a recording of an anonymous call made to police dispatch at 9:15 p.m. last night stating that you were acting erratically and that an officer needed to check on you. Brian Dixon responded because he was the closest officer to the scene at the time of the call."

Amber now saw how Holmes and Brian had planned to play this out. "But here's the problem, Detective Hackberry. Holmes or Dixon made that call anonymously. And don't you find it strange that a Grand Junction police officer just happened to be in Montrose and closest to the scene of the crime when dispatch was called? Don't you see how they schemed this out?"

Hackberry looked like he hadn't considered that the 911 call had been pre-planned. If her story was true, it would probably set Amber free, and he'd have two, possibly three dirty cops to deal with.

"All right, Ms. Downing. We need to confirm your story. It sounds pretty far-fetched, but I assure you, I will get to the bottom of this." And he did.

Forty-eight hours later, Hackberry walked into Amber's cell at the Montrose County Jail. She remained sitting on the cot in the corner as he stood in the doorway. "I believe you were telling the truth, Ms. Downing. I've been pulling cell phone records and corroborating your story with forensics. So far, everything you told me lines up. Last night, Officer Holmes was arrested by the state troopers. He was attempting to flee to Mexico in his RV."

He sat down beside her. "There's one thing I don't understand, though," he said, looking straight at her. "How did you find out the details of what happened in Iraq? That those teenagers and the old man were killed? There's nothing in the police reports or in Lopez's service record."

Amber figured this would come up. She'd promised not to let anyone know what Dr. Mankowski had confided in her. "I'm sorry,

Detective, but I gave my word to a confidential source. Even if you don't believe me and can't pin those murders in Iraq on Holmes, you have enough to lock him up for life, right? I mean, he conspired to kill Lopez, Arnold and me." Hackberry looked at her for a long moment. It didn't change the facts of this case, but he hated to leave a stone unturned in any of his investigations. He decided to let it go, for now.

"What about Hannah Livingston?" asked Amber reluctantly. She was afraid of the answer she might receive, but Hackberry hadn't mentioned her.

Hackberry remained silent for a few moments. What happened to Officer Livingston was confidential police business and not something he should share. Then again, Amber had been through a lot. "I can tell you this," he said, finally deciding to share something, "She was not part of the murder plot, I've confirmed that. However, she broke department policy in several ways. She's been suspended pending a formal inquiry."

Amber's spirit was lifted when she heard that her former best friend was not involved in trying to kill her or someone else. It was a huge weight off her chest. "So what do you think will happen to her?" Amber asked Hackberry.

He scratched his eyebrow, before speaking. "Well, I think it's likely that she will be fired and relieved for cause. She goes before a formal hearing this week that will determine her fate."

It was late in the afternoon when Amber was done tying up loose ends at the police station, she then called Tony and asked him to come get her. He loaded up Nikita and headed down to the Montrose County Jail to pick her up and bring her home. She was waiting in the lobby of the jail. She'd already checked out, turned in her orange jumpsuit and changed back into her slightly blood-spattered clothes from the night of the shootings.

Tony walked in with Nikita on the leash. Amber had almost never been happier to see anyone than she was to see the two of them. She bent down and rubbed noses with her best companion. Nikita licked her face and made a whining sound that she always makes when she's away from Amber for too long.

Amber stood up and reached to give Tony a big hug and kiss. He took the kiss, but was cold and rigid as she hugged him. "What's wrong, Tony?" she asked, fearing she already knew the answer.

"Nothing," he said, looking away before speaking. "It's just that all this is a lot for me to take in right now. Two dead men in your house and you killed one of them. I know it was self defense, but I'm still trying to process it all, you know?" he said, looking back at her with those dark eyes. "Let's get you home," he said, opening the door for her and Nikita. As Amber passed him in the doorway, she paused and looked up at him with a pained expression. He didn't say anything.

They were both silent on the drive home. When Tony pulled up into her driveway and stopped, she asked, "Do you want to come in?"

He held the wheel and turned to her. "I just think I need to work through all this right now, Amber. I was just getting over my wife's suicide when I met you. You are so beautiful and fun to be around, but I can't really handle any more stress in my life right now, you know what I mean?"

Amber wasn't sure if he needed a cooling off period to process things or if he was dumping her right there and then. Either way, she felt a knot in her gut. With Hannah probably out of the picture, she really needed a friend to talk to and lean on. This was not good. "OK,

Tony, I get it," she said. "I just want you to know that I didn't create this situation, it came my way and I dealt with it as best I could. I'm lucky to be alive right now. If it wasn't for Nikita, I'd be dead."

"That's kind of the other thing," he said hesitantly. "I'm not envious of Nikita, but it's clear she's the number one thing in your life." *He's not wrong,* Amber thought. "I don't know if there's a place for me in your heart. She seems to have it all," he said, looking down at the steering wheel.

Arguing that point with Tony would be futile, she realized. If he couldn't respect her relationship with her service dog, then there was not much she could do to repair their relationship.

"I'm sorry you feel that way," she said with a deep sadness, exiting the car and opening the back door to let Nikita out. She shut the car door and left Tony sitting there as she and Nikita walked into their home, a home that had been a crime scene, where two men had died in her living room. Tony waited until she was in the house and slowly drove back down the driveway.

She walked up the stairwell, kept her eyes averted from the living room, the scene of death, and headed straight for her bedroom. She curled up in her bed and pulled the fluffy comforter over her head. Nikita jumped up on the bed with her and burrowed under the covers, licking her face. Amber put her arm around Nikita's neck and slept for the first time in two long days.

40

OCTOBER 2008, BAGHDAD, IRAQ

I n Baghdad, the U.S. Army had set up an animal hospital within their military working dog kennels. This allowed the Army veterinarians to treat the working dogs for minor injuries and also perform major surgeries when needed. It was a noisy compound with dogs yelping, howling and barking at all hours of the day and night within their pens. Razor was a patient there, hanging on to life by a thread.

Following her rescue by Butcher's SEALs, Amber had gone through a special triage center to address all of the medical conditions she had incurred during captivity. She told the nurses and doctors repeatedly that she was fine, wanting to get out of there and visit Razor at the veterinary hospital as soon as possible. But they kept sending in hordes of doctors and nurses and performing a battery of tests. In between the visits by the specialists, she was interviewed by two Army intelligence officers, one male and one female. They hit her with a million questions about every aspect of her captivity. It was all necessary, she knew, but it seemed to never end. They would interview her for an hour, then come back later in the day with more questions. She could tell they were looking for any clues that would help them locate the Al Qaeda cell led by KAT. But Amber also couldn't help but sense that some of the interrogation seemed to question her actions: "Can you explain how you were captured? How did KAT get a jump on you?...Why did you leave the target area?" She felt like she might go crazy if they didn't let her out of there to visit Razor soon. *And where was her fiancé?* Even though she was in double secret quarantine, surely Chris would find a way to see her.

On a cold and windy Monday morning, the head doctor for her case, an Army colonel overseeing Amber's recovery, walked into her bare hospital room. She was up pacing the cement floor in her room, anxious to get the hell out of there.

"Can I ask you to sit down please?" the Army doctor ordered. He was not just a doctor, but a senior officer. She sat in the plastic chair in the corner, fidgeting with her hands. He remained standing.

"Sergeant Downing, I have come to the conclusion that you are suffering significant mental and emotional trauma following your captivity." *That's a no-shitter,* she thought. *You guys won't let me see my dog or my fiancé. Maybe that would help!* "Based on the analysis of our best experts, you are suffering from acute PTSD. This is entirely normal after what you have experienced, but we need to get you professional help right away. I'm sending you to Landstuhl Regional Medical Center at Ramstein Air Base in Germany on your way to Walter Reed Medical Center in the US. Your flight will depart at 2300 tonight. One of our travel nurses will accompany you to Germany. She will take care of all the logistics. Do you have any questions for me?" he asked, with his clipboard in hand.

She stood up and practically yelled at the doctor. "Yes, I need to see my dog and my fiancé! No one seems to understand that!"

He looked at his clipboard for a second, then back at Amber. "I have determined that you need to put all your energy into getting healthy. The military working dog you handled is no longer your concern, Sergeant Downing. You are going home and you need to focus on that. Please drop this notion of seeing the dog. As far as your fiancé is concerned, I'll see what I can do." He sounded like he was talking to a 10-year-old.

Amber stared at his blue eyes and jutting chin. She knew now that she wouldn't get any help from him. She turned her back and he quietly walked out of the room.

Even though visitors were not allowed during this time of her medical care and debriefing by the intelligence officials, the colonel intervened and made an exception for Chris, since he was her fiancé and they were shipping her off to Germany that night. So finally, on the third day of what she bitterly called her second captivity, Amber was allowed a visit from Chris. He came by after his shift was over. A nurse at the duty desk for the sensitive patients unit led him to room 302.

Before he opened the door, Chris closed his eyes and paused. The last month had been pure hell for him. Several of his friends and members of his platoon had been killed when their truck was hit by an IED on the way back from their mission at Umm Qasr in Western Iraq four days ago. Chris knew he should have been with them, maybe would have seen signs of the IED that blew up their truck. One of those killed was a young soldier from New Hampshire named Hutchins who'd just turned 19. The gangly kid had struck up an unlikely friendship with the tall, tanned surfer from California. The soft-spoken New England boy came from a small family farm and was terribly shy. He spoke with a lisp and some of the guys made fun of him, but Chris, the King of Cool in the platoon, had stood up for Hutchins and put a stop to the bullying. Hutchins had told his parents about his friend Chris in Iraq and his parents had sent Chris a box of homemade oatmeal cookies wrapped individually in white tissues. Now Chris was going to have to collect all of Hutchins's personal belongings and write his parents a letter.

During that same time, Chris had also been worried sick about Amber, trying not to think about what was happening to her in captivity. He couldn't imagine what she had endured at the hands of her captors. He knew how much she cared for Razor and how she was probably going crazy wondering how the dog was doing. The head doctor, who had approved Chris's visit at the last minute, had been explicit that he should not tell Amber anything about Razor's condition. Chris hadn't had time to check on the little guy, so he had nothing to share anyway. The doctor explained that Amber had experienced so much stress and strain that she might go over the edge if she heard bad news about Razor. He felt they needed to keep the bad news away from her until they had more time to help her deal with the PTSD.

In addition, Chris was dealing with regret about how he had betrayed Amber, his fiancé, and slept with Hannah on a night of weakness and despair. That demon of guilt and shame stood on the shoulders of the other devils in his life and pointed a huge bloody finger at Chris. He couldn't give Amber the care she needed with all these demons taking over his thoughts.

But these problems paled in comparison to the hell he had seen on one mission and the deal he'd made with the devil. That devil gnawed on his soul every night in the most bloody nightmares that played non-stop in his head. "I'll deal with you later," he mouthed a bargain out loud to the monster in his head, then opened the door and stepped into Amber's hospital room.

Amber lay on the hospital bed with her back propped up by two pillows leaning against the wall. There was no TV or window in the sparse room. She turned her head to look at Chris as soon as he opened the door. Her face softened and tears began to roll down her cheeks.

Chris rushed to the side of the bed and buried his face in her lap and started crying. Amber stroked his hair and said, "Hey look at me, Chris, everything's gonna be alright. I'm OK. Razor and some SEALs saved my life. It could have been much worse."

Chris looked up and stared at her beautiful face. He went to give her a kiss and closed his eyes at the last second. Amber kissed him back, but she felt in that shallow kiss that something was wrong with him, that somehow he needed more comfort than she did at this point, that he was holding something back. He pulled back and stood at her bedside, at a loss for words.

She took his hand and held it, again sensing that he was struggling with something. *Maybe it's just his way of dealing with what had happened to her*, she thought. "Chris, what is it? I've never seen you like this before."

"I'm sorry ... I just ... I was so worried about you, I thought you were gone from my life forever, and now you're back. I know I should be happy, but I'm just having a hard time." He paused, then continued, "Some of my friends in the platoon were killed this week in an IED attack. I should have been there for them. It's been a bad week for me."

"I'm so sorry, honey," she said, reaching up and stroking his face. Tears rolled down his cheeks and fell onto her hands. He bowed his head and started to cry uncontrollably, the hot tears of regret and mental pain escaping from his body like a severed steam pipe. He began to shake and buried his head again in Amber's lap.

There was something else, she thought, something beyond the stress of her captivity and losing guys in the platoon. He was different. She couldn't put her finger on it, but she sensed it. As she thought about it, a tall nurse stepped into the room. "I'm sorry, you two, but visitations are over," she said. Amber speculated that the nurse might have heard Chris crying and worried it would add even more stress to Amber. Chris kissed her on the cheek, then stood up to leave. He wiped his eyes with the back of his hands. "I'm sorry, baby," he mouthed as the nurse escorted him out of the room.

Twice a day at the hospital they let Amber walk and sit in a small grassy garden courtyard that was attached to the side of the hospital and bound by a high brick wall laced with razor wire. The nurse came and brought her down to the garden for her afternoon stroll. It was always an unsettling experience. She was surrounded by a beautiful garden and three lush palm trees, with the sounds of mortar and artillery shells exploding in the distance, constantly reminding her that the enemy was close and she was in a war zone, not a magical garden. She sat on a small bench in the corner and let the cool breeze blow her hair around, trying to ignore the big booms. She kept thinking of the short visit with Chris. *Had he said 'I'm sorry' before he left the room? If so, what did he mean? Sorry I was captured? Sorry about Razor?*

Suddenly there was a man standing next to her. She turned her head and looked at him, immediately recognizing his face.

"I just wanted to come and see how you were doing," Lieutenant Butcher said, sitting down next to her on the bench. "They wouldn't let me visit you so I came up with some BS excuse that I was visiting another soldier. I figured you might be out here."

Amber felt a wave of emotions rip through her body. The last time she saw Butcher, he'd lifted her off Razor and set her in the corner to be guarded by another scary looking Navy SEAL. All the terror, shock and sadness of that night seemed to hit her like a baseball bat in the gut. She rocked forward and put her head in her hands.

"Hey, hey," Butcher said, scooting next to her. "What you did surviving that captivity was nothing short of heroic. If you hadn't attacked that Al Qaeda maniac when we entered the room, he woulda shot me. You saved my life. I just wanted you to know how much respect I have for you."

Amber looked up at him with a faint smile. She'd never thought that maybe she'd saved a life when she stabbed KAT. She just wanted to kill the bastard.

She thought of something that had been bothering her, "Hey what happened to that little girl at the house where you rescued me?" Amber had been seeing the terrified little girl in her nightmares huddling in the corner of that horrible death room. Suddenly it came to her what *moral injury* meant. She saw KAT holding a pistol, clearly ready to shoot the frightened child to compel Amber to comply with his demands. It was a dilemma that had cut through Amber's heart, cleaving it and leaving a scar of moral injury. *Either watch this girl die, or allow KAT to behead me in front of millions.*

"We grabbed her off the site and took her with us. It turns out she was Yazidi, probably a slave, taken from her family up north. We had to turn her over to the Iraqi authorities after your rescue. Hopefully they'll reunite her with her family. Look, is there anything I can do for you or get you anything while you're stuck in this hospital?" he asked.

Amber looked over at this SEAL Team officer. He was clearly a warrior, but spoke with genuine concern and empathy. "I've *got* to see my dog. These idiots won't let me out of here," she said, looking at him with eyes starting to tear up.

Butcher smiled at her. "Sergeant Downing, just leave that to me. I've got you covered. I'll be in touch soon." And with that, Butcher stood up, nodded to Amber and walked back into the hospital. He passed a nurse who was standing by the window keeping an eye on Amber. On the way out of the hospital he stopped at the entrance kiosk. One of the duty nurses sat behind a counter awaiting the next patient's arrival.

"Is that you, Sally?" Butcher asked her with feigned shock.

The nurse stood up staring at him. "My name's not Sally. I'm afraid you have the wrong person," she said, eyeing him with suspicion.

"Oh my gosh, you look exactly like this girl I knew in high school! She was the prom queen," he gushed. "Do you mind if I take a picture of you? My friends back home won't believe the resemblance."

The nurse, somewhat flattered that she resembled a prom queen, could think of no reason to say no. "Sure, I guess," she shrugged a little hesitantly.

Butcher pulled out his phone and snapped a quick close up. "Thanks so much! Maybe you have a doppelganger in Kansas," he said, walking out the door. He took a few steps out into the dusty Green Zone street and looked at his phone. He zoomed in on the picture as far as he could until he had a good image of the security badge she wore around her neck. "Gotcha," he smiled to himself.

⸰

Two hours later, a Doctor Butcher entered the Green Zone hospital in Baghdad, wearing the drab green overcoat that most of the Army doctors wore over their fatigues. Under the overcoat was a baggy U.S. Army uniform with the insignia of a major in the U.S. Army Medical Corps. Butcher had tasked his platoon medical expert with "procuring" the uniform for him. Around Butcher's neck was a strap holding a security badge for the hospital. The face of a woman had been replaced with that of Butcher's, thanks to his platoon intelligence expert who was a hot shot with Photoshop. Butcher wore thick glasses and carried a clipboard.

The new nurse on duty at the entrance didn't give him a second glance as he walked into the hospital. He used the stairs and made his way to the third floor where he knew they kept the patients with PTSD. He walked straight out of the stairwell, took a right and headed past the nurse's station that supported the patients in the rooms behind them. Two nurses seated at the station looked up and saw a doctor walk right past them as if he owned the place. He looked unfamiliar, but he had a badge and the rank of major so they said nothing.

Butcher strode down the hallway and opened the door to room 302 where Amber sat in the corner on a plastic chair. She looked up at the doctor and it took her a few seconds to recognize him. "Butcher!" she almost yelled out. He put his finger over his lips signaling her to keep quiet.

"This is the second time you've rescued me!" she said.

He nodded solemnly, "Follow my lead and let me do the talking," he said to her quietly as she stood up, excited to have a chance to break out and see Razor.

Together they walked out the door and back toward the nurse's station. As they approached the two nurses, Butcher turned to them and said, "I'm taking her for another audiogram. We found some anomalies in her first tests." The two nurses looked at him and nodded, figuring everything looked legit. He didn't slow down, just kept walking out the door. He guided Amber down the stairwell until they came to the ground floor. Butcher's medical expert, who was very familiar with the hospital, having checked out controlled medicines for the platoon frequently, had told him how to get out of the building without going through the main entrance. On the first floor near the supply closet was an exit and entrance for deliveries only. Butcher guided Amber to the exit, looked around to make sure no one was looking, then opened the metal door and stepped onto the loading dock. Just then a tan HUMVEE rolled up from where it had been idling in the parking lot. Butcher opened the back door for Amber and quickly jumped into the front seat. Lone Wolf, the wiry pla-toon point man who had taken care of Amber and brought her to the MEDEVAC helicopter after the rescue, was seated behind the wheel.

"Well, fancy seeing you here, Sergeant Downing," Lone Wolf said, turning around with a wry smile on his deeply tanned and chiseled face. He stepped on the gas and off they went.

"How did you guys pull this off so easily?" Amber asked, almost giddy that she was out of the hospital and on the way to see Razor.

"Half our job is sneaking in and out of places," said Butcher, turning to look at Amber in the back seat. "This was a cake walk. You should've seen the operation last week when we liberated a case of New York steaks from the dining facility to celebrate your rescue. That was a thing of beauty, right Lone Wolf?" He turned to look at his point man, who was smiling.

"Second best op we've pulled off in Iraq so far," Lone Wolf said with a nod and wink.

After winding through several Green Zone barricades and check-points, they arrived at the military working dog kennels and clinic. Amber was very familiar with the compound since this was where she used to train Razor and pick him up each morning and drop him off at night. Her heart rate started to bang like a drum. She was about to see her most loyal friend, the one who had never given up on her.

The HUMVEE pulled up to the entrance of the veterinary clinic. Amber was about to jump out of the vehicle, when Butcher turned back to look at her, looking worried now for the first time. "I know why the doctors didn't want you to come over here. But I knew it was important to you, so we made it happen." Amber opened the door quickly and practically ran into the clinic. She shouted at the Army vet tech at the entrance, "Where's Razor?"

The poor vet tech looked over Amber's shoulder at the U.S. Army major behind her. Butcher nodded to the young corporal and he answered, "Third room on the right." Amber rushed past the corporal and pushed open the door. As she entered the room, she almost fell to her knees, gasped and put her hands over her mouth. Razor lay in a small wooden Viking ship complete with a little prow carved with the face of a dog that looked like Razor.

Amber rushed to him. He was lying on his right side in the tiny boat, his paws curled up and crossed in front of his belly. He was dead. Butcher came to stand beside Amber as Lone Wolf slid to the other side of her. "He died yesterday, Amber, from blood loss due to the stabbing and gunshot wounds. He went into a coma on the rescue flight off the target. The doctors here were amazed that he'd survived the loss of blood that long while running 40 miles through Iraq tracking you. We've been coming over here everyday checking on him. Since we're on R&R for seven days after the rescue mission, the boys decided to build a little Viking ship for this warrior. The vet clinic was just going to bury him out back, but we wanted to hold a ceremony for the little hero."

Amber looked like she'd been hit with a sledgehammer. She bent over the tiny boat and patted Razor softly on his head. "If only I could have been here yesterday," she said, sobbing, "I might have been able to save him."

"Amber, you can't think like that," said Butcher. "He was in a coma, the doctors here did everything possible for him. It was just his time. He went out a true hero. Think about that."

She looked at Butcher but didn't respond. She knew he was right, but those damn doctors should have let her come see him. "They're making me take a flight to Ramstein tonight at 2300!" she said, tears pouring down her cheeks. "I can't leave him like this."

"Don't worry, we'll do a ceremony tonight, right after dusk," Butcher said, gently patting her on the back. "Why don't we leave you here to spend some time with him. I'll be back in an hour to pick you and Razor up, OK?"

She turned to look at him and nodded. Butcher looked at Lone Wolf and motioned with his chin towards the door. The two SEALs walked out of the room and left Amber sitting in a chair next to Razor.

It was right after dusk when Butcher returned to the vet clinic as promised. Lone Wolf drove a big 6x6 truck with the rest of the platoon sitting on benches in the large bed of the truck. Butcher hopped out the tall passenger door and walked into the clinic. He had changed out of his phony U.S. Army Medical Corps uniform and into a set of US Navy SEAL cammies that were pressed and looking sharp. The vet tech on duty gave him a double-take as Butcher walked through the entrance and down the hall to retrieve Amber. He was sure he had seen the same guy in an Army officer's uniform an hour ago. He decided to keep his mouth shut. These didn't look like the kind of men he wanted to argue with. Lone Wolf and two of Butcher's SEALs jumped out the back of the truck and followed Butcher inside.

Amber was seated next to Razor with her head down and her hands inside the little boat resting on Razor's side. She looked up when Butcher entered the room with three big SEALs behind him.

"Time to go, Amber," he said quietly. She nodded and stood up slowly as two big men picked up the little boat and carried Razor to the back of the 6x6 as Lone Wolf led the way. Butcher gave Amber a hand and helped her into the middle bench seat in the front of the big truck, then jumped in next to her as Lone Wolf fired up the engine and rolled down the dusty road.

The sun set into an orange glow in the west as the truck wound through the Green Zone. Lone Wolf stopped near a compound that was used by the Iraqi Maritime Police. Butcher's men had trained the Iraqi police officers on riverine tactics and weapons so they had access to the small pier that was built over the mighty Tigris River. When Lone Wolf parked the truck, the whole platoon filed out the back, with four men carrying Razor up on their shoulders in a funeral procession walk. Butcher let the men pass, then spoke to Amber, "You ready for this?"

"Yes," she said, the old vigor back in her voice. Butcher nodded and they followed the platoon of SEALs down the pier. At the end, the dock split into a T-shape, allowing all of the men and Amber to face the river with Razor in the middle held by the four SEALs.

"Do you want to say anything, Amber?" Butcher asked. She walked over to the little boat to say goodbye one more time to her best buddy and savior. The SEALs lowered the boat so she could see him. She whispered into his ear, "I'll see you on the other side, soldier." Stroking his golden black muzzle one last time, she gave him a kiss, then stood up and nodded to Butcher, standing tall next to him.

"Do you mind if I say a few words then?" Butcher asked.

"I wish you would," she said.

Butcher looked down the line at his men then spoke in a loud voice, "This soldier, this canine soldier, is a hero. He fought for his country, never gave up, even though he was mortally wounded, he led us to

Sergeant Downing and saved her life and mine as his last act. He will forever be one of us, a warrior!" With that, Butcher nodded at Lone Wolf who took a U.S. Navy SEAL Trident, the coveted insignia of the SEAL Teams, out of his pocket and placed it gently on Razor's side as the four SEALs lowered the little boat.

Suddenly Lone Wolf let out a booming roar, "Razor!" which was followed by all the men yelling in thunderous unison, "HooYah Razor!" It was the highest form of recognition in the SEAL Teams.

Butcher nodded and the four men set Razor's boat gently in the river. Before they let the boat drift away, Lone Wolf reached down and lit a fire in the back of the boat, which quickly started to blaze. They pushed the little burning craft off the dock and out into the dark, swirling river. The red glow of the fire on the boat set off shadows on the water, illuminating the starless night. The current of the great Tigris carried the heroic warrior out of their sight and down the mighty river toward his final destiny.

41

OCTOBER 2012, RAMSTEIN, GERMANY AND SAN DIEGO, CALIFORNIA

Chris called Amber on her cell phone, but she didn't answer. She had left for Ramstein Air Base in Germany the night before and was undergoing further tests and treatment there before being sent on to Walter Reed Hospital in Washington DC. Chris left her a short voicemail, telling her that he would be redeployed back home from Iraq in a week. The unit let him go home one month early after the loss of his buddy, Hutchins, and the captivity of his fiancé. Everyone in his unit noticed that he was not the cool, upbeat guy he used to be. He was quiet, reserved and unwilling or unable to communicate with the other soldiers in his unit.

He was back in the small bungalow he had inherited from his parents in the Ocean Beach area of San Diego now, trying to adapt to a normal life. He kept the place on short term rental while he was in Iraq. The idea of mowing the lawn, shopping at the grocery store, surfing and having a carefree life without mortars going off and trucks rolling out of the compound headed for battle seemed meaningless now. He looked out the window of his 1940's stucco home and saw a young lady walking her poodle, cell phone in hand. The poodle was wearing a pink jacket. *This is all bullshit,* he thought, *a superficial life, no consequences for your actions, no sense of the darkness lurking just beyond the shadows.*

He, like all U.S. soldiers, hadn't been allowed to drink alcohol in Iraq. But now that he was home, he'd been drinking heavily. He hadn't been a drinker before Iraq, but now he found that the liquor blanched his brain, made him forget the pain for a moment, and knocked him out. He'd been putting down an entire bottle of Jim Beam daily. It had been two days since his last shower, and he now resembled a homeless veteran with his scruffy beard and stinky clothes.

The letter he'd written to Hutchins' parents was among the hardest things he'd ever done. To lose your son, your only child, to an IED in Iraq was just terrible for Chris to contemplate. The thought weighed even heavier on him, knowing he hadn't been on that mission where he could have potentially averted the disaster. He'd tried to say good things about Hutch in the letter, but in the end, he felt the guilt of not being there for the kid haunt him and permeate the letter. If he hadn't been so bloody weak when Amber was captured, the lieutenant might have let him go with the platoon to Umm Qasr. He was the best in the platoon at seeing the telltale signs of an ambush or IED attack. He had the knack of seeing things out of place, the slightly different color dirt off to the side of the road, the stranger in the abaya who looked nervous, the wires sticking up out of the ground. The letter felt more like a confessional than something to make the parents proud of their son. They hadn't responded.

He sat in his dark living room, the shades drawn. His thoughts kept pulling him down with heavy weights of guilt and shame. When he wasn't thinking of Hutchins, he thought of Amber undergoing PTSD treatment after captivity, completely ignorant that her fiancé had been unfaithful, was unfaithful. There was no way he could undo that. The email he'd received from Hannah yesterday only reinforced what he thought of himself: weak, shameful and guilt-ridden. He found that the booze couldn't erase that, couldn't erase any of it.

Amber had been held captive for over 48 hours. Chris's operations officer, a strict former enlisted Marine, now Army lieutenant, came to tell Chris the news right away, knowing he and Amber were engaged. Since he'd heard about Amber's captivity, Chris had barely been able to function. His best friend, his fiancé, held by those maniacs! What would they do to her? How long would they hold her? He heard the operations officer telling some other officers in the hallway that if she was not recovered quickly, her chances of being rescued at all would diminish.

His master sergeant took Chris off the duty roster for a while. He saw how badly Chris was taking the news—it wasn't a good time to put a weapon in his hand in the very dangerous and uncertain circumstances they found themselves in as infantry soldiers in a country where it was nearly impossible to tell the difference between the insurgents and the populace.

Chris sat in a small room that he shared with another soldier who was on a mission out to Umm Qasr. His roommate would be gone for at least a week. His platoon lived in one of the palaces that was formerly owned and periodically occupied by the late, crazy, murderous Saddam Hussein. The wild contrasts of the palace were not lost on Chris. He slept in an Army issue folding cot in a room with marble floors hand inlaid in gold letters with some sort of Arabic symbols. The palace designed for a dictator king was now housing U.S. Army grunts who were used to sleeping on the ground, or in a tent when they were lucky.

There was a knock on his door. "Come in," he said glumly, not wanting to get up from his cot.

The door opened and Hannah stepped in. She was off-duty from her security patrol in the Green Zone and was wearing tight jeans and a sweatshirt. Amber had introduced her to Chris several months back while they were all stationed in Iraq together.

"How are you taking all this, Chris?" she asked, sitting down on the cot next to him.

Chris sat with his bare feet on the floor and his head in his hands. He sat up straight, turned his head and looked at her for a moment. She wasn't as striking as Amber, but somehow, she radiated sex appeal. It just rolled off her like clouds rolling off a high snowy peak. There was something in her eyes, her touch, her voice, the way she moved. She put her hand on his back as if to say, "I'm here for you." The gesture was meant to convey sympathy and support from a friend during a tragedy, but the touch electrified Chris. She kept her hand there on his back and began to rub it in small circles. It may have been all well-intentioned, but the dam of heartbreak and anxiety that Chris was feeling began to break, and it was replaced by something else—a deep need for love, for human connection in the midst of this terrible war. He turned to Hannah and buried his face in her shoulder, quietly sobbing. Hannah wrapped both her arms around Chris and held him tight. "It's gonna be alright, Chris, you'll see."

After 10 minutes, his sobbing stopped, and Chris pulled back and looked into her green eyes. She brushed her long black hair back and quietly stood up, walked over to the door, locked it and slowly pulled her jeans and sweatshirt off. She waited to see Chris's response. He continued to stare at her, wide-eyed, silent. Holding his gaze intently, she released the bra strap behind her back and let it fall to the floor. Again she waited, watching his response. He said nothing. She slipped off her panties and walked back to his cot and stood over him. He was frozen, unable to think or move. She pushed him down onto the cot then slowly climbed on top of him, one inch at a time. A demon of regret began to scream in his chest, but it was crushed by the weight of her milky white, smooth body.

But the biggest stain on his soul was the horrible scene playing over and over in his head from that one terrible mission. The gruesome things he saw, unspeakable scenes, had become like an eclipse on his soul, covering up and blocking any chance of light or happiness in his life. The deal he'd made with the devil, the terrible dilemma, was the final straw in what he felt was a cursed deployment. He reached for the bottle on his counter and downed the last three fingers in two big gulps.

There was only one way out of this mess, he thought, forcing himself back to the present. One way to make things right and shut down the fiends who were screaming in his head day and night. He headed out to the garage. It was time to close the deal with the giant demon on his terms and face accountability for his actions, once and for all.

He walked out the front door, down the cracked wooden steps he had neglected to re-stain for so long and out to the battered garage alongside the house. He hesitated at the door, then finally opened it and closed it gently behind him. It was dim inside; the sun had just set. Walking over to his toolbox on the workbench, he opened the bottom drawer and took out a black Beretta pistol. It was like a lead weight in his hand. He sat down on the hard cement floor and looked out the western window to watch the flash of orange and red blaze one more time. He thought of her. He laid down on the cement floor and finally let the gates to his mind swing wide open. He'd been holding them at bay for so long, but he no longer had the strength to resist. The terrible thoughts came crashing through like a back door was left open in hell. A hoard of devils ran through his head, but they all stopped and fell to their knees trembling as the last demon sauntered in with huge red eyes. He slowly lifted a finger and pointed it at the man, and in those dark eyes Chris saw what he had been dreading. He put the pistol to the side of his head and pulled the trigger.

42

Amber returned to work at the VA hospital five days after she was released by the Montrose County Sheriff. Her boss, John, had offered to let her take a leave of absence, but she was anxious to get back to work. The first thing she did was email Dane Hutchinson, her counterpart from the VA hospital in San Diego. Hannah mentioned something had been bothering Chris from a mission he had been on, though he had never spoken of it to her. Maybe Dane or Chris's mother had information about the mission. Despite all she had been through, her desire to understand Chris's suicide was always right below the surface.

Hutchinson emailed her right back. He didn't have the information she was looking for, but he sent her Chris's mother's phone number. Amber had never met Chris's mother, Janet in person. Chris and Amber had made Zoom calls to Janet in San Diego to introduce her to Amber and to announce the engagement. But after Chris's death, the two had hardly spoken.

Amber hesitated before contacting Chris's mother, but her drive to understand why Chris left her life was stronger than her fear of upsetting Janet. She picked up her phone and dialed.

"Hello," Janet answered.

"Hello Mrs. Hawkins, this is Amber Downing. I know we haven't spoken in a while, but I was wondering if I could ask you something about Chris."

There was a pause before Janet spoke, "Nothing will bring back my son, Amber."

"I know Janet, but I need to understand what happened to Chris, why he took his life, could you please help me?" Amber pleaded.

"What is it you need, Amber?" Mrs. Hawkins said after a moment

"I heard from another soldier that Chris was on one very bad mission, where maybe he saw something that he couldn't deal with. He never mentioned anything to me about it and I thought we shared everything. We were about to get married. I was wondering if you knew anything about that or had any of his papers or military records that described that mission?"

Again, there was a long pause before Janet spoke, "Before Chris died, he mailed his Iraq journal to me. He'd kept a day-by-day account of his tour in Iraq. When I received it in the mail, he was already dead. I think he wanted to keep it private." Amber's heart rate picked up at the mention of an Iraq journal and everything Chris must have included in it, things that might help her understand.

"I never shared it with you," Janet continued, "At first I didn't understand why he didn't send it to you as a fellow Iraq soldier and his fiancé, but then, after reading it, I understood." Mrs. Hawkins hesitated, "I don't want to tarnish my son's memory. Do you understand Amber? He was my only son."

Amber was confused but answered, "Yes, of course, Mrs. Hawkins. I loved your son, I would never hurt him."

"I am going to send you his journal, Amber, but I have one request in exchange."

"Sure, Mrs. Hawkins, anything you ask."

"I want you to destroy the journal after you read it. Can you do that for me Amber?"

Amber, even more confused now, answered, "Yes, of course Mrs. Hawkins, I promise to do that for you."

Amber sat back in her chair and reached for her service dog, thinking about what she had just heard. Nikita stood up and put her head in Amber's lap with that look that said she needed to go outside. But before that, there was someone she needed to contact, someone she had made a promise to.

She called Mrs. Lopez who picked up immediately. "Hola."

"Mrs. Lopez ... um, Maria ... this is Amber Downing from the VA." Amber assumed the police had already been to visit Maria and told her that her son's suicide had been a cover up for his murder. *I'm not sure which is worse,* thought Amber.

"Si, si Amber, how can I help you?" she said.

"I wanted to come and talk to you about Henry. I'm sure the police have already told you about his death, but I have more information for you." She hoped Maria would be willing to meet, but she wouldn't be surprised if Henry's mother had had enough already.

"Of course, Amber. I be home now."

"OK, give me thirty minutes," Amber said, checking her watch.

"Si. Adios."

She pulled up to the Lopez home and let Nikita out of the back seat. She was going to need her service dog for this meeting. She wasn't sure how Mrs. Lopez would react, and Amber needed Nikita's comfort and presence.

Maria let her in the front door and led her and Nikita to the small living room, where Amber sat on the couch and Nikita lay at her feet. As she had for their last meeting, Mrs. Lopez had made Mexican coffee with cinnamon and offered Amber a biscuit before they began to talk.

Maria kicked it off, sensing that Amber was having a hard time getting started. "Now what new information do you have about my Henry, dear?"

Amber took a sip of the tasty hot coffee. "The police informed you of how Henry died?" she asked. Maria nodded, but said nothing. "What I want to share with you, Maria, are more of the details of why your son died, details that the police did not fully know."

Maria put a hand on the back of her neck, trying to disguise the sorrow in her wise face. "Go on, please," she said.

"It began on a mission in Iraq. Your son was in a convoy that was hit with an IED, an explosive device. The vehicle in front of Henry's vehicle was destroyed and the three soldiers inside all died from the blast." Amber paused to see if Maria had heard this before. She doubted Henry would have confided this to his mother and the police did not know all the details. She continued Henry's story in Iraq until she came to the hard part.

"At that point, the leader of the soldiers shot the old man dead. Then he tried to force Henry and Henry's friend Jerry to kill the two teenagers. Henry refused, Mrs. Lopez. He knew in his heart it was not right, that it was murder, no matter what the teenagers had done." Mrs. Lopez put her hand over her mouth in shock as her eyes widened.

"The other soldier, Jerry Arnold, shot both teenagers." Mrs. Lopez shook her head in disbelief.

"You see, Maria, this is what Henry was struggling with the whole time, a type of moral injury, seeing that and being a part of it. This is why the other soldiers killed your son. They were afraid he would talk to the authorities, let them know what really happened and send them to prison. They plotted together to kill Henry and make it look like a suicide."

Maria broke down, lowered her head into her hands and began sobbing. Amber sat in the chair across from her, trying to figure out how to comfort this woman, this mother who'd lost so much. That's when Nikita stood up and did something she'd never done before. She walked over to Maria, even though this was not in her training, put her paw on Maria's knee and began to lick her face. Amber was stunned. Maria sat up, smiled at Nikita and touched the soft brown paw that perched on her knee. Maria had never owned a dog and was in fact scared of them. She had been chased and bitten by a dog as a young girl in Mexico.

Amber kneeled next to Nikita and looked up at Mrs. Lopez in her chair. "Maria, you raised a good son, who became a good man. He did what was right and tried to protect life. You should be proud of his actions. He was a hero." Amber immediately thought of Razor. "He was a good soldier, Maria. He didn't kill himself and he didn't deserve to die. I'm so sorry for your loss."

Maria sat back in her chair and wiped her eyes with a tissue she'd pulled from a box on the small table next to the chair. Nikita kept her paw on Maria's knee. Mrs. Lopez patted Nikita on the head and said, "Gracias, Amber, for this knowledge about my son. You promised me you would find out what happened to him, and you kept your promise. This means the world to me. And thank you for bringing this beautiful animal into my home. I have much to be grateful for."

Amber stood, sensing that Maria needed some time alone to process everything. Nikita put her paw down and moved to Amber's left side as Maria showed them out. She opened the door for them and Amber and Nikita walked out into the bright afternoon sunlight.

43

JUNE 2012, GRAND JUNCTION, COLORADO

After a day back at work, her boss, John Hutson, asked Amber to come up to his office. His receptionist seemed to frown when Amber appeared, Nikita at her side. She wasn't sure what to expect from John, but the receptionist's manner was a bad sign.

John was typing when Amber walked into his office, but stopped as she entered. He looked her up and down again like she was a runway model, unconsciously licking his lips. "Please sit down," he said after taking a long hard look at her chest.

"We're all glad you're back with us, Amber. I didn't know what to make of your arrest. A detective from the Montrose County Sheriff's Office came up here and interviewed me about you and the project you were working on. I must say, I was shocked that you had drifted so far away from the intent of the work I gave you. He even called you a suicide detective!" John was clearly setting the stage for an ass-chewing.

"Do you know how embarrassed I was to have one of our employees arrested for murder? To find out you were working lines of inquiry that were clearly out of bounds? But I stood up for you, Amber, I want you to know that." Amber thought he was trying to appeal to her in some way, like she was supposed to feel guilty and grateful to him at the same time.

"Do you have anything to say for yourself?" he asked, sitting back and crossing his fat arms. Amber hadn't expected this ambush, but she'd taken enough shit from John. Her blood was boiling.

"Yeah, I have something to say, John. I don't care if you were embarrassed by the interview. I'm innocent of any crime. Two police officers and an Army veteran who was supposed to be dead tried to frame me and kill me. So I don't care if that bothers you." She saw John's eyes widen. He hadn't expected this reaction from her. "I performed the task you assigned me. When some things didn't add up on two of the suicides, I dug deeper. Isn't that what you expected me to do? Try to find out why these veterans committed suicide? That's what I did, John. No one else was going to look into these suspicious deaths, so I did." She sat back, looking across the desk at her boss, who was now red in the face and trying to come up with a response.

"Well, I never—" he tried to say more but Amber cut him off.

"And here's the other thing, John. I'm sick of you leering at me like I'm a piece of meat. That's textbook sexual harassment, in case you didn't know."

John slapped his hands on the table. "That's ridiculous, I've never looked at you in anything but a professional manner."

"You and I both know that's bullshit, John. I don't know if you're a womanizer or just have a problem, but you constantly look me up and down, checking me out. Believe me, a woman knows." His red face now turned white with anger. "I've already drafted up a sexual harassment complaint, John," she continued, leaning forward and staring directly at him. "How do you think that's going to go over?

The head of the VA in Grand Junction accused of sexual harassment by a decorated veteran. I'll bet I can find a bunch more women here to back up my complaint. Just think how thorough the VA Headquarters investigation will be, the interviews, the articles in the newspaper." She leaned back now as John looked deflated, the anger replaced with fear and dread.

He wiped the sweat from his brow with a handkerchief before speaking in a quiet voice. "Okay, Amber, I'm sorry. What is it you want?"Amber hadn't really thought of this moment, hadn't planned to chew out her boss, had been bluffing about having drafted up the complaint. But then it came to her. "Here's what you're going to do, John. You're going to change my job description to Suicide Detective. From now on, I will look into any and all veteran suicides in this area and conduct detailed trend analysis and investigations."

He nodded, thinking this was an easy out for him.

"And two days a week I will be accompanying my service dog to provide support and comfort to the inpatient veterans at this hospital who are sick and most in need of care." She had been unconsciously petting Nikita on the floor as she said this last bit. What Nikita had done for Maria was remarkable, and Amber now planned to extend that out to the veterans in need at this hospital. She hadn't thought of that in advance, either, but John's ambush had set her mind to work.

"You mean like a therapy dog session?" John asked, his tone returning to normal.

"Call it what you like, but yes, she will provide comfort, a friend, and hope to sick veterans in this hospital."

"Well, I certainly support that, Amber," he said, beginning to regain his composure and sensing he had a way out, even a good deal. "It looks like we have a deal. You drop those sexual harassment allegations and I'll make all that happen."

Amber realized she couldn't let him off that easily; she had to stand up for all the women in this hospital. "And one final thing, John," she paused to see the fear return to his face. "I will be creating an anonymous sexual harassment survey for the employees here at the hospital and sending it out every six months. If your name comes up in this survey six months from now, this deal is off, and I'll submit my complaint and help every woman here submit theirs too."

His jaw opened like he wanted to say something, but there wasn't much he could say. Amber stood up and walked out of the office, Nikita at her side.

Back at her desk, Amber logged onto the computer, but her hands were still shaking after the confrontation with her boss. If he had just been cordial and welcomed her back to work, nothing would have happened, but he had to try and confront her, dominate her—she was not going to let that happen.

She tried to get started on the next case in her list, but her mind was elsewhere. There was one person she hadn't visited, told herself she would not visit, that there was nothing she could provide. Jerry Arnold's mother. Amber had put the woman out of her thoughts, refusing to consider visiting her—what could she add that the police hadn't already told her? In the back of her mind, Amber knew she should visit Mrs. Arnold, give some information to this poor woman, a mother who'd lost her son twice, once to suicide, so she'd thought, and now to murder and complicity in another murder. Amber thought she must be a wreck right now.

She closed her laptop. She couldn't work on the next case. She had to see Mrs. Arnold, knew it was the right thing to do even though she dreaded the encounter, remembering how angry Mrs. Arnold had been on her first visit. She decided to skip the call and just show up unannounced, suspecting Mrs. Arnold would've told Amber to take a flying leap over the phone.

On the drive north on the I-70 bypass, Amber went over everything she knew had happened to Arnold. The police would have briefed his mother on the murder and conspiracy, but they would not have had the detailed knowledge of what had transpired in Iraq—maybe something there could help her understand what had happened to her son.

She parked out front on the dusty gravel road, let Nikita out and walked up to the house that badly needed a paint job. Before knocking, she took a big breath and reached for Nikita's ears for comfort and confidence. "We can do this, girl," she whispered to Nikita. She knocked on the door.

After two more hard knocks, Mrs. Arnold opened the door. Amber tried not to show shock. The woman looked like she had come off a three-day bender; her hair was a mess, her clothes wrinkled and Amber could smell booze on her breath.

"Go away," she said, trying to close the door on Amber.

"Wait, Mrs. Arnold! I have to talk to you about your son. I know the police spoke to you, but I want to give you some additional information they don't have," she pleaded.

Mrs. Arnold looked down at her bare feet for a long moment then opened the door. As expected, the place was a mess with food wrappers, beer cans and dirty dishes spread across the table and kitchen.

Mrs. Arnold didn't even try to apologize. She plopped on a chair across from a small table, leaving Amber the couch with room for Nikita at her feet.

"Well, I guess you're the reason my son is dead," she said, shocking Amber with the accusation. "If you hadn't stuck your nose into all of this, my Jerry might be alive right now." Amber sensed that Mrs. Arnold didn't really believe that. It was merely the terrible grief of a mother who'd lost her son, again. Amber decided not to argue with the woman, since it would only make things worse.

"I don't think you really believe that, Mrs. Arnold. The members of this conspiracy were not going to let Jerry live either way. He knew too much. It just happened at my home," Amber said, waiting to see Mrs. Arnold's reaction. Nothing. She continued, "I want to tell you how this all got started. Maybe in hearing that, you will find some comfort, or at least understanding."

Mrs. Arnold sat back in the overstuffed chair and nodded. What mother would not want to hear more about how and why her son had died?

Amber walked her through the story of the convoy ambush in Iraq, leading her to the point where Holmes, Arnold and Lopez entered the second floor room with the old man and teenage boys. "Master Sergeant Holmes, who you now know was a Grand Junction police officer, shot the old man, murdered him in cold blood. Here's the hard part, though. He then ordered your son and Henry Lopez, your son's buddy, to kill the two unarmed teenage boys, even going so far as to point his own weapon at your son and Lopez and threaten to kill them if they disobeyed. What happened next is hard to imagine, but your son shot and killed one of the teenagers, then as Holmes pointed his weapon at Lopez, trying to force him to kill the second one, Jerry pulled the trigger on the second boy." Amber let that sit for a moment, noting that Mrs. Arnold seemed even more deflated and broken after hearing it. She slumped in her chair and shook her head in disbelief.

"But here's the thing, Mrs. Arnold. I believe Jerry did that to protect his buddy Henry. He'd already killed one boy under duress, maybe he thought it was not much more to kill the second. I think he was protecting his friend and fellow soldier. Either Holmes would have shot Henry for failing to kill the boy or Henry would have had to shoot the other boy and live with the memory and guilt of killing an unarmed teenager. This is the only thing that makes sense to me: your Jerry tried to save Lopez that day. Don't get me wrong, I'm not condoning his actions, I'm just saying that in my heart, I think Jerry was trying to do the best he could in a terrible situation." Tears began to roll down Mrs. Arnold's cheeks.

Nikita stood up and did it again, putting her paw on Mrs. Arnold's lap. Amber couldn't believe it. Mrs. Arnold didn't react to the touch of the dog. She wiped her eyes with the back of her hand, looked at Nikita then back to Amber. Nikita pulled her paw back and lay down at Amber's feet. *It's not for everyone,* thought Amber.

Mrs. Arnold regained some of her composure. "The police told me Jerry was killed in your home and that one of the crooked police officers shot him. Can you tell me any more about that?"

Amber was not planning to bring this scene up, as there was not much she could pull out of it to provide comfort to Jerry's mother, but she did her best. "I'm sure the police told you how it all happened," Amber said, bracing herself to relive that night again. "What I can tell you is that Jerry was beginning to have questions, doubts about how this whole thing would end. He had a plan to escape to Belize, but I think he started to see that wasn't going to happen. That's when the police officer Brian Dixon shot him. I think that was the plan all along, to use Jerry, then get rid of him." She knew it was a lot more than that, as Jerry had played an unwitting part in Lopez's death, but she didn't need to rub this into Mrs. Arnold's nose. Jerry, too, was a victim of Iraq, of unspeakable tragedy, pain and loss. He'd never recovered from killing the two boys, part of him had died in that upstairs room in Iraq. Somehow it had warped him and made him vulnerable to this crazy plan to kill Lopez.

Amber did have one final morsel of comfort she could share. "That night at the house, I asked Jerry what would happen to you now that he was caught up in this mess." The thought came to tell Mrs. Arnold a lie, to tell her that Jerry had said he loved his mom. But she couldn't do it. Instead she said, "Jerry thought the world of you, ma'am. He told me he had no choice. I think his perceptions were altered, his decision-making skewed. He was suffering from moral injury, and PTSD, no doubt. Like so many other veterans, he was a victim of the war in Iraq. He was put in a situation none of us can even imagine. I don't hate your son for trying to kill me, Mrs. Arnold, I feel sad for him and for you. He was a victim of the war, too."

44

It was Monday morning and Amber was on her way to work. There was a light mist falling from a slate sky. She had picked up a coffee and blueberry muffin from The Coffee Trader on the way and was listening to Native American flute music on her phone. The soothing flute and nature background sounds helped keep her mind off the events of last week. She was always searching for something to bring peace to her fractured thoughts. The music suddenly stopped as her phone rang. She looked at the caller ID — Montrose Police Department. Her pulse jumped as she wondered why they were calling. "Hello," she answered cautiously, pushing the button for the speakerphone.

"Hello, is this Amber Downing?"

"Yes."

"I'm officer Aribe from the Montrose Police Department. First I want to say that I'm very sorry for the ordeal you went through," he paused, giving Amber the opportunity to respond.

"Thank you, that's kind of you to call," she replied, wondering what else he was going to say.

"The other reason I called is to ask if you would be willing to attend a hearing for Officer Hannah Livingston. The Disciplinary Review Board would like to hear from you as they make a determination on Officer Livingston's fate. They would like to understand the impact of Officer Livinston's actions and decisions on what you had to endure."

Amber was momentarily shocked, she hadn't expected to have to relive that night again, or face Hannah at a tribunal.

"Can I have some time to think about this Officer Aribe?"

"Yes, of course, I understand how difficult this could be for you. The hearing is on Thursday. You could let me know by Wednesday afternoon."

"OK, thanks Officer, I will let you know." Before Aribe hung up, he gave Amber his cell phone number.

The inner quiet Amber was feeling with the flute music was shattered. She punched the steering wheel and turned to Nikita, "Why do I keep getting dragged through these messes?" Nikita turned her head trying to understand her master. "I want to put this behind me, not wallow in it!" She realized the real stressful part would be confronting her ex-best friend. Part of her wanted to rake Hannah over the coals and make sure she got fired, but the other part of her wanted nothing to do with this police inquisition, that was the part of her that just wanted to move on and forget.

For the rest of the drive, Amber tried to decide what she should do. As she pulled into the VA Medical Center parking lot, she was no closer to a decision. *I wish I could talk to Tony or even Hannah about this,* she lamented to herself. But then she knew exactly who she needed to talk to.

Instead of heading straight to her dungeon office, Amber turned left at the entrance and walked down the hall to the cafe. A lone veteran with a red ballcap cocked to one side was rolling himself in a wheelchair in front of her. Nikita turned and looked at him. Amber paused and let Nikita walk over to the veteran. He didn't say anything, just stopped pushing his chair and reached out a frail hand. Nikita sniffed it, then let him pet her on the head. The veteran nodded thanks to her and continued slowly wheeling his chair down the hall.

The cafe was busy this morning. The hospital had advertised some sort of free vaccine for veterans this week and the normally quiet cafe was bustling with veterans drinking coffee, sharing stories and eating pancakes. Amber stood in line so she could speak with Sheri without cutting in front of the veterans in line for food. When it was Amber's turn to step up to place an order, Sheri greeted her with a big smile and quickly reached under the counter for a biscuit and handed it to Nikita who crunched it down to the delight of the older gentleman behind Amber. Amber had already told Sheri about the incident at her home with Hannah, Brian and Jerry. Sheri had again listened with patience and had allowed Amber the space she needed to talk that night out and begin to process everything. "Hey, Sheri," Amber said leaning forward across the counter, "I see you're really busy today, but do you have some time for a chat?" "Sure, Amber, I'll probably be swamped all day, but I get off at 1:30. Will that work? You want to meet me down here? I'll save you a sandwich."

"That'll be perfect," Amber said, stepping back from the counter and letting the next customer order. She looked back at Sheri one more time and noticed that Sheri was taking the order from another veteran, but looking at Amber with an expression of concern.

On the way downstairs to her office, Amber had the thought that maybe it was unfair to dump her problems on Sheri, but she brushed off the notion, realizing that she would do the same for Sheri if needed, it was just that Amber seemed to be the one with all the problems lately.

Amber had blown off a lot of the training requirements that were mandated by the VA while she was engrossed in the Lopez and Arnold cases. She figured today would be a good day to catch up on her on-line training courses. She opened her computer and clicked on the training folder. She saw five courses that needed to be completed: Computer Security, *that will put me to sleep*, Sexual Harassment in the Workplace, *my boss better have aced this one*, Maintaining Patient Medical Record Confidentiality, *at least this looks interesting*, and Suicide Prevention. She slammed her laptop closed after seeing the last course.

"Suicide Prevention! Are you kidding me!" she said loudly to no one but Nikita. "This is fate giving me the big finger, never letting me forget!" She closed her eyes for a few moments and felt Nikita nudge her arm with her wet nose. "OK, girl, I get it. Time to get on with it," she said, scratching Nikita's ears. She opened the laptop, clicked open the first training course and got after it.

At 1:30 Amber locked up and headed to the cafe to meet Sheri. The place was empty except for the rather large cook in the back of the kitchen who was scraping the hot grill. Sheri was wiping down tables and looked up when she saw Amber and Nikita walk in. "Hey, Amber, I've got your sandwich back here," she said while walking behind the counter. Amber and Nikita sat at a table near the window and Sheri brought out the sandwich wrapped in white paper, and a bottle of water. Amber scarfed the sandwich down quickly while Sheri petted Nikita. Finally Amber finished and turned to her friend.

"I got a call this morning on the way to work from the Montrose Police Department. They asked me to speak at a disciplinary board about what happened last week and the impact of Hannah's actions on me. Can you believe it?" She paused to see what reaction she would get from Sheri—there was none. "I was just starting to see the tiniest light at the end of the tunnel and they're to drag me back into the dark. I don't want to relive all that and if I do go in there, I'm dreading having to face Hannah. I'll throw her so far under the bus, that they won't find anything left of her. So what should I do, Sheri, fight or flight? Ignore them or go in there and blow Hannah out of the water?"

Sheri took a sip of her lukewarm coffee and looked at her friend who was so upset, a friend who had been through more than most could imagine, a young woman who looked up to Sheri as a kind of mentor and kindred spirit. "Did I ever tell you about how I lost this arm?" Sheri said after a long silence, lifting her arm and showing Amber the stub below her elbow? Amber shook her head, suddenly feeling that her outburst about the disciplinary review board was childish.

"I was driving home after a long shift at work," Sheri began in a soft tone, "A car swerved at me on the two-lane road, forcing me into the ditch where I hit a tree." Amber unconsciously covered her mouth in dismay. "I had a fractured hip, a broken leg and my arm was almost completely severed from the elbow down. They had to amputate it." Sheri paused for a moment before continuing, looking straight into Amber's eyes. "I also lost the son I was pregnant with at the time." Amber shook her head and tears began to roll down her cheeks. The pain that her friend had endured was too much. She had always looked to Sheri as a calm voice of wisdom in her life, but she couldn't square that with the tragedy that had befallen Sheri. Sheri should have been bitter, angry and resentful.

"I am so sorry," Amber said, reaching across the table and gently grasping Sheri's hand.

Sheri looked at Amber with cloudy eyes then continued, "It turns out the driver of the swerving vehicle was a young man driving drunk. Three months after the accident, I was called to testify at his trial. The prosecution wanted me to play to the jury, explain in detail my injuries and push for the maximum sentence." Amber's gut began to tighten.

"To the consternation of the prosecutor, I stood up and said that I forgive the young man, and wished him no harm. I asked the judge to take into consideration that he was only 18 and that I thought he'd learned his lesson and didn't need to have his life ruined." Amber was shocked, "You mean they just let him go?"

"No, he was given probation, a fine, a felony charge and community service," said Sheri.

Amber thought for a moment trying to formulate a question that was bubbling up in her head. *How did this humble woman in front of her, this cafe worker and single mom who had lost a baby and an arm, find the ability to forgive that young man.* Amber realized she wasn't interested in the *why, but the how. How did Sheri find the ability, the courage and character to forgive the man who had taken so much from her?*

Sheri saw the look on Amber's face and anticipated the question her friend couldn't put into words. "The thing is Amber, I didn't do it for the young man, I did it for myself." She paused, letting that sink in. "I didn't want to live with resentment, hatred and anger. I just wanted to let it go and get on with my life. I realized somehow at the time that I could either seek revenge or I could forgive the young man and move on, but not both. Revenge would never make me feel any better. It was like a bad dream where you're about to find gold, but you wake up, realize it was all a dream, but find yourself chasing the gold again every night, never to find it. I just wanted to get off the treadmill of anger I had been feeling and start a new life."

Amber looked at her dear friend, stunned. She hadn't expected this from Sheri. The story cut Amber to the bone, most of all because it shined a mirror back at Amber, forcing her to recognize how much she wanted revenge for Hannah's betrayals, how she could taste the retribution and see the look in Hannah's eyes when the hammer dropped. But now she had doubts, tiny cracks began to form in her plans for seeing her friend suffer. Finally she realized, in her gut, that like Sheri, she wanted to get past this too. In her heart she knew anger and revenge would haunt her like a two-headed hydra unless she found something deep within herself. She was already fighting two monsters from Iraq, she didn't need three.

Suddenly Sheri reached across the table and took Amber's hands in hers. "Do you mind if I pray for you Amber?" Amber was taken aback.

"I'm not religious Sheri," Amber responded, not sure what to say.

"It doesn't matter honey," Sheri replied, "I just want to pray for you."

"Uhm, OK," Amber responded, not sure what to do. Sheri closed her eyes and bowed her head for what seemed a long time to Amber.

While Sheri prayed, Amber suddenly had a wave of gratitude wash over her for this dear woman who had been through so much and yet had been there for Amber every time she needed a friend. *I'm so blessed for her friendship,* thought Amber, as Sheri opened her eyes and smiled at Amber.

———◦———

On Wednesday Amber called Officer Aribe and told him she would give a statement to the board. Aribe gave her the time and location of the meeting on Thursday. "I know this is hard, but you're doing the right thing here," Aribe said before hanging up. Amber wasn't so sure.

Amber parked her truck on the street outside the new Montrose Police Headquarters building downtown. She had stared at her closet for 20 minutes that morning as if a hidden oracle would reveal what she should wear. Finally she settled on a calf length blue dress and low flats. The receptionist inside the building took her ID then pointed to a conference room down the hallway on the left. Her gut tightened as she stepped into the room.

Several senior police officers had just entered the room and were taking seats at a long table. Facing the panel of senior officers, Hannah sat at a smaller table alongside a man with a shock of gray hair and a tweed suit. Amber figured he was either a lawyer or union representative for Hannah. Amber was about to take a seat in the row of chairs behind Hannah, when a man approached her and introduced himself as Officer Aribe.

"You'll be the only witness called," he whispered to her as they sat together in a row of folding chairs behind Hannah. He was wearing his Montrose Police uniform. Amber turned to look at him and saw a tall man with a hawkish nose, jet black hair and prominent crow's feet around his eyes. Amber guessed he was in his early forties. He was about to say something else to Amber when a senior officer at the long table called the meeting to order. He introduced himself as the Deputy Police Chief for Montrose then introduced the other four officers, one being Hannah's direct supervisor. Apart from Amber, there were seven or eight other people seated behind Hannah. She figured they were supporters of Hannah who might be called to give some testimony like herself or friends of Hannah.

The Deputy Police Chief started the meeting and called on an officer at the end of the long table to go over each of the infractions that Hannah had been accused of breaking. He acted like a prosecutor in a trial, laying out the rules Hannah had apparently violated and the results of those broken regulations. He went over several seemingly minor rules that Hannah had broken, but he saved the kicker for last. He laid out how she had gone to the Grand Junction Police Department and checked out the records on the deaths of Lopez and Arnold without any official need to know about those cases. He explained that she had done this act at the request of her disgraced and now deceased boyfriend, Brian Dixon, a former Grand Junction Police Officer and by extension the other disgraced and now imprisoned officer, John Holmes.

Amber could sense the mood of the panel of senior officers shift as the prosecutor-like officer laid out the impacts. "Based upon the actions of Officer Livingston, the two conspirators in this heinous crime against Ms. Downing and Mr. Arnold solidified their motive and hatched their failed attempt to murder two people." He paused for effect, then continued. "It is my opinion that had Officer Livingston not given in to the unauthorized request to check out those files, the plan to kill Ms. Downing would not have happened. By her poor judgment she became an unwitting accessory to a murder plot." The room fell silent as the officer sat down and nodded to the Deputy Police Chief.

"Ms. Downing," the Deputy said in his deep voice, "I understand you will make an impact statement here today. Would you please step forward and address the panel?" The Deputy pointed to a spot next to the small table where Hannah sat. During the proceeding, Amber had seen nothing but the back of Hannah's head, now she turned to look at her ex-best friend before speaking to the panel. Hannah wore her police uniform and had her hair tied up in a tight bun. She returned Amber's quick glance with an empty expression.

Amber's heart was thumping as she started, "Today you've heard a lot of testimony about Officer Livingston, I'd like to fill in some of the blanks for you." Amber gulped and continued, "Hannah and I served as Military Police Officers together at Fort Bragg. Hannah was selected as our squad leader because of her leadership, dedication to the mission and acumen. I considered myself a good military police officer, but I was not half the officer that Hannah was." Amber could see a few looks of concern on the faces of the senior police officers. They had not expected Amber to start like this.

"Later we were both deployed to Iraq at the same time, me as a military working dog handler, Hannah as a security officer within the Green Zone. She was responsible for a squad of 10 other military police officers, training them and leading them from the front every day. Just to give you an idea of her bravery, at one point a vehicle blew through the vendor gate to the Green Zone. Officer Livingston was standing in front of the vehicle as it broke through the security, she drew her weapon, stood in the middle of the road, putting her life at risk and fired continuously into the vehicle until the driver was neutralized. Her actions that day undoubtedly saved hundreds of lives as a bomb was later found in the trunk of the vehicle. For her actions Officer Livingston was awarded The Bronze Star." Amber paused to survey the panel. They were frozen like statues.

"In terms of the records being removed from the Grand Junction Police Department, I hold myself partly to blame for this. I was overzealous in my pursuit of some anomalies in the suicides of two Army veterans. I should have gone to the Grand Junction Police and let them investigate the things I discovered. With the exception of a personal matter that I know we both regret deeply I have nothing negative to say about Officer Livingston." Amber took a quick glance at Hannah and saw that her friend was crying and looking up at Amber with reddened eyes.

"There is no one I would trust more to put her life on the line for me than Officer Livingston," Amber continued. "She and I and others experienced things in Iraq that I can't describe for you today. As Military Police Officers we were desperately trying to protect our soldiers and civilians from terrorists in a bloody conflict that defied all the rules of war and norms of Western societies. Almost weekly we had to confront women or children who had bombs strapped to their bodies by insurgents." Somewhere deep in her gut, Amber realized she was also speaking for herself, for Chris and all Iraq veterans as much as she was for Hannah. "Today I'm not asking you to excuse Officer Livingston's actions, I'm just asking you to give her a small break, realize in your hearts what she has had to deal with as a soldier in combat and ask yourself if you can find a way to keep her in this job she loves and is so good at, while also giving her the correction and punishment that she deserves."

Amber looked at all the faces of the senior officers on the panel before she sat down. She could sense that they had been moved by her remarks. She stole a glance at Hannah and saw her friend nod at her with watery eyes and a tight smile.

"Ladies and gentlemen, I want to thank you for your presence here today," the Deputy Police Chief said to the assembled audience. "We will adjourn and continue our deliberations in private."

Amber stood up and looked at Officer Aribe standing next to her. "Well, that was not what I expected," he said, turning to face her, "But it was powerful. I think you might have saved her job today." And with that, he walked away.

Amber turned and headed for the exit. She was physically and emotionally drained. She didn't want to face Hannah at this point. She'd done what she could to save her friend's career, but what happened between her and Chris was another issue. Amber knew she needed to get over that too, but she'd done enough forgiving for one day she thought.

45

Two weeks later

The last few weeks at work had been good for Amber. Two days a week she and Nikita had been visiting inpatient veterans at the hospital. Nikita wasn't trained as a therapy dog, but it surprised Amber how quickly she adapted to the added mission. The veterans, especially those in critical care, absolutely loved Nikita's visits. They would hang a frail arm over the side of the bed and Nikita would lick the back of their hand and put a wet nose on the bed to say hello. The old veterans would pet her, scratch her ears and reminisce about a dog they had when they were a kid, or just bask in the joy of interaction with an animal that was a lot like they had been—fierce when needed to defend the innocent, but otherwise loving and kind. Amber thought she was actually getting more out of the encounters than the veterans.

The panel of senior Montrose police officers decided to allow Hannah to continue as a Montrose police officer after she finished her suspension and completed additional training. Hannah tried to reach out to Amber several times, but so far Amber had ignored the calls and texts. She planned to sit down with her friend one of these days, but she needed to work on more forgiveness. She had been meeting with Sheri a couple of times a week and it was really helping Amber sort through her emotions. Sheri never pushed her religion, but Amber always felt the peace that Sheri radiated. "I want to feel like she does," Amber thought often.

She also hit a milestone on the suicide project, reaching the halfway point of the names on the spreadsheet. It was a big step and she was proud of her work so far. She hadn't discovered any more anomalies, but she had been able to visit a few more families, hear their stories, and when she felt it was appropriate, share something with them about Chris.

It was Friday afternoon and this weekend she'd planned to take Nikita backpacking on the Uncompahgre Plateau west of Montrose, now that the snow had mostly melted. She would pack her gear tonight, drive up Saturday to the Spring Creek Trailhead, head off for a long hike, find a campsite, spend the night and hike back to her car on Sunday. The weather was looking fine, with crisp evenings and a warm, sunny day. Up on the Plateau at 9,000 feet it would be cool hiking amid the tall pine and aspen forests.

There was a little ceremony she planned to conduct at her campsite to mark the halfway milestone in the suicide project. She felt it was important to recognize progress, however small. It was one of the tools she'd picked up from her doctor at the Walter Reed Medical Center on her way home from Iraq.

She was driving home after work on Friday when her cell phone rang. She picked it up and saw it was Tony. She ignored the call and let it go to voicemail. She'd tried not to think of him the last two weeks, and when she did it was usually with anger at the way he'd left things after her arrest. When she was honest with herself, she knew she had feelings for him, but she couldn't get past those hurtful things he'd said to her.

Her phone dinged and she knew Tony had left a voicemail. She thought about deleting it without listening, but cooler heads prevailed and she played it.

"Amber, it's Tony. I just wanted to tell you that I've come to realize what an ass I was to you after your arrest. I don't expect you to forgive me, but I just wanted to apologize. I was wrong about all of it and about Nikita, I know that now. I should have known then. I'm really sorry."

"Shit," Amber said under her breath. She hadn't expected that. She was sure Tony was out of her life. She looked in the rearview mirror at Nikita, who was poking her head out the window, sniffing the breeze. "What do you think, girl, should we give him another chance?" Nikita turned to look at Amber with her soulful eyes, but remained silent.

She dialed Tony's number and he picked up almost immediately.

"Hey," he said.

"Hey," she replied cautiously.

"Did you get my voicemail?"

"Yep," she replied, still not knowing exactly what she planned to say. Then it came to her. "Nikita and I are going backpacking tomorrow on the Plateau if you want to join us. We'll hike and spend a night in the woods, then come back Sunday."

Tony didn't have to think twice about the offer. He had to work Saturday, but he could get someone to cover his shift. "I would love to come," he said.

"OK, meet me at the Spring Creek Trailhead at 9 a.m.," she said, still not sure what she was doing, but following her instincts.

"Sounds great, see you then," Tony replied, seeing that Amber wasn't in the mood for a conversation over the phone.

That night she packed her backpack and prepared for the hike tomorrow. She packed kibble for Nikita, along with a folding rubber bowl for her water and food. She thought about taking a pistol; she was still dealing with anxiety after the shootout in her living room, but decided against it.

Saturday morning broke clear with a few high clouds, but other than that it looked like a good weekend for backpacking. Amber walked downstairs to let Nikita out for the morning and that's when she saw the package behind a potted plant. It must have arrived yesterday, but she didn't see it. She picked it up and noted the sender, Mrs. Janet Hawkins. Her mind spun in a million directions—*maybe this journal held answers to Chris's death.*

She arrived at the trailhead early, let Nikita out to sniff around, set her backpack next to the truck and waited for Tony. She was more than a little anxious about taking him on the hike. It had been a spur-of-the moment decision on her part. She had an idea that she would include him in the little ceremony she had come up with. *Even if things don't work out between us,* she thought, *at least I can do this for him, and end the relationship on a positive note.* A few minutes after 9, Tony rolled into the trailhead parking lot.

Amber didn't want him to get handsy, or give her a hug, so she quickly asked, "Ready to go?" as Nikita bounded over and ran circles around Tony in excitement. *If Nikita likes him that much, he can't be all bad,* thought Amber.

"I'm all set," he said, slinging his backpack over his shoulder and grabbing a walking stick from his back seat.

"Was I supposed to bring the beans and weenies or was that you?" he joked.

Amber smiled, "We'll have to catch rabbits for dinner," she said.

They set off on a narrow path from the trailhead with Amber out front and Tony taking up the rear. Nikita ranged ahead, sniffing and exploring. In a few hundred yards, the trail widened and Tony moved up to walk beside Amber. A few high clouds were building to the west, but it was still a fine sunny day. Tony kept quiet and let Amber talk if and when she felt like it. He had given his mea culpa on the voicemail. The ball was in her court.

They walked through tall pines and were starting to see stands of aspen as they gained elevation. After a mile or so, Amber turned to Tony and asked, "What are your plans for the summer while school is out?"

"I'll work a few more shifts at the bar, do some landscaping on my home and maybe take a trip somewhere in August," he said, looking up at the pines towering over them. "How about you?"

She was silent for a moment, then said, "I've got some vacation days coming up, and I'd like to see the ocean sometime. I love the mountains, but it's good to see the salt water, get my feet wet, do some swimming, that sort of thing." Tony nodded and they continued hiking in silence.

Nikita chased a large squirrel up a tree and stood at the base with her paws on the trunk, looking up and barking at the terrified squirrel who perched on a branch and squealed at her. Tony pointed out a large woodpecker that was drilling into a branch on the same tree. At one point two dirt bikes came up behind them on the trail. The two riders slowed way down and waved as they passed the hikers. Amber made Nikita sit down as the dirt bikes passed them by.

At 5 o'clock they reached a clearing in the woods up on the top of the Plateau that was level and littered with available firewood. With the sun low on the horizon blocked by the tall trees, it started to cool off. Together they gathered sticks and built a small fire ring from rocks and started a fire. Nikita lay next to the fire as Amber and Tony fiddled with the poles, bungies and nylon while they put up their tents. Tony waited to see where Amber put her tent, then moved his site a respectful distance away on the other side of the fire ring.

Amber heated up a pot of water and produced two dehydrated meals from her pack. "Which one do you want?" she asked, holding up the two bags for Tony. "Chili mac or pad thai?"

"I'll take whatever you don't want," he said, sitting down next to the fire in a folding chair he'd pulled from his backpack. Amber, poured hot water in both of the bags and handed Tony the chili mac with a large plastic spoon. They let the meals soften for a few minutes before digging in. Amber went back to her pack and brought out a folding bowl and Nikita's food. Nikita licked her lips and wolfed down the kibble like it was her last meal. Amber and Tony had hiked 9 miles, but Nikita had run at least twice that far, bounding through the forest in search of new smells. Now she lay down next to Amber, who was sitting in a folding chair seated in front of the fire as the trees filtered the last beams of daylight.

Tony made instant coffee from the remnants of the hot water and handed Amber a small steaming plastic cup. "Thanks," she said, sipping it. They sat staring at the fire for a few minutes, then Amber reached into her pack and brought out the binder she had been keeping on all of the suicide cases she had finished.

"What's that?" Tony asked.

She paused then answered, "I've collected the pictures, names, and additional details of each of the veteran suicides I've researched. I've completed 71 of them, which is halfway through the project. That's a milestone for me to acknowledge."

She pulled the first page out of the binder, using a headlamp to illuminate the pages. She looked like an angel with the beam of light on her face and her golden blonde hair falling around her neck.

She read the title of the first page out loud, "Corporal Anthony Deluca, United States Marine Corps, from Palisade, Colorado. Born 1995, died 2018." She looked up at Tony and said, "Say his name with me," and together they both said, "Corporal Anthony Deluca." Although there were 71 cases, Amber knew them all. She'd spent many hours on each case and could see their picture in her head or remember something their mother or family member had told her about their life. She placed Deluca's page gently onto the fire, where it was slowly set aflame and returned to the earth. She pulled out the second card, "Petty Officer Angel Martinez, United States Navy, from Moab, Utah, born 1993, died 2016." In unison they said, "Petty Officer Angel Martinez," then Amber gently put the paper into the crackling fire.

It took almost 45 minutes to make it through the binder. Tony was shocked that there were so many veteran suicides in the area and Amber was only halfway finished with the project.

Finally Amber came to Henry Lopez and Jerry Arnold. Although it turned out that these young men had not committed suicide, Amber included them in her ceremony. Their lives were torn apart by the war and now they were dead. Suicide or not, they were victims of the war, as were their families.

When she finished, she sat back in the chair and looked across the fire at Tony. His eyes were glassy in the flickering of the dying fire as he thought about all those young men and women who had taken their own lives. He looked across the fire at Amber and saw that her face was aglow in the beam of the headlamp. It shone on her soft features and he could see that she had been crying too. As she was looking at him, she reached into her pack and pulled out three more papers. She held them in her hand but froze for several minutes, unable to move past the moment. Tony picked up his camp chair and moved next to her. He reached over gently and took her hand in his. It was trembling and warm. She shook her head in consent, she couldn't do it.

Tony slowly reached over and took the three papers from her hands. He held them face down and looked at Amber, making sure she was OK with it. She lifted her gaze, looked at him and nodded with gratitude. He turned over the first page and read, "Chris Hawkins, Sergeant, United States Army, from San Diego, California. Born 1979, died 2008." He paused, then turned slowly to Amber. "Say his name with me." He said, "Chris Hawkins," aloud and Amber mouthed the name as tears streamed down her face. He gently laid the paper in the embers of the fire, reached over from his chair and wiped her tears away with his dirty fingers. He'd inadvertently made her look like she was wearing war paint under her eyes, with the black soot of his hands smeared on her face.

He looked at Amber, silently gaining her permission before he turned over the next page. She nodded, looked down at Nikita asleep at her feet and scratched her fuzzy ears. Tony turned over the page and was momentarily confused. There was a picture of a black-faced dog wearing a military vest standing next to a dark helicopter. The heading on the page said, "Razor, born 2003, died 2008." Then it hit him—he had never seen a picture of Amber's military working dog from Iraq. He looked over at Amber, and knew now without a doubt why Nikita held a special place in her heart. He nodded in understanding to Amber and said, "Say his name with me," then said, "Razor," as Amber wiped a tear from her eye and spoke his name in unison.

He was about to turn over the last page when Amber reached across and gently took it back from him. He had no idea what was written on the last page. She read it aloud, "Angelica Nichols, from Crested Butte, Colorado, born 1992, died 2018." Tony was both shocked and surprised to hear his wife's name. He thought he was over her death, but now he realized with surety, after hearing her name, that he would never be completely over it. He could only live a life that would honor her memory. "Say her name," Amber said quietly and they looked at each other. "Angelica Nichols," two voices whispered into the dark night.

Amber then reached into her pack and brought out Chris's journal. "What do you have there?" Tony asked.

"It's a journal that Chris kept in Iraq. His mother sent it to me. It might help me understand why he killed himself," she said, turning to Tony who was putting another log on the fire.

Tony stood up, "I'll take a little walk, give you some time." He called for Nikita who was lying down by the fire. Nikita, unsure if she should leave Amber, looked to her master for direction. "Go ahead, girl," Amber said, motioning for Nikita to follow Tony.

Amber skimmed through the journal, until she came to June 10, 2008. There she read:

Yesterday I was tasked to augment a platoon in Charlie Company of the 157th Infantry Battalion as they were short on personnel for a mission. We were ambushed in an alley by a large EFP, and the HUMVEE behind us was completely destroyed and three soldiers were killed. I was ordered to provide security back down the alley as three soldiers from the platoon entered a building to neutralize a threat from above. When the soldiers came back downstairs, two of them were white as ghosts. The Master Sergeant didn't want me to go up and recover the enemy weapons, but that's what the Captain ordered me to do. Once the Master Sergeant left, I went upstairs and saw the most horrible thing I could even imagine. An old man and two teenage boys were dead with their brains splattered on the wall.

After the mission was over and we returned to base, I found the Master Sergeant and confronted him about what I saw. He said he had to take care of his soldiers, and file reports first and that we could talk the next day.

I went to see him the next morning in the chow hall. He had a cup of coffee and was waiting for me. I told him that I had seen what they had done to the old man and boys. He listened to me then spoke in a low voice, "I heard you have a fiancé working here in the Green Zone, a military working dog handler. If you breathe a word of what you saw to anyone, I will find your fiancé and kill her. I'll make it look like an accident, but you will know it was me. No matter where you live after Iraq, Hawkins, I will find Amber Downing and kill her."

So this is the deal I made with the devil. I kept my mouth shut about the most grisly murders I could ever have imagined to keep the love of my life, my dear Amber alive and safe. Did I make the right choice? Did I sell my soul to protect her? I don't know, all I know is that I would do it again in a heartbeat to protect her. My life came undone on that mission, the image of those boys haunts me every day and night—it is the terrible demon of my life. The only thing keeping me going now is Amber, my dear sweet Amber, the love of my life.

Nikita bounded out of the darkness followed by Tony. As they both approached the camp, Amber gently set the journal on the fire. The black cover curled, the final answer, the terrible moral dilemma and demon haunting her fiancé, burned, turned to smoke and drifted through the ancient pines and up to the stars.

As the crackling fire turned to glowing dark embers, Tony and Amber slept side by side in Amber's tent. It was barely big enough for one. Nikita lay on Amber's legs asleep. Somewhere a coyote yelped and Nikita poked her head out the opening of the tent, sniffing the dark forest. She turned her head to look at her master then stared back into the blackness. A shooting star flashed across the sky and a sliver of moon shone on their campsite as the bugle call from a bull elk pierced the silence of the night. Nikita put her head on her paws, closed one eye and kept her eternal watch, ever alert, ever ready to defend.

Acknowledgments

In writing a book, as in life, you don't get very far without help. Throughout the writing of The Suicide Detective, I've been supported by a wonderful team. Special thanks to Lisa Messinger for her masterful grasp of the English language and to Randall Surles for assisting me in so many ways, giving freely of his time. I also want to thank Gary Dickson for graciously volunteering to do a final proofread.

I want to thank Rich Pierce, Chuck Fowler, Erin Henley, Care Gerland and Eric Bach for taking the time to read the manuscript and give me feedback. They truly helped me shape this story.

My wife, Sergina Bach was a huge help, kicking me in the butt when needed and dedicating countless hours to editing and research.

I have to confess that my German Shepherd, Nikita, stole her way onto the pages of this story.

Finally, I want to acknowledge those intrepid members of our United States military whose teamwork, dedication and professionalism inspired me to write this story.

Black Dog Escape

On a clandestine operation in Afghanistan, US Navy SEAL Jack Thibideaux accidentally shoots a 12-year-old girl, forcing him to make a life-changing decision to abandon the mission and navigate a gauntlet of enemies to bring the girl to safety.

You can purchase a signed copy directly from the Author at
wlbachauthor.com

Scan or click on the QR code for a direct Amazon link

Please Leave A Review

I hope you enjoyed reading *The Suicide Detective*. Stay updated on new books and events by signing up for the newsletter on my author website. Thank you for your interest.

https://www.wlbachauthor.com/

Your feedback matters! If you've enjoyed, *The Suicide Detective* please consider leaving a review by scanning the QR code below. Your thoughts help others discover the adventure. Thank you very much!